Kensho was a death trap, until the coming of the Way-Farer.

Then the people of Kensho learned to live in the Way, and prospered.

Now the warships of Earth have come, to seize in prosperity the world they were happy to ignore in its time of trouble.

Earth reckons without the power of the Way.

SATORI

At last, the long-awaited sequel to WAY-FARER and KENSHO

This book is dedicated to

Edward Wilson
Ludwig Wittgenstein
Martin Heidegger
and my parents

SATORI

DENNIS SCHMIDT

SF
ace books
A Division of Charter Communications Inc.
A GROSSET & DUNLAP COMPANY
51 Madison Avenue
New York, New York 10010

SATORI

Copyright © 1981 by Dennis Schmidt

An ACE Book
First Ace printing: November 1981

Published Simultaneously in Canada

2 4 6 8 0 9 7 5 3 1
Manufactured in the United States of America

Other Ace Science Fiction titles by
Dennis Schmidt:

WAY-FARER
KENSHO

PROLOGUE

The probe slid cautiously toward the fifth planet. All its sensors were extended to their fullest, sending out wave after wave of careful electronic questioning. Aside from the usual background whisperings of interplanetary space, only a dead silence returned. Nevertheless, the probe remained tensely alert, ready to run at the slightest sign of hostility.

It paused as if in surprise when it detected the five starships that hung in geosync orbit above the cloud-speckled surface of the world it was approaching. A series of inquiries in various modes and frequencies failed to elicit any response. All five appeared to be dead lumps of orbiting metal. Four were even partially dismantled, showing gaping holes in their hulls. Only one, a dead black monster, seemed completely intact. Visual identification showed it to be a Class B Command Ship of a design at least eight hundred years old! The probe checked its memory cubes for the exact call numbers and tried to contact the ship's computer directly. Again, its efforts were met with a total, death-like silence.

More confidently now, the probe moved toward the planet. The Class B, which could have squashed it as easily as a human could squash an ant, remained totally inactive, perhaps even defunct. The four Class F Arks (identification had finally been achieved despite their condition) that orbited with it were empty—and didn't carry weaponry in any case. There were no indications of dangerous or hostile activities anywhere within the system. Even the surface of the planet was quiet.

The probe took up a position behind the largest of the four moons. The light reflecting from the vast ice fields that covered the satellite showed the intruder clearly for the first time. It was no more than forty feet from end to end. Its center was dominated by a large, dead black globe, some fifteen feet in diameter. At either end, four more globes, equally black, about five feet in diameter, clustered together. In between the three groups stretched a thin, weblike tracery of cables and girders that held the pieces together.

Twice the probe followed the moon around the planet, always keeping position on its far side. The third time around, the smaller globes detached them-selves, one by one, moving slightly inward, to form a loose ring just inside the orbit of the moon and keeping pace with it. Two more orbits and they began to move closer and closer, tightening their ring, until they took up positions well within the path of the smallest, closest, and fastest of the four satellites.

Reaching their final orbits, they hung there silently for a while. Then they began to chatter, sending streams of information to the large globe that still hid behind the moon. Every few revolutions, the heart of the probe aimed its antenna outward and squirted a high-speed data-crammed message toward the stars.

Deep in interstellar space, another antenna received the messages. And slowly a huge, dark shape began to move in their direction.

PART ONE

In every serious philosophical question uncertainty extends to the very roots of the problem. We must always be prepared to learn something totally new.

—Ludwig Wittgenstein

I

"She's quiet as a suspension vault, Worship."

The tension on the bridge relaxed just slightly, but every hand stayed poised over its switch. "All sensors are operational?" The question came from the small, purple-robed man standing in the center of the bridge area.

"Aye, aye. All functioning within six decimals of optimal."

"No sign of electromagnetic discharge?"

"Minor, Worship. Nothing that can't be accounted for by natural sources."

"What about visible wave lengths on the night side?"

"Marginal. Something that appears to be an active volcanic chain. Nothing indicating large population clusters."

"How about the longer wave lengths? No radio at all?" queried a tall, well-formed man in a deep blue military uniform. He wore several medals on his chest and there was gold braid around the brim of his cap.

"No, sir. Not a peep. Just random discharge from a large storm centered over the northern continent and minor whistles from a few others scattered here and there."

"Evaluation," demanded the man in the robe.

A young woman in a brown robe responded with a crisp, "Yes, Worship" and began to punch at lighted squares on the console in front of her. After a moment she looked up. "Evaluation, Worship. Point four chance of human habitation. Class Three optimal, Class One minimal."

"Class Three," he murmured. "Preindustrial. Transitional, if I remember correctly."

The woman nodded. "Yes, Worship. Approximately equivalent to Earth, Western European Sector, around the turn of the nineteenth century A.D. That's, let's see," she punched quickly at the squares again, "ummmm, about fourteen hundred years ago. Industry was just beginning. Small scale, family owned. Most water powered. Some steam. Petrochemicals still unused and . . ."

"Weapons technology?" snapped the military man.

"Ummmm . . . well, sir, primitive. Gunpowder-propelled missiles. Muskets, cannons, nothing much more than that. I don't even think they were repeating weapons. But that's not my specialty."

"No matter," he dismissed her with a wave, turning to face the man they all referred to as "Worship." "Bishop Thwait," he began with a slight inclination of his head, "if Your Worship agrees, I think we can stand down from full red alert. It seems that if this colony survives at all, it's degenerated to the point where it offers no threat."

The bishop raised one white eyebrow and asked, "The flagship?"

Immediately a second brown-robed figure at a console across the bridge responded. "Quiescent, Worship. Seems dysfunctional. All vital power readings zero. Evaluation: dead, Worship."

"Hmmmmmm. Well, then, yes, Admiral, I agree. I think yellow alert is sufficient. Do you concur?"

The admiral nodded. "Sufficient. Yes." He turned to an orderly standing nearby. "Stand down from full red alert, mister. Establish yellow alert."

"Aye, aye, sir." The man walked over to a console, pressed down a lever and spoke into a grid. "Now hear this. Now hear this. All hands stand down from full red alert. Stand down from full red alert. Crew Block Two establish yellow alert. Crew Block Two establish yellow alert. That is all." He turned to the admiral and saluted. "Sir, report crew standing down from full red alert. Report Crew Block Two establishing yellow alert. Sir."

"Good. Worship, I think we should confer on this situation and our planned course of action, soonest. My cabin."

"Agreed, Admiral. The time seems propitious." He turned and spoke to the robed figures who made up about half of those manning the consoles scattered about the bridge area. "My children, you will stay alert and on duty until relieved. Churmon, I want the sensors in farther, just within the atmosphere for several turns. Calmanor, break out the photo-probes and send them in for low-level scan. If this is a Class Three, that is about the only way we will get any data short of landing. And remember, all of you, collect and correlate as much data as possible, as soon as possible. No guesses, no errors. Data."

Although their eyes never left the dials and meters on their consoles, a murmur of obedience rose from the robed ones. For a moment the little man stood and watched, a musing expression on his sharp-featured face. Then he lifted both hands into the air, joining forefinger with forefinger, thumb with thumb to form a single large circle. "In the name of Reality, in the name of the Circle, in the name of the Power, in the name of Humanity," he pronounced with ritual solemnity. Even as they continued to watch their instruments, everyone on the bridge, robed and unrobed alike, raised their right hand, forming a small circle with forefinger and thumb and intoned, "So be it and so it shall be." A slight pause, a slight satisfied nod, and the bishop turned and followed the admiral from the room.

The cabin directly adjoined the bridge so they didn't have far to walk. "Care for anything, Andrew?" the admiral asked as the bishop settled into one of the chairs in the front sitting room.

"No, Thomas, no thanks. A bit too early for me. But go ahead. I guess the major strain of this contact procedure rests on your shoulders. After all, you are the one in charge of fighting or running."

"Huh," snorted the military man. "Not much of either here. No way to build a career contacting Class Threes. If it's even that! Damn. She did say only point four, right? Damn planet might be empty. I'd hoped for a little action."

"Like at Quarnon?" Andrew asked softly.

"Yes, damn it! Like Quarnon!" the other man snapped back in sudden anger. "I know you priests didn't approve of that action, but I still believe we had no choice. We had to smash those bastards before they smashed us."

"But the whole planet, Thomas, the whole planet? Was that not a bit extreme? It might have been useful unburnt, you know."

"I lost two ships in that battle," the admiral answered grimly. "Good men, all of them. Damn near bought vacuum myself." He paused, his face harsh with remembered hatred and anger. "Bastards got what they had coming to 'em. They asked for it."

Andrew Thwait, Bishop of the Power, looked carefully at the man who stood glaring down at him over the top of a glass filled with the finest whiskey Earth could offer. Thomas Yamada, Admiral of the First Expeditionary Fleet, was a man of action and ambition. How else could one explain the presence of such a high-ranking officer aboard a scout ship? Thomas wanted to be in on the excitement, the contact, the possible battle and subjugation of every new colony world they found. Unlike most other men of his rank, he refused to stay behind a desk back with the rest of the fleet. Simple blood lust and a zest for adventure demanded that he be out front, taking the risks and getting the thrills himself. Everyone called him the Fighting Admiral, and he loved it.

He's well-suited for the role, Andrew thought. Tall, broad-shouldered, narrow-hipped, muscular, handsome, he was everyone's vision of the brave soldier. His black hair was precisely cut and seemed almost like a dark, shining helmet. Two calm, midnight eyes challenged the world with an unwavering stare. An aquiline nose, firm mouth, and strong chin completed his face and gave him the commanding look of a recruiting-poster model or vid-program hero.

Yet he had faults, and serious ones, as far as Andrew was concerned. First and foremost was his strongly militaristic mind-set. For Thomas, every conflict, no matter how minor, took on the character of total war. The only method he had for dealing with a problem was to destroy the cause of it.

Not that Bishop Thwait saw anything wrong with destroying one's enemies. Far from it. Killing was often the simplest and the most efficient method. But Thomas liked killing in large quantities. He talked of mega-deaths, even planet-deaths. And killing was always the admiral's first, if not only, approach to the solution of conflicts. The bastards always asked for it.

Actually, the bishop realized, this simplistic view of the world was probably the result of the admiral's other fault: Put succinctly, Thomas wasn't terribly bright. Oh, he was intelligent enough in a limited way. But obviously he hadn't been smart enough to enter the Temple for training in the Power.

Perhaps it was this lack of real intelligence that accounted for Thomas's tendency to reduce every question into one of "Surrender or I shoot." Perhaps he simply had a bloodthirsty nature. In either case, the man utterly lacked subtlety. His thoughts went in straight lines . . . and usually ended in collisions. He was incapable of seeing that there were other ways of overcoming barriers than just smashing them down.

Andrew sighed. And I have to be saddled with him as my co-commander on this expedition, he thought. I'd much rather have had Davidson, especially for this particular situation. She was most reasonable, for a military type, and capable of clever, subtle maneuvering. The Power awed her, or at least she pretended it did, so she was quite tractable and open to suggestion. Altogether the sort of person needed for this potentially touchy contact. But no, Thomas had smelled glory and demanded it for himself. Ah, well, Andrew sighed mentally, there are ways. Thomas will do. Not as pliable a tool as some, but he will do all the same. The Power always triumphs.

Devious bastard, the admiral thought, returning
Bishop Thwait's cool scrutiny over the top of his whis-
key glass. They're all devious, these priests of the
Power. If I had the power they control . . . Damn!
Who'd need to be devious? Just demand what you
want. If anybody objects . . . zaaaap! All that science
at their command. Shit. The Power is well named!
Wonder what he's thinking right now?

Searching for some clue, he scrutinized the figure
sitting so calmly before him. The ice blue eyes were as
cold and closed as ever. The sharp, straight nose
pointed to the grim line of a mouth that indicated
decisiveness and efficiency rather than emotionality.
The pale skin was smooth, unwrinkled, lacking either
smile or worry lines. Closely cropped pure white hair
completed an appearance that yielded nothing, remaining cool and aloof. Long, slender hands lay quietly in
the lap of the purple robe. Beneath that robe, the rest of
the figure must be equally spare and simple, Thomas
thought. And tiny. The man was so tiny! Barely five
feet tall.

Physical size didn't really matter in a priest of the
Power, though, and Thomas knew it. Brains were all
that counted. Sheer intelligence. And tiny little Bishop
Thwait had more than his share. The man had worked
his way up through the hierarchy by exercising a combination of pure brilliance and breathtaking ruthless-
ness. His schemes were so devious, so involute and
multilayered, that no one over knew exactly what he
would do next, or why. All one could depend on was
that the bishop would accomplish whatever it was he set
out to do and that anyone who stood in his way was
doomed.

And that's why the Committee sent me on this mission, he thought. Something's up when a bishop of the Power, especially Thwait, goes out on a scout ship to make contact. Something special, something worth keeping a close watch over. Perhaps even something that could be useful to the Committee, could serve in the struggle against the Power.

He frowned. But now I'm beginning to wonder. That planet's nothing. Oh, maybe rich enough in resources. But hardly important enough to rate the attentions of a bishop. It doesn't even look like the colony made it, might not even have any human life at all. Strange, he mused. Very strange. Because I'm sure Andrew was expecting something. Ordinarily he's as cool as deep vacuum. But he was excited about this contact. He even looked nervous on the bridge just now, picking and fiddling with the sleeve of his robe.

Damn it, there's got to be something here! I smelled it. I knew it. What the hell is it?

The bishop cleared his throat. "Ummmm, Thomas. I think we should proceed with caution. I know there are no signs of activity, hostile or friendly, on the planet, and that the flagship seems to be incapacitated. But let me urge care even now. Until we are sure that what seems to be true is indeed so."

Sitting opposite the bishop, Admiral Yamada took a long, thoughtful sip from his glass. "How long?"

"Oh, well, several turns to establish all the basic parameters. Then, say, forty-eight standards for an analysis, perhaps another forty-eight for full evaluation. By that time we should be ready to set up a definite plan for contact with whatever Pilgrims have survived on the surface."

"If any've survived. Hell, Andrew, we don't have to wait that long. Even if any of 'em did make it, they've got nothing to match us. Easiest thing is to find some big population center, blast it, and lay down the law to 'em. No need for all this analysis and evaluation nonsense.''

Andrew rested his elbows on the arms of the chair, steepled his long fingers, their tips just touching his nose, and gazed abstractedly at the floor. "Perhaps, perhaps not, Thomas, but, you see, there may be a few things about this particular pilgrimage you do not know.''

His eyes lifted and met the admiral's for a few moments of cool appraisal. ''I take it you have read the briefing on this planet? Good. Then you know the leader of the pilgrimage fleet was a man named Arthur Nakamura, a full fleet admiral.

''What you aren't aware of, because it wasn't in the report, is that Nakamura was a High Master of the Universal Way of Zen.''

Thomas looked surprised. ''A military man and some kind of priest?''

The bishop smiled. ''Not as impossible as it sounds. Before the Readjustment many strange religions abounded on Earth. Zen was one of them. And there was nothing in their tenets to keep a man from combining warfare with high religious office.''

''Huh. Sounds sensible to me.''

''Hmmmmmmm, yes. Well, the Zenists were one of the most stubborn groups opposing the Readjustment, Thomas. There are none left on Earth. We had to readjust them all. Terrible loss, really. Many were quite brilliant.''

The admiral shuddered inwardly. And they call us bloodthirsty, he thought. They ''readjust'' their enemies, destroy their minds, turn them into slobbering, pissing, shitting hulks that starve to death because they haven't enough sense left to feed themselves. That's civilized, clean, scientific; in keeping with the Power. Because some damn machine of theirs does the dirty work for them. Hell. At least I give my enemies a clean, quick, honorable death.

"Ah, well," the bishop mused, "the lessons of the past, and all that. It is a pity we did not keep a few of them around. They knew so much we would like to know.

"Anyway, I drift from my purpose. Nakamura was a High Master. I know you have no idea what that means, but imagine it as the approximate equivalent of a Cardinal of the Power. But with abilities of his own that went beyond the Power in some way we do not understand. That was the kind of man that led this pilgrimage."

Thomas shrugged. "So? Your own man said it. It's quiet as a suspension vault down there. If this fighting priest of yours was such a damn genius, what happened? Looks to me like he blew it."

"Yes. And that is exactly what worries me." He shifted position and leaned quickly forward, fixing the other with his sharp stare. "Thomas, the man's success probability quotient on that pilgrimage has been estimated at ninety-six percent. Ninety-six percent! I have never seen such a high figure!

"And yet, from a first look at things, it does indeed seem he failed. Utterly.

"Which can mean one of several things. First, things are exactly as they appear. He failed. Totally, or at least so badly that the colony has degenerated almost to the point of being uncivilized.

"But the major question one must then ask is 'Why?' After all, he had a ninety-six percent chance of success,

he led a fully equipped pilgrimage with a flagship and
four Arks. You know the firepower of that ship hanging
out there, Thomas, and the amount of technology
crammed aboard those Arks. What could have happened to them? Was there some unsuspected enemy
lurking in the system, or even down on the planet?
Some enemy capable of overcoming a ninety-six percent rating and a fully armed flagship? I do not like it,
Thomas. There are just too many unanswered questions. Anything that could defeat a Class B would have
to be big and powerful. Why have we not detected it?
Or anything else, for that matter? Is there still an enemy
skulking about? What could it be? And where is it?
Still here, somewhere, waiting, waiting for us?''

He paused for a moment to let the words sink deep
into the admiral's mind. Then, in a sudden swish of
robes, the bishop stood and began to pace about the
room. ''But some things just do not fit that kind of an
analysis. There are no signs of any struggle, let alone a
major battle. That flagship may be defunct, but it is
intact. It has never been blasted and the hull has never
been breached. And even though those Arks are in bad
shape, it's because they were purposefully dismantled
so the materials could be used on-planet. So,'' he
continued, ''we are left with the obvious alternative.
Some eight hundred years ago the pilgrimage led by
Admiral and High Master Nakamura landed here and
succeeded.''

Thomas straightened up, carefully placing his now
empty glass on the arm of his chair. ''Shit,'' he said
softly. ''If that happened . . . then in eight hundred
years they'd have . . .'' He paused for a moment.
''They were state-of-the-art on leaving, right?'' The
bishop nodded. ''Huh, even allowing for a bit of

backsliding, they should be at least a Class Six by now. Like Quarnon.''

"Yes, Thomas. Like Quarnon.''

"So that's why you wanted this one to yourself, eh, Andrew?''

The bishop nodded silently.

"I realize it's classified material, Power business and all that, but I think I've got a justifiable need to know in this case: Did the hierarchy ever achieve contact with this colony?''

"A message was sent, Thomas. And receipt was acknowledged by the flagship. No reply was ever received. And new inquiries weren't even acknowledged.''

The admiral studied the floor for a few seconds, then raised his eyes and met the other man's quiet gaze. "You think this might all be a trap?''

Andrew shrugged. "Who knows? By all the odds we should have found a flourishing colony down there. The initial readouts from our own probe sensors give the planet a rating in the high nineties. They had all the right equipment. And exceptional leadership. Plus eight hundred years in which to develop.

"Yet all we find is silence. No indication of anything above a Class Three, if even that. It just does not make sense. And I neither like nor trust things that do not make sense.''

Thomas Yamada leaned back, closed his eyes, and gently stroked his temples with his fingers. "Should we return to full red, Andrew? They could be suckering us into relaxing, just waiting until we're off guard.'' He opened his eyes and began to rise.

The bishop held up a restraining hand. "No, no. Yellow is sufficient for now. We know something is wrong, but we still do not know what. So far we've discovered nothing immediately threatening, so I see no sense in exhausting the men by keeping them on full red. No, I think we have to play a careful waiting game. Move slowly and precisely. Leave nothing undone, no option uncovered. We should send probes to every planet, every large rock, in this system. If they are hiding, they could be anywhere. And we should keep collecting data on the planet itself. Perhaps even send a team down. That is the key, Thomas: careful data-gathering. Once we have the right information, the answer will appear."

He paused for a moment, his expression turning thoughtful. "Hmmmmmm, yes. The answer will appear. Thomas, I have a growing feeling we are fighting a battle of wits with a very subtle and brilliant opponent, one, moreover, who has been dead for eight hundred years."

"Nakamura?"

"Nakamura. This may be the final, ultimate confrontation between the forces of the Power and last remnants of our enemy. Fascinating."

There was a knock at the door. The admiral barked out a *Yes*. The door opened and a brown-robed acolyte stood there, embarrassed to have interrupted, but obviously brimming with news.

"What is it, my child?" the bishop asked, taking a step toward the young man.

"Worship. Pardon for interrupting. But we've just gotten the surface-scan photos in."

"And?" questioned the bishop.

"The planet's definitely inhabited, Worship. There are humans down there. Lots of them. And they're not primitive!"

II

The sun's first rays leapt over the horizon and soared westward, brushing Myali Wang's still face as they passed. More and then more light poured toward her until her whole body was wrapped in the warm, glowing cloak of morning.

This is the day, whispered a silent voice in her mind.

I am ready, she replied. *I await the others.*

There are five candidates, the voice continued. *They have entered the Judgement Hall and are being prepared. Come when the others arrive.*

Soon, she answered. *I sense the approach of Mind Brothers.*

She gazed down the hill on whose crest she sat and spied four darkly robed figures moving softly through the morning dimness that still clung to the narrow, tree-filled valley below. We always wear black for Judgement, she thought. How much nicer bright yellow would be.

The Mind Brothers she tended pulled gently against her restraints, attracted by the approach of others of their kind. Go, Brothers, she silently allowed and then laughed out loud as they tumbled invisibly down the hill to meet the newcomers in a swirling dance of welcome. To think our ancestors actually feared and hated them, she wondered, amused by their playful exuberance.

There had been good reason for their fear and hatred, of course. When men had first found the planet, it had seemed so perfect they called it Kensho after one of the stages of Enlightenment. They landed at First Touch and began to set up Base Camp. Quickly they shuttled down the Pilgrims and their equipment, delighted with the apparent tranquility and promise of the new world.

Their joy had been short-lived.

Suddenly, from nowhere, the invisible enemy had struck: the Mushin—unseen, undetected creatures that drove men mad so they could feed on the emotive energy that burst from an insane mind. They would take a mild emotion, like annoyance, feed it back through the mind in a feedback loop that spiraled it higher and higher, until it became an uncontrollable rage that blew the mind apart. Then they would swarm about in a frenzied feeding orgy, and leave nothing behind but a mindless, drooling hulk.

In a flash, the peacefully working Pilgrims turned into a howling, fighting, murdering mob. Every man, woman, and child fell on every other, clawing, striking, stabbing, killing. Over ninety percent of the Pilgrims died in what became known to future generations as the Great Madness. The shattered remnant would have perished too, if it hadn't been for Admiral Nakamura, the leader of the pilgrimage. Nakamura noticed that most of the survivors had one trait in common—they were devotees and practitioners of one or another form of mind control. From that informa-

tion, and his own profound knowledge of the Universal
Way of Zen, Nakamura had guessed the nature of the
Mushin and devised a way to combat them. Mankind
had been unable to leave the planet, and the mind
leeches had made it impossible to stay, but there had
been a Way—and the admiral had found it.

The fate of humanity on Kensho had had its ups and
downs since that time, but thanks to people like Jerome,
Chaka, Edwyr, Yolan, and many others, the Mushin
had first been neutralized, then conquered, and finally
tamed. Now, rather than the invisible terror that drove
men mad, they were the Mind Brothers, partners in a
new relationship that was still being explored.

Myali came out of her reverie as the four emerged
from the trees and walked up the hill toward her. She
didn't know any of them, would have been surprised if
she had. People seldom performed Judgement more
than twice in their life and then never with the same
partners. It was too much to ask of anyone. Especially if
there was sorrow . . .

They arrived and stood around her, waiting. She was
the senior judge this time, and it was up to her to begin.
With a fluid movement, she rose and bowed to each
one, giving them her name and receiving theirs in
return. The two men were Hiroshi and Karl; the wom-
en, Ulla and Marion.

"Gather the Mind Brothers," she said once the in-
troductions were finished. "The candidates are waiting." One of the women, Ulla, hesitated and Myali
turned to her with a gentle smile. "I know," she reassured, "the first time is difficult. But Judgement is a
service required by the Way. And joy is always a more
likely outcome than sorrow. So walk with us, Sister,
and hope." The other woman nodded, sighed, and

joined them as they moved off westward, down into a broad valley where a low, rambling building lay in the distance.

A brisk fifteen-minute walk brought them to the door of the building. A knock was unnecessary for they were expected, and the door swung open as they reached it. The front room was empty of everything but a few simple pieces of furniture. In the next room five women and five men sat in twosomes, trying to look calm. As the judges entered, though, all eyes turned and followed them. Myali could still feel them on her back as they passed into the inner room.

An old, gray-haired man stood tall and silent in the center of the room. At his feet lay five babies, wrapped cozily in blankets. He pointed each of them to one of the children. Myali picked up the bundle on the far left and pulled back the cloth. A tiny, solemn face, mostly big blue eyes, looked up at her. *Hope,* she greeted it without speaking. *Hope, little one.*

When all the babies had been taken from the floor, the old man bowed to each of them in turn. Then he smiled and said softly, "The garden is lovely this time of the morning."

Myali bowed back. "Does the ko still bloom?"

The old man laughed. "The chill is in my bones. I will go sit in the sun in front of the Hall." With that, he bowed again and left by the door through which they had just entered.

Hiroshi looked down at his bundle and the room fell quiet after the old man's departure. "Come," he said to the baby, "we will go view the ko." The others all nodded and Myali led the way to the other door, the one that opened into the garden that lay at the rear of the Judgement Hall.

Once in the garden, they wandered off in different

directions until each seemed to be alone. Myali found a moss-covered stone next to a small pond. A water lizard squeaked annoyance as it scurried out of her way and landed in the water with a plop. After a second, its head popped up and it watched her with dark, suspicious eyes.

Sitting, she bent over the child again, pulling back the blanket so she could see more of it. Chubby, healthy, altogether a beautiful child. Peace and hope, she thought at it. I wish you joy.

She sighed deeply. But this, my little one, is Judgement. And I cannot guarantee joy. We face the moment of truth this day. And truth and joy have no necessary relationship.

It was time, she knew. She held the Mind Brothers in readiness. Now, she thought. Don't wait any longer. If there is joy, there is joy. If sorrow, sorrow. It is the Way.

She let the Mind Brothers loose. In sick dismay she felt them swoop down on the child, felt the little body convulse in agony as they struck, heard the strangled cry of anguish ripped from the tiny mouth. Twice the child twitched, arching its back, beating the air with helpless fists. Then with a silent scream of mental horror, it died.

Weak and shaken, Myali slumped over the now still form, tears pouring down her face. Sorrow, her mind wailed, oh sorrowsorrowsorrow. Great sadness flowed through her.

After a few moments she straightened up, wiping at her eyes with the sleeve of her robe. Yes, she thought, bright yellow would be better. Even for sorrow. She looked down at the dead baby. I'm sorry, little one. But you would have died anyway. Judgement is final. But it is the Way. And it is right.

Joy! Hiroshi shouted into her mind. *Joy!*

Joy! warbled Ulla. *Oh, happiness and joy!*

Joy! Joy! came the ringing cries of the other two, their minds overbrimming with gladness.

Sorrow, she wept again. *Dark and deep as blackest night, sorrow.*

For a few brief moments she felt the grief and mourning of the others surround her, enclosing her in a wailing anguish that stripped all pain from their minds and souls. They would always feel the sadness of the loss of the little life. But once the initial impact had been experienced and purged, no one of them would cling to it, not even Myali. It had to be. It was done.

The sweep of life and the victory of the four could not long be repressed by the sorrow of one. In a sudden flood their gladness returned and lifted her up and up in joyous celebration. One by one they appeared, gathering to her in the garden, cradling their precious bundles, crooning to the gurgling, smiling babies.

Once together, they walked slowly back to the inner room, then through the door to the next room where the five pairs of parents waited. "Joy!" called Marion and stepped up to a radiantly smiling couple, handing back the lively bundle. "Joy!" sang the other three and returned the babies to their parents.

Myali approached the last couple, two who stood close and solemn, a cold, weary sadness growing in their eyes. She held out the small, limp bundle to them. "Honor," she said softly. "Honor but sorrow. I'm sorry."

The mother took the dead child and cradled it gently against her chest. Tears filled her eyes and ran down her cheeks. A slight sob broke from the man and his eyes also streamed his grief. Myali spread her arms around both of them and held them together and wept with them, the sobs racking her body, but freeing her mind.

Eventually they all ceased. The man and woman looked calmly at Myali, gave her one final hug, then stepped back and bowed. She returned their bows and watched as they turned and left the room.

The other couples left, too, then the four she had shared Judgement with bowed their farewells. She stood alone in the room until the old man returned and walked up to her. For several moments they simply stood and gazed into each other's eyes. Finally, he spoke. "Judgement is. Joy is. Sorrow is. Ko is."

Myali nodded. "The Real Aspect is."

"Where does the child go when it is no more?" he asked.

"They will bury him."

"Where does the child go when it is no more?"

"The bright eyes will grow on his grave."

"Where does the child go when it is no more?"

"It is cool in here. I would like to sit in the sun."

"Ah," the old man sighed. "Would you share breakfast with me? It is simple."

"I am hungry. And hunger is simple."

"Good. Let us sit in the sun and eat."

A bowl of boiled cereal grain and a cup of scalding hot tea helped to warm her insides while the sun did its work from the outside. Gradually her mind calmed and became serene. She hadn't realized how deeply the child's death had affected her, how far down into the center of her being its last cry had echoed. Judgement is, she admitted. But . . .

As if he read her thought, the old man said, "For many months now all has been joy. That is the first sorrow we have had for some time."

"How much longer, Father? Will we always need it?"

"To stay what we are, to follow the Way set down by Nakamura and Jerome and Edwyr, Judgement must be. But every year there is less sorrow. The genes change quickly here on Kensho and we do our best to encourage the change." He looked at her questioningly and she nodded slightly, encouraging him to continue. The old man who tended the Judgement Hall had been a Keeper when younger and only in later life had entered the Way as a Seeker. The depth and breadth of his knowledge was well known.

He shifted slightly, settling into a more comfortable position. Once in place, he began to speak again, his voice shifting to the deep, compelling tone the Keepers used when passing along the Knowledge. "Under environmental stress, any population with sufficient phylogenetic pliability can move relatively swiftly from one mode of existence to another. Especially if the genotypes appropriate to the new mode can be assembled from the material already existing in the current gene pool. And if by chance the population possesses some kind of preadaptation—say, a behavioral pattern which is already functional in another context and applies in a new way to the new mode so it can act as the basis for a modified behavioral pattern—the changeover is even surer and swifter.

"Selection, however, isn't on a gene-by-gene basis. It's individuals that survive, and any single person contains on the order of thousands of genes. Furthermore, the kind of behavioral modifications that are likely to increase an individual's chance for survival are seldom the result of a single gene. More often than not, they derive from a combination of and interaction between several genes. Which is why the simple weeding

out of 'undesirable' alleles (even if they could be
identified) isn't enough. It's perfectly possible to have
all the right genes, but in the wrong combinations, and
end up with the opposite of the results you want.

"So it's the development and spread of a complex,
polygenetic structure that allows the population to shift
its behavioral pattern to the new mode and survive in
the new environment.

"Usually, the kind of stress we're talking about is
gradual and selection takes place over a long time span,
allowing many genotypes to survive alongside the fa-
vored ones. But occasionally stress is sudden, sharp,
and final. A population can crash then, only those
individuals surviving who by chance have the proper
polygenetic complex to meet the requirements of the
changed conditions. But even under such severe circumstances, it's possible for many alleles of the necessary genes to continue in the pool since minor variations
may survive almost as well as the optimal arrangement.
In addition, especially if the adaptation is in the form of
an altered social behavior, the benefits of the new
pattern may extend even to those who do not have the
complex, increasing the likelihood of their survival
despite that lack. In more intelligent species, there's
even the possibility that the pattern may be mimicked
or learned through experience. Although behavior
achieved that way can't be passed on genetically, the
individual survives and his genes continue in the pool,
perhaps even as a complex which makes his offspring
good at mimicking or learning."

The old man cocked his head to one side and gave
Myali a quick, apologetic smile. "I know all this seems
like a rather roundabout and complicated way of
answering your question. But it wasn't a simple question and there is no simple answer." He sighed.

"That's the trouble with the wholistic sciences. They lack the virtues of simplicity and elegance. But, no matter, I wander from your answer.

"When we came to Kensho and landed at First Touch, we suffered just such a sharp environmental stress. Yes, I imagine the death of ninety percent of the Pilgrims can be considered a 'sharp' stress! The unforeseen and unexpected presence of the Mushin, with their ability to feed on our emotions and drive us into the Madness, made a shift in our mode of existence necessary if we were to survive on this planet.

"Luckily, as Nakamura realized when he analyzed the data, the kind of stress the invisible mind leeches created was one for which a well-established preadaptation existed in a number of the Pilgrims. Put simply, those who made it through the first onslaught were predominantly those trained in some technique of mental and emotional control.

"But two problems immediately became apparent. First was the fact that barely ten percent of the original twenty thousand Pilgrims were left alive. The human population on Kensho had suffered a disastrous depletion. As a result, the number of effectives left to rebuild the race was precariously small. And the gene pool subsequently available for adaptation to the new situation was limited.

"Second, the preadaptation that had made the survival of even a fraction of the Pilgrims possible was not a genetically encoded one. It was a learned behavioral pattern, requiring years of study and effort. There was no way to pass it on to the next generation at conception.

"Nakamura understood that his first task was to provide the race with a breathing space, a chance to multiply our numbers to the point where we were no longer in danger of becoming extinct before we could adapt to the new environment. He saw there was no way we could maintain even a slightly sophisticated technological society, given our scant numbers, so he devised a simple agriculturally based system of semi-self-sufficient farmsteads with scattered trading-manufacturing centers located in the Brother-and Sisterhoods.

"But the most important, and brilliant, part of his plan was the creation of the Way of Passivity. At one stroke, he minimized the danger of the Mushin, secured the time we needed, and shaped the future direction our evolution would take. The Passivity provided a method of emotional control that allowed almost everyone to escape the full impact of the mind leeches. It gave us enough immunity to the Madness to assure we wouldn't be wiped out before we had a chance to increase our numbers.

"By gathering those best able to withstand the stress of the Mushin into the 'hoods, he provided the creatures with a sure and stable food source which they could control through the Grandfathers. The Madness still came, of course, even to those in the 'hoods. But it came in smaller doses which didn't threaten the existence of the whole race. Individual humans died, but humanity lived.

"The 'hoods served two other critical functions as well. First, since the vast majority of the Mushin tended to gather about the 'hoods as their food source, the rest of the countryside was relatively free of the creatures, making it safer for the breeding and raising of children. Minimum contact with the mind leeches during the younger years assured that more had a chance to survive until they could learn the defenses of the Passivity. It also meant that more survived to breeding age and that the gene pool suffered as little reduction as possible.

"The other function of the 'hoods was equally important. They served as testing grounds to establish the degree of Mushin immunity the Brothers and Sisters had achieved. Naturally, those with any level of genetically determined immunity fared better than those depending strictly on learned behavior. And although most of those in the 'hoods never bred, enough deserted to form families so that the superior polygenetic complexes were added back into the pool.

"Genetically, the whole scheme was optimal under the circumstances. By dividing the population into relatively isolated clusters centered about the 'hoods, Nakamura created a situation where substantial genetic drift could occur, thereby enhancing chances that the proper polygenetic complex would develop. Of course, the higher radiation level of Kensho's sun increased the rate of spontaneous mutation as well, and the system improved the possibilities that any positive mutations would have a chance to develop without being submerged in a massive gene pool, while at the same time canceling out detrimental mutations before they could spread."

The old man paused and looked musingly off into the distance for several moments. "I've often thought," he finally continued, "that Nakamura's koan was a hint to us that his entire plan had a genetic basis." He chuckled at Myali's look of surprise. "Oh, I know that's hardly an orthodox view, my dear. But it's not as foolish as it sounds at first hearing. The man was a bona fide genius. A high master, an admiral, and an accomplished scientist. A regular polymath. Let's see, his koan goes:

To be free, a man must follow the Way
that leads to the place where he dwelt
before he was born.

"What and where are we before we're born? We're a
genetic potential, half our future written in the chromo-
somes of the ova, half carried in a sperm. When they
meet, we become what we are to be, a genetic whole, a
realized possibility. Our freedom on Kensho lies there,
in the genes, where the changes are being made that will
fashion our being to fit our world. I like to think
Nakamura knew all that and left his koan to remind us
of that truth.

"Ah, but I drift from my purpose again. Excuse an
old man. Yes. The Judgement. I imagine by now its
purpose is clear. When Edwyr unleashed the Mushin to
stimulate the continued evolution of our race, he
switched from Nakamura's original survival stra-
tegy—based on rapid expansion of the population into the available habitat—to a new one, based on increased selection pressure focused on developing in-
nate immunity to the Mushin. Since Jerome's time, the
Great Way had degenerated into a learned behavioral
pattern. Many people didn't even bother to follow it any
longer because they felt secure from the threat of the
mind leeches who were tightly confined in the 'hoods in
the Home Valley. The polygenetic complex that con-
ferred immunity to the Mushin was in danger of becoming lost in the greatly expanded gene pool.

"The freeing of the Mushin caused many deaths. But
it also led to a rapid improvement in the race's adaptation to the environment. The Council of Twelve, led by
Edwyr, soon realized, though, that there was still a
major loophole in the system. The existence of the Way

allowed individuals without the proper polygenetic complex to survive the Mushin and live long enough to breed and perpetuate their genes in the pool.

"Since the Way was the basis for our whole civilization, it wasn't possible to totally disband it without causing utter chaos. Besides, we'd already suffered enough from the renewed attacks of the mind leeches. With great reluctance, the Judgement was instituted. Babies, at an age before any learned behavioral patterns could develop, were exposed to the Mushin. Those with the complex survived. Those without, died. When the survivors reached breeding age, *their* genes were the ones available.

"Our progress from that time on has been very rapid. Oh, the losses at the beginning were steep and tragic. But the failure rate dropped dramatically after the first generation. Now sorrow is much rarer than joy. And we face an almost unimaginable future. We are changing, my dear. And only the Gods know how much further we have to go."

The old man fell silent, his eyes quiet and hooded as his mind and attention turned inward. The two of them sat there, unspeaking, in companionable self-contemplation as the sun rose higher and higher, warming the day.

Eventually, Myali stirred and broke the stillness. "Thank you," she said softly as she saw his awareness focus outward once more. "Sometimes acceptance is easier if I know why." He nodded and smiled self-consciously at her praise.

She hesitated for a moment, then made a decision and spoke.

"Father, why did you leave the Keepers and come here to tend the Judgement Hall? You were brilliant in your field, one of the most respected on Kensho.

Why?''

The old man sighed. ''My daughter, I'm not completely sure. Ah, but then,'' he said, as if struck by a sudden realization, ''you have a special reason for asking, don't you? Excuse my forgetfulness. Yes, yes indeed. A special reason. For you have left your work and become a Wanderer. Am I correct?''

She bowed her head in silent admission.

''And you're probably not too sure why you've chosen as you have either.''

A slight nod indicated her affirmation.

''Then I suppose I have an obligation to share my ignorance with you. Indeed, yes, I do. Well. I was a population geneticist. A holistic science, filled with *it*'s, *and*'s, *or*'s, and *but*'s, quanticized to a degree— and to that degree both mimicking and mistaking Nature.

''I did my best to seek out the rules that reality runs by, to bind and hold the world so I might nudge it to useful ends.

''But one day I awoke to find myself like a man who has been standing in the cold outside a warm house, measuring and contemplating the door rather than knocking and asking to be let in. I sought to put a purpose on nature when its very essence is merely that it is. I searched out the names of things and took them for the things themselves and ended speaking into emptiness.

''Only a fool would try to live without names, but only a bigger fool would try to live by them alone. Suddenly I knew it was not enough to know something from outside. It wasn't enough to know how to manipulate a thing. So I sought the inside of reality, the experience of being.

''Now I seek the ground of my existence. I try to find

the place my perceptions come from, to pierce the veil of what seems to be and find what is. I search for knowing rather than knowledge.

"Someday I may succeed. And then I can return to the names and naming. But I will know them for what they are and will see, really *see*, the things they stand for.

"More than that I can't tell you. And I've only one small piece of advice to offer: The only way to find wisdom is to plumb the depths of your own ignorance." With that he rose, bowed to Myali, and disappeared back inside the Judgement Hall.

After a few moments, she stood and looked about. Which direction shall I take today? she wondered. She shrugged. Since my answer is as likely to lie in any one as the other, it makes no real difference. She began to walk toward the north.

For a while she followed the floor of the valley in which the Judgement Hall lay. Then, feeling a sudden need for wider horizons, she began to climb the valley wall to her left. The way was steep, but she finally made it, only to see more hills, steeper yet, stretching off to the edge of the sky.

She was about to begin moving again when a faint voice sounded in her mind. *Myali?*

Josh? she answered in surprise.

Yes, the voice became stronger. *We've been searching for you. You've run far.*

Not run, walked. I'm not escaping anything. I'm looking for it.

Whatever, came the reply. *But this isn't a personal call. It's taking five of us to hold the network open over this distance. Myali, the Way-Farer has called the Council to meeting at First Touch.*

The girl's mouth fell open in surprise. *Meeting?*

Ay, immediately. All twelve.

But, she began to protest, *I'm Wandering. I . . .*

Myali, this is your fiveyear on the Council, Wanderer or not.

Yes, but why a meeting?

Girl, they've arrived.

Stunned, she was incapable of even answering. Finally she pulled herself together enough to ask, *Truth?*

She felt the mental shrug. *As much as anything. They're behind the Slow Moon. They've got a ring of sensors around the planet and have even sent in low-flying photo-probes. You've got to come now, Myali. We have a lot of planning to do.*

God! she cried. *It'll take me a week to get there, even if I run most of the way!*

We're going to snatch you.

Dismay filled her mind. *Snatch me? That far?*

Josh chuckled. *There's a first time for everything. I think we can manage it. We're going to try it with the full Council in the network. Minus you, of course.*

And if you fail, I end up Between.

We won't fail. Ready?

Now? Right now?

Now, he answered. And she disappeared.

III

The young woman's sobbing had finally turned to mere sniffling and sighs. And not a moment too soon, thought Bishop Thwait as he patted her shoulder reassuringly. Damn, how I hate it when they snivel this way. What's done is done. And she'd have wailed a lot louder if she hadn't informed on him and had gotten herself mindwiped along with him! Weakness, weakness. How he despised it.

Pity, though. Dunn was one of my more promising acolytes. He sighed. Ah, well. Heresy is heresy, and improper use of the Names of Power is one of the worst sins possible! Besides, anyone foolish enough to commit a crime like that and then tell his mate about it obviously wasn't all that promising after all. No loss, really.

Not true, he corrected himself. What Dunn did requires a good deal of intelligence and imagination. Or just plain luck. His fault wasn't stupidity. It was weakness. An inability to bear the burden of his secret by himself. If the man had kept silent, simply continued in his crime, amassing more and more data, more and more Power, who knows what he might have accomplished? But weakness in any form is dangerous. And despite his intelligence and daring, it was the man's weakness that destroyed him. Remember that, Andrew, he told himself.

Yoko, the young woman, was looking up at him, a pleading look in her tear-damp eyes. "Worship," she barely whispered, "what will happen to him?"

"Child, I will talk to him to discover the nature and depth of his sin. Perhaps he will receive only a mild rebuke. I cannot say until I have spoken with him." Mindwipe at the very least. Total readjustment most likely. "But do not fret, my child. There is no blot of sin on your soul. You have done as the Power requires. For the good of yourself, for the race, and indeed even for his own good. Your errand was one of mercy and compassion for his soul." You betrayed your mate of seven years. You've doomed him, destroyed him. "Now go in peace, child. Stop by the infirmary and ask the Brother there to give you something to settle your nerves. And thank you for your service to the Power."

The young woman rose to go, then hesitated and suddenly knelt in front of the bishop with her head bowed. Her voice was heavy with misery as she mumbled, "Please, Worship. Your blessing before I go." With a mental sigh of exasperation, Andrew lifted both hands to make the Sign of the Circle over the kneeling woman's head. "May the Power guide and protect you," he intoned solemnly. "May the Word of the Power be ever on your lips and in your heart and your mind. Be with the Power and it shall be with you. In the name of the holy Kuvaz, so be it and so it shall be." Without looking up, Yoko rose and silently left the room.

For a moment, Bishop Thwait stood gazing at the floor where the young woman had knelt. Then he spun on his heel and moved swiftly to his comm-unit. He punched in Security's code, waited for a second or so as the computer put him through.

A face he knew well came on the screen. "Worship," the man said, no flicker of surprise or emotion showing on his harsh features. The inclination of the head in greeting was barely proper, but respectful enough to allow no valid grounds for complaint. Andrew smiled inwardly. Chandra had been his chief of security for some thirteen years now. They understood each other thoroughly.

"Acolyte Yoko Rabb is on her way to the infirmary. I want her sedated and probed. When you've completed that, we'll decide if any restructuring is necessary."

"Yes, Worship. What are we looking for?"

"Hmmmmmm. Seeds of heresy. She just informed on her mate."

"So. It will be done. And the mate?"

"Dunn Jameson, Acolyte Third, Drive Engineer."

"I know the man. Stubborn. Secretive. Few friends. Seldom participates voluntarily in activities. Spends inordinate amounts of time in hookup. We've been watching him."

"Bring him to me in the Room, Chandra. Whole, unharmed, but sedated. Use alpha seventeen."

"You're preparing for readjustment?"

"Possible, possible."

"It will be done, Worship." Chandra bowed, more deeply this time, a look of grim satisfaction flashing briefly across his features.

As Andrew blanked the screen, he chuckled. The man is a monster, he thought. But he so enjoys his work. The only problem is that sometimes his enthusiasm carries him away a bit. Hmmmm. Best have the girl checked later for conception. No sense in allowing any unauthorized pregnancies. Chandra does love his work. Especially *that* kind of work.

He looked longingly over at the piles of sensor readouts and probe photos that littered the floor around his favorite chair. Data was still pouring in, and although he knew the computer was totally capable of correlating and analyzing it without his help, he still felt compelled to go over everything personally. After all, he reasoned, there was always an outside chance that some low-order probability, something the computer would ordinarily rate as of minor importance, might actually be the key to the whole situation. And furthermore, the culture below, despite its Earthly origins, had been isolated from those origins and had been developing for many hundreds of years in response to an alien environment. So the possibility existed, however slight, that some of its aspects might also be alien and hence outside the parameters the computer was programmed to handle.

So far, he had to admit, aside from a strangely mixed technology, everything seemed pretty straightforward. But something continued to bother him about the whole setup. He had a nagging feeling he was missing some crucial piece of information. Call it a hunch, or overmeticulousness, or whatever, he knew he'd never rest easy until he'd resolved it. Besides, playing hunches and paying close attention to details was how he'd built his career. He wasn't about to change his style now.

Shrugging off his frustration with this inconvenient delay in his studies, he walked slowly over to his bookshelf. What must be must be, he thought. Best get it over and done with so I can get back to more important matters. He stood in front of the bookshelf for a few moments, gazing fondly at the twenty or so volumes sitting there in neat rows. My one luxury, he admitted. Lovely, lovely, but inefficient. Yet I enjoy their mass and feel. So much better than cubes and a reader. So different from hookup. He reached out and pulled one massive tome from its place. So much more impressive to conduct a questioning with the Book actually in your hands, he thought. Just the kind of thing that will unsettle Dunn. He hefted the weight of the book, savoring its solidity.

Turning, he moved to the door, palmed it open and stepped into the corridor. He paced along at a stately rate, nodding to the hurrying novices and acolytes who stopped dead in their tracks and bowed deeply as he passed. It was a relatively short walk to the Room, so he took his time.

The entrance to the Room was slightly wider than the average door, since many arrived there unconscious, on powered gurneys. But it was unremarkable in any other way. He paused briefly before it, then palmed it open and entered.

Lights came on as he stepped across the threshhold. The banks of instruments sprang to instant life and a subtle, almost imperceptible hum filled the air. Subsonics, he knew. To unsettle those being questioned. The training necessary to control the vague fear they engendered was given only to those high within the hierarchy.

He put the Book on a table which stood almost dead center in the room. He would sit behind it during the questioning. Directly in front of it, some five or six feet closer to the door, was the chair. Carefully he checked

it over, making sure that all the hookups were clean and
ready to be attached to his subject. Finally, he went
over to the instrument panels and did a routine check of
all the readouts. He punched Dunn's name and number
into the machine through a keyboard and then hit the
"Ready" button. Everything was set.

As he turned back toward the center of the room, he
heard a knock at the door. He moved quickly to take up
his position behind the table, then, settled, he called
out, "Enter." The door slid back and revealed
Chandra. Behind the security chief was Dunn, his face
slack, flanked by two guards.

"Ah, Dunn, my child," Bishop Thwait called out.
"Come in, come in. How nice of you to stop by."
Chandra grinned viciously as he ushered the young
acolyte to the chair and strapped him in. As he began to
attach the hookups, however, Thwait waved him away.
"Not yet, Chandra. The straps are enough for now. He
is quite immobile. Not to mention sedated. I want to
talk with him a while first. You may leave now." The
security chief scowled briefly, but bowed and then left
with the two guards.

Bishop Thwait sat silent for several moments after
the door closed, staring solemnly at Dunn. What makes
this one so different from all the rest? he wondered.
About six feet tall, he estimated, with broad shoulders
and a lean, athletic body. He obviously takes his man-
datory physical-conditioning workouts seriously. The
face was a strong one, square, solid, with a firm,
straight nose and a mouth even now set in a line of
stubborn determination. The eyes were an intriguing
shade of bluish green, the short, curly hair blond with
a slight reddish highlight. A rather handsome face, in a
rugged way, Andrew thought. But open, naked to the

world. He doubted the man could hide even the mildest
emotion. Happiness, grief, doubt, confidence, hate,
love—whatever he felt, he would announce to the
world through his expressions. I'll probably learn as
much by watching this one as by listening to him, he
decided. All the more reason to question him without
drugs.

Completing his appraisal, Andrew rose, came
around from behind the table, and stood squarely in
front of the young man, gazing down at him with a calm
and benign smile on his lips. "Ummmmmm," he began, "Chandra has been overly enthusiastic again, I
see. That is a nasty bruise on your forehead. Also, too
much sedation. You are so numb you cannot even
respond." He snapped his fingers and spoke to the air.
"Equipment." At his command, a small column suddenly rose up out of the floor near his right foot. The top
opened and inside lay several instruments, including a
number of syringes filled with pale amber and green
fluids. He picked one up and held it out for the other
man to see. "Old fashioned, isn't it? Imagine, using
syringes nowadays! But the symbology is so fraught
with horror that it appeals to me and is ideally suited for
questioning. Now this one is really nothing to be afraid
of. It will simply counteract the sedative you have been
given. So we can talk." He took a swift step to Dunn's
side, and jabbed the needle into the man's neck right by
the jugular vein. "Swifter this way, if harder on your
system," he muttered. "But then, no need to worry
about that if you are to be readjusted."

Watching Dunn carefully, he moved back to his chair
and sat down. The young man's eyes brightened
quickly and he shook his head as if trying to clear it.
With a start he looked around, fear growing in his gaze.

Finally, his eyes settled on Bishop Thwait and turned hard. "Worship," he muttered automatically.

"You know why you are here, Dunn?"

"I imagine because my loving mate informed on me," he answered, his voice heavy with anger at the betrayal.

"Then you realize there is no hope? No reason to hold back any of the truth?"

Dunn barked a harsh laugh. "The truth? What do you care about the truth?"

Andrew was startled by the young man's attitude. "My child," he said smoothly, "your immortal soul is in great peril."

Dunn laughed again, bitterness transforming his face. "You can have my 'immortal soul.' Just leave my mind alone."

"You have sinned," the bishop sighed. "You have misused the Names of Power, sought unauthorized data, diverted the privilege of hookup to your own ends. Surely you know the severity of what you have done. And the penalty." Dunn simply stared at him with open hostility. Andrew sighed. "No repentance. I suspected such would be the case."

Suddenly he changed his tone and manner. "You have your choice, Dunn. You can tell me about it willingly or I will rip it out of your mind with the machine," he snarled.

The young man didn't bat an eyelash. "You haven't asked me anything, yet. I've no reason not to answer. Try me."

"All right. What did you do? Exactly."

"I stumbled over three Names of Power that gave access to restricted areas of data. I think at least two of them are part of the Ten. But the third was the most interesting. He was a historian of the period just before the Readjustment.''

"Hmmmmmm,'' mused the Bishop, his right fingers stroking his chin. "I was unaware the computer on this scout contained such information. The names?''

Dunn responded with a feral grin. "Gone. After I told Yoko and saw her reaction, I realized what a stupid thing I'd done. I went into hookup and had them erased. If I can't have them, nobody else will either,'' he finished defiantly.

Thwait was quiet for several moments. His eyes studied the seated acolyte's features with a considering gaze. "Very clever, Dunn. I admire your resolution. I could use a man like you. Indeed I could.''

"Never. After what I discovered about the Power and how it rose to ascendancy, I'll never work for you of my own free will. Readjustment would be a blessing compared to that.''

"The establishment of the Power saved the Earth from destruction by the forces of regression.''

"Bullshit. The Power *is* the force of regression.''

"The Power is all the knowledge mankind has gathered in its lifetime, used wisely and carefully for betterment.''

Dunn laughed out loud. "How you twist words and shift meanings! The Power controls knowledge, keeps it under lock and key. It's stopped the gathering of any new knowledge and totally destroyed the scientific effort that created the knowledge in the first place. It lives off the wisdom of the past, has a stranglehold on the present, and by killing science, it kills the future.''

"Not so, my child. The science of the period before the Readjustment ruined our planet. It made Earth such a stinking waste that the Great Pilgrimage became a necessity. And even then, even surrounded by the evidence of its own destructiveness, it went on and on, seeking more and more power. We broke that power, for the good of all, to save the immortal soul of the human race. We have enough knowledge, more than we can possibly even digest. It will take centuries to sift through all of it and evaluate what is good and what is evil. In the meantime, the Power protects us from ourselves. It gives the people that part of the knowledge they need to make their lives better.''

''And what if the data you've got is wrong? What if you're off on false leads? What if further research would uncover a new theory, one that might make vast areas of current theory obsolete? What if—''

''Impossible,'' interrupted the Bishop. ''Unthinkable. Such a thing cannot happen.''

Dunn smiled slowly. ''If you believe that, really believe it, you're a fool.'' A flicker of anger passed across the other man's face and Dunn's smile widened. ''Final answers don't exist, Bishop. The most we can achieve is a momentary, state-of-the-art solution that's always open to revision and even replacement. The followers of Ptolemy once thought they had it all figured out, but Copernicus proved them wrong. Newton revised Aristotle and the whole Middle Ages. And a host of men revised Newton. Oh, the list goes on and on, around and around. Nothing is ever final, the results are always still coming in.

''Do you realize, Worship, that if Sarfatti and Aspect had blindly accepted Einstein's dictum that the speed of light was the limiting velocity in the universe, they never would have conceived or proven superluminal connectedness, and we wouldn't even be here? Tachyons never turned up, spinning black holes gave random destinations with no way back, and sub-light velocities simply took too long. Only the Sarfatti-Aspect effect gave us the key to the stars.'' He snorted derisively. ''If the Power actually believes it holds the final word, the ultimate answer, you're fools!''

''Your mind has been warped by what you have experienced in hookup, my child. You no longer see clearly. I greatly fear you are a hopeless heretic. But it is my holy duty to try and make you see the error of your way . . .''

''Before you blot out my way forever!'' shouted Dunn. ''Damn you, get on with it! Hook me up to your stinking machine and wipe my mind! Readjust me!'' His voice dropped to a husky growl. ''But know that by doing that you lose. You can't really change what I am and what I know. You can only destroy it and put something of your own making in its place. But it won't be *me*. It'll just be another shadow of yourself!''

''You lack faith, Dunn.''

Dunn shook his head. ''Rubbish,'' he said scornfully. ''Faith has nothing to do with it. Unless, of course, by faith you mean a simple feeling of confidence in the scientific method. But faith itself, faith as a way of viewing the world, as an expectation of reality, is irrelevant. Faith is no substitute for science. It doesn't contain within itself any method for self-contradiction, any mechanism which allows it to change and evolve through time. Faith, especially blind faith, simply is.

''Science, on the other hand, takes the form of a series of approximations, a fluid and constantly changing movement toward reality. But since reality is always greater and more complex than any approximation or model of it can ever be, science can never do more than reflect its outlines.''

''How little you understand the power of faith, my

child," Thwait interrupted smoothly. Before Dunn could protest again, he hurried on. "It was the betrayal of the faith mankind had placed in them that led to the downfall of the scientists of old. And it was the strength of mankind's faith in the Power that allowed it to triumph over that cancerous evil and save our race."

The bound man smiled cynically. "Oh, I don't doubt the 'power' of faith for one instant, Worship. I'm quite thoroughly aware of the important part it plays in justifying the whole system of beliefs that comprise the Power. After all, I've been a part of that system for years. At the beginning I even had faith myself.

"No, I'm not questioning the power of faith. What I'm questioning is its validity as the guide and control for science. I doubt . . ."

The bishop gave the table top a resounding swat with the flat of his hand. "You blaspheme!" he shouted angrily. "By doubting faith you call into question the very foundation, the motivating force, of the Power itself!"

Dunn cut right through the other man's objection, pressing home his argument. "Yes! I question the Power! By basing itself so completely on faith, the Power has become rigid, monolithic, and static. Oh, I admit it's got a lot of damned fine engineering triumphs to its credit. But since it refuses to allow science to continue the exploration of reality, sooner or later it's going to run out of steam and stagnation will set in. Hell, it already has in most areas of physics.

"The Power owns and controls science now. But it's a dead, useless thing you own. And no amount of blind faith will bring it back to life. Only freedom can revive it."

"When science was free, it destroyed," the bishop

said sternly. "It destroyed because it never developed a true perception of the nature of reality. It saw the universe as consisting of separate, independent objects interacting in ways determined by their individual natures. The interactions followed patterns that repeated themselves. And these patterns, when carefully observed, could be formulated as laws of nature which held true in all places at all times. Science set itself the task of discovering those laws.

"But such a view of reality had devastating consequences. It moved man from the center of creation to its periphery and made him just one more independent, separate object interacting with others in accordance with the laws of nature. Human nature, with all its beauty and ugliness, was reduced to a series of mechanical reactions to external stimuli. Our laughter and our tears, our very sense of wonder, became nothing more than sociobiological adaptations to environmental stress or more chemical equations. Morality was exposed as a set of cultural rules based on convenience or self-interest.

"What a terrifying place the universe became! A vast mechanism, it ticked away in time with the impersonal laws that drove it, but drove it to no purpose since it lacked any transcendental significance. Mankind found itself in an echoing emptiness, dancing to the tune of cold reason and the meaningless rhythm of the cosmic logic.

"And what was this mighty force, this vaunted science you cherish so much, based on? Human reason!" The bishop laughed harshly. "As if reason itself was not rooted just as deeply in the dark places of the soul as the most ferocious and irrational passions! As if the conscious, rational mind was the major driving force in human history! As if there was not vastly more to nature than the philosophers of reason ever dreamed of!

"Is it any wonder that a monstrosity like science could offer no ultimate answers and found itself incapable of developing its own restraining morality? And what else could prevail against its power? The old moralities, tied as they were to discredited views of reality, lay impotent beneath the burden of their own rigidity. The new 'isms,' proliferating to fill the vacuum in men's souls, were too shallow and limited to offer any real hope. And the ethics of expediency, so beloved by mankind's leaders, only brought on the disaster all the sooner.

"The result was inevitable. The people, finally realizing the dangers of an all-powerful, uncontrollable science and beginning to understand the dreadful price they were paying for the questionable benefits of science and technology, lost their faith in the good intentions of scientists and in the value of reason. Even within science itself there was a protest against the iron rule of reason. Quantum theory punched the standard view of reality full of holes. Men of foresight and wisdom like Heisenberg, Bohm, and Finkelstein tried to make their comrades see the error of their ways. But it was too late, too late. Ruin came down on all alike.

"If the Power had not come along when it did, my child, the destruction would have been complete. The Pilgrimage was not enough. It only spread the disease of the old science to new worlds. It took something greater than that, something basic.

"The Power provided that something. It gave us a new view of the universe, a new way of understanding reality. The holy Kuvaz himself revealed the truth to us with his perception that reality is circular and based essentially on faith." Solemnly he made the Sign of the Circle with the forefinger and thumb of his right hand. " 'We believe in reality because we have faith in our perceptions and we have faith in our perceptions because we believe in reality,' " he quoted in a heavy, ritualistic voice. "In truth we create the universe through our continuing act of faith and in turn are created by our own creation. We are not separate and independent from it. We are it.

"Nor does the power of faith stop there, my child. For it is the simple faith the people have in us that provides the strength we need to control science and transform it from the ravisher of our planet and our race into the gentle and beneficent Knowledge. It is the faith mankind gives us that allows us to give them peace and security and happiness in return.

"Yes, Dunn, faith is essential. And, I fear, faith is exactly what you so sorely lack."

Dunn had been staring at the floor throughout most of the bishop's monologue, slowly shaking his head back and forth. Now he raised his eyes to the other man's and gazed at him in stony silence for several moments. "Words," he finally muttered in a dispirited tone. "Words, words, words, words. And all of them so twisted and turned that even though they seem to mean something, they don't." His voice began to gather strength as he spoke. "You forget, Worship, I've read *other* histories, *other* viewpoints than the official one. Oh, I admit there's a grain of truth in almost everything you say. Sometimes more than a grain. But it's that very speck of truth, mixed in so cleverly with so many lies, that makes what you say all the more vicious and deadly.

"You speak of faith. But you really mean blind

obedience. You speak—" He stopped himself abruptly, snapped his mouth shut, and looked down with
sudden intensity at the straps that bound him to the
chair. His head swiveled toward the blinking lights and
glowing dials that covered the wall to his right. He
swallowed and shuddered involuntarily.

When he turned back to face the bishop there was a
slightly wild, frightened look in his eyes. A brittle
laugh tinged with hysteria broke unexpectedly from
somewhere deep inside him and ended just as suddenly
in a long, sobbing intake of breath. "I'm wasting my
time," he muttered in a dazed, slightly desperate voice.
"It doesn't make any difference what I say. You don't
give a damn. You aren't even really listening to me.
Your mind's already made up." His words came in
pinched bursts. "Four hundred years ago you people
decided you knew the Truth. Since then you haven't
heard a word anyone has said!" His voice cracked on
his last word and he broke off his monologue with a
violent shake of his head. Sweat beaded out on his
forehead and his chest heaved against the straps that
held him to the chair back as he sucked in panting gasps
of air.

Bishop Thwait gazed at him, his face devoid of
expression, his eyes hooded and cold. Gradually
Dunn's breathing returned to normal and he slumped
slightly, his eyes drifting down to stare listlessly at the
floor again.

Andrew let out a long, heavy sigh. His gaze fell to the
volume that lay on the table in front of him. Slowly he
reached out and drew it toward him. Lovingly he
stroked the cover, tracing the golden Sign of the Circle
embossed there. Then, at random, he opened the book.
Closing his eyes, he stabbed down at the exposed page
with his finger. He looked to where his finger pointed,

reading the passage it indicated to himself. Pleased, he nodded.

"Dunn," he said, staring with bright eyes at the bowed head of the man in the chair, "this, as you know, is the Book." He gestured toward the volume that lay open before him. "It is here you have your last appeal, your final hope. For the Book was written by the holy Kuvaz himself, the Readjuster, the Founder of the Power, Protector of Humanity. It is the Revealed Truth. If you harken to its word, your immortal soul may yet be saved." Dunn didn't stir or give any other indication that he even heard the Bishop. "Listen then to the word of Kuvaz and let its true meaning shine on your soul and bring you back to the Power." He cleared his throat and began to read:

> "And in those days there were others who
> said, 'Let us change men to fit the world
> rather than change the world to fit men.'
> And they went into the secret places of the
> cell and they manipulated it and gave birth
> to monsters. Then went the monsters out
> into the world and spread evil and sickness.
> The people cried out in their fear and an-
> guish. Yea, they raised their voices in sup-
> plication and said . . .

"Enough, enough," Dunn interrupted wearily without raising his head. "Let's cut the ritual crap. I'm not impressed any longer. Get on with it, Bishop. I'm weary to death of waiting to be found out, sick of hiding and sneaking, tired, tired, tired of the whole damn thing. There's no room for truth in the Power. No room for me. To hell with it all."

Andrew shut the Book with an annoyed snap. Why does he make me so angry? he wondered. He's right, though. There's no hope for him. Clearly a waste of my time. An unrepentant heretic if ever I saw one. Oh, there are ways, he thought, ways to bend and twist his mind until he crawls across the floor to kiss the hem of my robe. But they take time and right now there are more important things for me to attend to than readjusting scum like this. Total mindwipe is quicker and easier for the moment. Then, when things aren't quite so hectic, I'll spend a few days and do a complete readjustment. And create another willing servant for the Power.

He rose and walked over to Dunn. The man closed his downcast eyes as Andrew approached, a slight tic beginning to twitch in his right cheek. He's frightened, but determined not to break down and beg, the bishop noted. Great strength of character. Pity he's a heretic. With reverent slowness, he made the Sign of the Circle with both hands over the seated man's head.

Methodically, the bishop attached all the necessary wires to Dunn's body, then called for the helmet. It lowered smoothly down from the ceiling to fit precisely over the man's head. Checking everything a second time, Andrew finally stood back and snapped, "Isolation." Instantly a circle of shimmering light surrounded Dunn, making him hard to see. The bishop returned to his place at the table and spoke one final word. "Begin."

The dim figure in the chair suddenly stiffened and convulsed, straining violently against the straps. Its mouth snapped open in an unheard scream. The bishop watched for a second. Then, bored, he opened the Book and began to read.

An hour later Chandra returned with a gurney and roughly dumped the drooling, empty-eyed hulk that had been Dunn on it. As he wheeled it out the door, Bishop Thwait said, "Suspension, Chandra. Vault Seven. No sense in wasting even flawed material. We are a long way from home and replacements."

Chandra nodded and disappeared down the corridor.

IV

"No use grumbling, Myali." Josh chuckled as he walked along beside his sister. "You know we figured it had to happen sooner or later. Just dumb luck it took place during our lifetimes."

"And during my fiveyear," she replied sourly.

The young man laughed. He laughed a lot at the things Myali said and it annoyed her, brother or not. But then, she sighed to herself, Josh laughs a lot at everything. At times I'm convinced he perceives the whole universe as a colossal joke. Suddenly she remembered once when she'd accused him of exactly that view. He'd laughed then, too, loud and long, shaking his head in agreement. She'd gotten very angry and had asked if he thought even the Way was a joke. He'd nodded vigorously, declaring that a joke was probably as good a description of the Way as anything else. She hadn't known how to reply to that, so she'd simply stomped off in a huff. Josh had been teasing her ever since she could remember.

"Ah, little sister, so serious! Always so serious! Are

you angry because we interrupted your Wandering, because we snatched you all that way, or because the whole infinite universe seems to be conspiring against you?''

"I was just at Judgement," she responded darkly. "And there was sorrow. My sorrow."

His face changed and became solemn. "A tragedy, then. A reason for being serious. I apologize. But surely you don't hold the anguish to you still?''

"No," she admitted. "I'm sad, but only in a general way."

He brightened up instantly. "Then smile, Myali! Smile at the sun that shines after two days of rain."

Myali turned and glared at him, her fists on her hips. "Josh, there are times when I think you're the shallowest, silliest person on all Kensho! How in Jerome's name can you be so damned cheerful knowing they're hanging up there? Damn it, Josh, they're here! And we're not really ready for them yet. Not by several generations."

He shrugged. "Way-Farer doesn't seem too worried. Oh, all right, all right," he protested, holding up his hands to ward off the comment he saw forming on her lips. "Here. Is this better?" His features became serious, a slightly worried scowl settling on his forehead. He held the expression for several seconds, then cast a quick glance upwards toward where the Slow Moon hung, dimly shining in the daytime sky. "Are they gone yet?" he muttered in a loud stage whisper.

"Ohhhh, you're hopeless!" she responded, throwing up her hands in exasperation.

Josh grinned. "No, Myali. Not hopeless. Just trying to point out that all the worrying in the world won't make them go away or change the fact that they're here. No matter how you or I feel, worrying is irrelevant to the real problem. It just uses up mental and emotional energy and gets in the way of our ability to think and act clearly. We're not going to accomplish a damn thing by grumping and groaning. Especially not before we've even been to the meeting and gotten all the details.

"Remember what Edwyr said about a true warrior being someone who knew how to wait? That's the attitude we have to adopt now—waiting. The battle will come to us sooner or later in any case. In the meantime, best we keep our minds bright and ready rather than darkening and weakening them with useless worry. We might as well laugh and sing as we sharpen our swords.

"So smile, little sister. It's a beautiful day. And only the Gods know how many such we have left."

Chastened, she fell in beside him once again as they strode toward the mound that marked all that was left of the Basecamp at First Touch. As they walked, Josh stole a sideways glance at her. Little sister, how you've grown, he thought warmly. He remembered the tiny, freckled little imp that used to plague him with endless questions about everything in the world. "Why is there a sky? What holds the moons up? Why don't they bump into each other?"

Then there was the day he'd left to become a Seeker. He recalled her brave smile and the tear-filled eyes that ruined the pretense. She'd run off and hid somewhere until after he'd left.

That was all years ago. Myali was a woman now, tall, slender, and graceful. Her long brown hair framed a delicate, finely chiseled face. The eyes were a rich brown, the nose slightly arched and narrow, the mouth firm and decisive. Josh supposed she was beautiful. At least that's what other people told him. But to him, her real beauty lay deep inside in the special place that was her. There she was still that wide-eyed, wonder-struck child with a million questions and a bubbling love of life. And despite the serious facade she had built over the years, he knew that that was what really stood just behind that frown of concentration.

Yet for some time now he had glimpsed a shadow in her usually clear glance. It was a darkness he knew only too well, having experienced it himself many years ago while seeking the Way. Yes, he was sure it was the black demon Doubt that chilled Myali's mind and spirit and was the cause of her Wandering. They had never discussed it. One just didn't question another's desire to Wander. Every since Yolan had felt the need, shortly after the Re-Establishment, and had gone Wandering to re-establish her own contact with herself and her world, Wandering had become an accepted and honored institution on Kensho. Any time anyone had a personal problem that needed resolving, the life of a Wanderer offered the leisure, the privacy, and the time necessary to work it all out.

Whatever it is that's bothering Myali, Josh thought, it must be pretty basic. Because she's not the confident, constantly excited girl I've always known. He stole another quick glance. No. Now she's nearly a stranger. Hesitant, unsure, almost fearful, she always seems to be miles and miles away, lost somewhere in her own world, uncertain of the next step she has to take in this one. Ah, well, he sighed, the Master once said that uncertainty was midwife at the birth of all serious philosophical problems. And if I know Myali, what's bothering her is a "serious philosophical problem."

Serious philosophical problems indeed! he thought. Patent nonsense posing as profundity behind a mask of misused and misunderstood words! But real, he reminded himself, very real for those suffering from them. We no longer suffer very much from the Mushin. But our own confusions still plague us.

They arrived at the mound, the last of the Twelve. The others were standing about in loose groups, talking quietly, no evidence of any strain or concern in their manner. Gods! Myali thought, how can they all be so calm? My stomach's churning at the very idea of Them hanging up there, peering down at us, watching our every move.

The Way-Farer, Father Kadir, motioned them all to sit and form their circle. Myali searched the man's darkly handsome face for some indication of how things stood. His black eyes, hooked nose, and thin lips gave no hint of his inner state of mind. He seemed peaceful and regal. The slight graying at the temples of his black hair merely added to the stateliness of his appearance. Long, slender hands swam gracefully through the air as he spoke, following his words, pushing them, leading them, shaping their meanings into motions.

"Ah," he began once they were all seated, "welcome, my friends. Such lovely weather. There is a small patch of yellowfire blooming on the other side of the mound. You really must view it before leaving.

"But I know you have all come long distances for this meeting, so I will not delay. If you will join me in the network, it will facilitate the passage of background information to each of you. Our discussions, however, should be conducted verbally. Prepare."

Myali and the others settled themselves in half lotus

position, left leg folded over right, hands lying in the lap, palms up, left over right. The right hemisphere of the brain was the conduit for the network, so the left side of the body was given dominance in preparing for it. Myali began to calm her mind, controlling her breathing and bringing herself into a state of open receptivity.

Suddenly she felt the warm melting that indicated her Mind Brothers had merged with those carried by the others and had come under the control of the Way-Farer. Then, equally as suddenly, he was there, in her mind, sharing his knowledge with her. She experienced it exactly as he had, losing nothing of his feelings and insights. Wordless, beyond height or width or depth or time, it simply was part of her own being at the very instant of its arrival from elsewhere.

She blinked at the slight snap with which the universe returned to normal. It always surprised her, that shift that took place after a deep sharing. It was almost as if she had actually been somewhere else, Between perhaps, while the exchange was taking place. She shook her head. She had decided long ago that there was simply no understanding it. Best just to accept.

Father Kadir smiled at them. "Well?" he asked, arching one black eyebrow.

An older woman, from one of the PlainsLord clans by her dress, cleared her throat and said, "A great many objective data, Father. But nothing that really gives a clear indication of their intentions. Do they come as friends or as foes? If as friends . . . well, that creates a whole set of special problems we should discuss. But if they're here as enemies . . . Master, that scout vessel could do quite a bit of damage if they decided to be nasty, right?"

"I think we can safely assume that the primary mission of this ship is reconnaissance," the Way-Farer answered. "Technically, then, it doesn't represent any immediate physical threat in and of itself. Of course, it *is* a potential source of danger, since they could always decide that a major military action is required and call in a battle fleet, but I don't believe they're here to start a shooting war on their own.

"On the other hand," he continued, "even a scout ship has awesome weapons at its command. Once they discover that we have no defensive or offensive capabilities that even approach their own, they may decide they can handle the situation all by themselves. And indeed, as you suggested, that ship could do quite a bit of damage."

"The flagship has vastly more power than that scout," offered a tiny man with the long, delicate fingers of a master artisan. "Couldn't we reactivate it, blast the scout, and end the whole problem?"

The Way-Farer sighed. "I wish it were that easy. It's true that the flagship outguns the scout. But there's no way we'd be able to knock it out before it was able to send an emergency call. Then we'd have the whole fleet bursting in here, shooting as they came. No, the flagship is a last resort, a secret weapon to be unleashed only in utter desperation. If we use it against an enemy as small as the scout, we've wasted it."

A young Brother spoke up eagerly. "But couldn't we send a boarding party to the scout by way of the Mind Brothers? I mean, we snatch people here and there all the time. Couldn't we snatch them to the scout for a surprise attack? They wouldn't be expecting it."

Josh shook his head. "Sorry. Snatching doesn't work that way. You can only snatch to a location where the Brothers already are. Both ends of the journey have to be nailed down. It's more like pulling than pushing.

Gods only know what would happen to you if you just leapt off with no destination. No, unless we somehow managed to get some Mind Brothers on the scout, there's no way we could send a party up there.

"And even if we could, it wouldn't work for exactly the same reason activating the flagship won't work. No matter how much of a surprise we achieved, there'd still be plenty of time to send off a call for help."

"Obviously," a man in a Seeker's robe spoke up, "we should avoid doing anything to antagonize them until we've found some way to defend ourselves." A general rumble of agreement passed around the circle. "But does anybody have any idea of what will or will not make them angry?"

"Seems to me," began a very old man dressed in the simple clothes of a Home Valley 'steader, "best thing to do is ignore 'em. Let 'em make the first move. Right now all they're doin' is watchin'. No harm in that. But sooner or later, they're gonna act. You can bet on it. Seems to me, best thing to do is try an' figger out what they're gonna do then. Get ready for as many diff'rent possibilities as we can. Not much else we can do."

A heavy man dressed in the formal robes of a merchant vehemently shook his head in disagreement. "No, no. Look, we're all approaching this thing from the wrong angle. Sure this is a crisis. Hell, could mean the destruction of Kensho as we know it. Or just period.

"But damn it, it's more than that. It's an opportunity." The others stirred at that and looked toward the man, obviously wanting him to continue and explain himself more fully. He cast a quick glance at the Way-Farer. Then, receiving an encouraging nod, he began once more.

"Look, we've been here on this planet some fourteen

generations. Since Jerome's time, and especially since Edwyr and the Re-Establishment, we've spread over most of the world and developed a technology unlike anything Earth ever saw.

"Sure, I admit most of the *techniques* were borrowed from the home planet. It's the *system* that's different. It's the way technology relates to us and to our planet that's unique.

"Take energy, for example. We don't shred the landscape strip-mining coal. Or smear our waters and our skies with oil dragged up from the bowels of the earth. Instead we've found substitutes for all those things our ancestors ripped from the ground. We use wind turbines on the Plain; hydro power in the mountains; solar where the sun shines; geo where the crust is thin; tidal on the coasts . . . hell, it goes on and on.

"The key, though, is that we've learned to tailor our technology to fit our world rather than twisting and warping our world to fit some artifically determined technological requirements. We've kept things small, local, within the ability of ordinary individuals to grasp and comprehend. What industry we do have is limited in size and located where energy and raw materials are naturally available. We don't have any vast industrial complexes or huge population concentrations to service them. We've refused to let ourselves get caught up in that destructive spiral of uncontrolled technological growth and population explosion that characterized the home world—and destroyed it. We've kept human control for the sake of our humanity."

He looked proudly around the circle. Then a considering look clouded over his features and he became solemn. "Yeh. The only trouble is that the road we've picked doesn't ever lead off this planet. We'll create a

paradise here where we'll be able to live happily for
many, many generations. But there'll never be any way
out of that paradise, never be any way off Kensho.
Because, like it or not, starships take heavy industry.
Metal, lots of it, torn from the earth. Incredible
amounts of energy from sources we couldn't even develop without destroying our environment. Yeh,'' he
mused, ''it's almost like you have to ruin your world to
be able to leave it.''

With a deep sigh, he looked morosely down at the
ground. ''Living a happy, secure life is a wonderful
idea, something to really strive for.'' He paused as if
hesitating to make his next point. ''But,'' he finally
continued, almost in a whisper, ''I wonder if it's really
enough?''

He looked up then, fixing them all with a defiant
glare. ''Damn it, there's a hell of a lot of universe out
there,'' he declared with a broad sweep of his arm.
''But we'll never see it if we continue on our present
path.

''Oh, don't worry. I'm not some kind of modern day
Mitsuyama wanting to introduce heavy industry to
Kensho. But I can't help but think that some day, if we
don't have new horizons to walk toward and new skies
to watch at night, we'll stagnate and die.''

For several moments, it seemed as if he had stopped,
for he sat perfectly still, his eyes staring off into the
distance. But then he lifted his gaze up, up toward the
sky. When he spoke, his voice was husky with longing.
''But they've got them. Lots of them. Whole fleets of
them. Starships. More than they know what to do with.
Enough to take us anywhere we want to go.''

He drew himself up decisively. ''That's the opportunity I'm talking about. Those ships. Oh, I know
there's only one scout up there right now. But more are

coming, you can bet on it. A whole fleet, maybe, depending on what the scout reports back. When they arrive, they could be bringing us our death. But they could also be bringing us the universe!''

Stunned, they sat and stared at the heavy man until an elderly woman across the circle from Myali rubbed her eyes with the palms of her hand and muttered loud enough for everyone to hear, "Lovely, lovely. All we have to do is snatch a fleet of starships from their warlike owners. But how to do it? Especially since we're weaponless?''

"Not completely weaponless, Mother,'' murmured the Way-Farer. "Just unsure of our own power, unversed in the use of the weapons we hold.''

"Ah, yes,'' she replied, a sweet, innocent smile playing about her lips. "Of course. How foolish of me. We're armed like a young swordsman, new to his art, unsure of his techniques, but brave, oh so brave, and willing to face the Ronin to save his people.

"Bah!'' she snarled, her face suddenly changing and becoming hard. "Fools die that way! So do races. Snatch starships, indeed. 'Not weaponless,' nonsense! One false move and they'll bring a whole fleet, all right. To burn this planet and all our fine ideals into cinders!

"And that's the real danger of the path we've been on for so long. It's not just that we can't reach out and grab the universe, it's that we can't stop the universe from reaching out and grabbing us! Right now, after fourteen generations, after conquering a world and the Mushin, we're virtually back where we started . . . defenseless in the face of any enemy that threatens our very existence. We can't fight because we haven't prepared ourselves to fight any more than the Pilgrims were prepared to fight the mind leeches.''

Silence greeted her statements as their truth pierced

deep into everyone's mind. Josh was the first to recover and ask, "Then you'd have us give up?"

"Give up? Don't be a double fool, young man! Give up and they'll come marching in here and take over. Then you can kiss everything we've ever worked for goodbye. Oh, it'd be nice to believe they've changed. Grown wings and haloes or whatever. But they obviously haven't. They're out there hiding, sneaking and skulking around in a manner that's hardly angelic. Initial caution is to be understood. But they've been here long enough to know we pose no threat. If they had good intentions, they'd have shown themselves by now rather than lurking in the dark. Huh. They're just trying to decide how to go about the rape, not wondering whether to rape or not.

"No, giving up isn't the answer any more than trying to fight them on their own terms is. Stop thinking in black and white, all of you! Haven't you learned anything from Nakamura's example? He faced an impossible choice of alternatives, just as we do. And rather than chosing either one, he found a totally unexpected way out." Her face grew crafty. "We have to start thinking like Nakamura. Things are happening. The universe is flowing. The key is to do as he did and find how it's flowing so we can go with it to achieve *our* purpose through *its* effort. There are an infinite number of possibilities from this point on, not just two! How we choose to act will open some options, close others. We need to scheme and plan to make sure we pick the right ones to reach our goal."

"Are you proposing a seeing?" Myali asked in wonder.

"Damn right I am. Oh, I know how dangerous that is. Don't bother with scary tales about shifting possibility lines and observers affecting reality. It's all irrelevant in this case. We don't have any choice. It's a seeing, or we stumble on and bump right into disaster."

"A seeing is no guarantee of success, Mother Illa. It only shows the multiple probabilities. Everything is always shrouded in the mists of uncertainty," the Way-Farer warned solemnly.

"Bah," she retorted. "Don't forget who you're talking to, Robert. I know as well as you do what's involved in a seeing. Remember: A man with only one eye sees better than a man with none. So, vague and uncertain as it may be, a plan based on seeing is vastly superior to one based on the blind hope everything will turn out happily because the universe loves us."

The Way-Farer looked at each of them in turn, his gaze moving clockwise around the circle. "Do we all agree with Mother Illa, then? Do we all feel a seeing is called for?" Silent acquiescence greeted his questioning glance. He sighed. "Ah, well, then. A seeing. I remind you all how personally dangerous it can be. Once confronted with the multiple universes that a seeing reveals, many minds are incapable of finding their way back home to their own probability line again. Of course, those of us who are more adept at the technique will lead and guard you, but the peril still exists. No one is compelled to join, although admittedly, the more who do, the stronger the seeing will be."

Myali glanced at the others out of the sides of her eyes. Everyone seemed to be stolidly accepting the idea of going ahead with it! No one even hinted at a desire to step out of the circle. Are they all fools? she wondered. People die in seeings. That's why they're restricted, even on an individual basis. And this, this was a mas-

sive one—one that had to explore the possible futures of
the whole planet!

Her eyes flashed around the circle once more, wildly
hoping to see someone else who doubted and feared as
she did. If even one of them felt it, she knew she would
stand and leave. Even one!

But the rest appeared calm, some of them already
beginning the quieting exercise that preceded any group
effort. Gods, she thought. I've got to go through with it,
then. But my mind is so confused, so unsure. How will
I ever find my way back when I'm not any too certain
where I'm starting from?

Myali felt someone's eyes on her. Looking across the
circle, she saw that Mother Illa was watching her intently. "Young woman," she said sharply, "are you
sure you're really up to this? You're a Wanderer, you
know, and that indicates a certain unsettling of the
mind."

"Yes, Myali," Josh added. "Maybe you should sit
this out."

The suggestion from others, especially her big
brother, that she might not be fit enough to participate
in the seeing, stiffened her resolve. How dare they? she
thought. Haughtily, she returned Mother Illa's stare. "I
can handle it," she said in an icy tone.

"Damn stubborn," muttered the old woman. Then
her face softened and she smiled. "Damn stubborn, but
damn brave, too. You'll do, my dear. But I'll keep my
eye on you just the same."

Father Kadir nodded to them all. "Thank you. I think
we might as well begin." He settled himself firmly into
full lotus, left leg over right, hands palm upward in his
lap, left fingers over right, thumb tips touching. The

others followed his example, closed their eyes, and began rhythmic breathing.

Myali felt a sudden yearning for one last look at the world before closing her eyes. Surprised by the urgency of her own need, she was almost overwhelmed by the flood of sensations that poured through her hungry senses. There was so much beauty! The sun blazed like a vast smile in a sky whose blue intensity was only heightened by the occasional fluffs of cloud that bumbled across it. A warm breeze played light-fingered games with her hair and snuggled joyfully in the loose folds of her robe. The grass around her gave a blue-green shout of sheer exuberance and then crept softly off to cover the hills. Josh is right, she realized with genuine delight. How could I have missed it? It *is* a beautiful day!

With a sigh of reluctance, she began to disengage her attention from the outside, refocusing it internally. Duty, she thought. I had a chance to avoid it. Wisely or not, I made my choice.

Her eyes lightly closed, she began breathing deeply, letting her body and mind relax. In, out, in, out, her breath traveled. She allowed her attention to follow it, in, out. Gradually she became aware that she was following the breath of the others, in, out, matching and merging with the common rhythm.

Slowly the shared rhythm passed on beyond mere breath and became the beat of her whole body, brought into harmony with that of those seated in the circle with her. Her heart beat with theirs, her blood surged as theirs surged, until at last there was no her or them, but only One that was All.

Unbidden, the words of a chant suffused her whole

being and vibrated throughtout her body-mind, once
more changing the pattern and meter of her existence.

> Moons, moons, shining down on waters,
> waters moving slowly, moons moving
> slowly,
> yet being still.
> Still the waters, still the moons.
> Movement, strife, all longing is but
> reflection, passing to stillness
> when the mind is calmed.

Quiet stilling, then slowing of all rhythms, all motion. Almost, almost movement ceased. Then began
again in a new pace, one not belonging to any of them,
or even to all of them, but coming from someplace
Beyond. The words of a new chant washed across her
awareness.

> Flowing, flowing, timelike flowing
> through the spacelike frame of being,
> flowing to the stable center,
> to the place of ceaseless stillness,
> to the moveless heart of motion,
> inward, inward to the center,
> inward to unbinding chaos,
> release of meaning, form, existence . . .

Time slowed, stopped. Space collapsed. The two
melted into one, then compressed, all points becoming
a single event.

In a blinding explosion, possibility suddenly surged
outward, spreading all the richness of spacetime out
and out and out.

It was like looking down from a height on a series of

transparent planes, infinite in number, each emerging from another and then flowing on to branch yet again and again. From Now they rippled off in all directions, filling the whole volume of time, right to the dark horizon of the future. On some of them, Kensho bloomed in the distance, a bright ball of angry flame. In others, the sun that warmed the planet bulged and burst in a torrent of bright destruction. Here and there, the planet charred and died. Or part of it did. Or it remained green. Or iced over. Or . . . or . . . or . . . or . . .

And then she saw a path, twisting out through the planes from one to another, down, over, around, right , left. Others appeared. Infinitely others. They tugged at her awareness, pulled at her being, whispering things and futures she had never guessed at. From the height she felt herself slipping, beginning to fall down and through those endless possibilities. Terror seized her and she struggled, flailing about wildly for something to hold on to. But as soon as she grasped anything, it melted and flowed away. She screamed. And sensed a presence, calm, firm, strong. Hysterically, she made a grab for it. It held. With a gigantic effort she hauled herself back up. Then she felt the thing she clung to slipping, slipping, pulled off balance by her tugging. Bracing herself, she heaved, trying desperately to keep it from falling. Straining with all her might, she simply wasn't strong enough. She felt a rending and stumbled back, clutching a part of the thing to her while the rest wailed off into vastness.

With a snap, she found herself back on the grass at Basecamp, weeping hysterically. Several others were sobbing as well. A few sat dazedly, holding their heads in trembling hands. Two lay sprawled in twisted positions.

The Way-Farer, his face gray with fatigue and pain, rose and went to one of the figures that lay so quietly in the afternoon sun. He bent down and placed his head against the chest. Myali wiped the streaming tears from her eyes and tried to make out who it was. She knew, though, in a way she couldn't explain. As he leaned back, his face more drawn than ever, dark eyes heavy with grief, she saw the ashen profile of Mother Illa. "Dead," he said simply. As he spoke, the other prone body stirred. "Alive," he declared with equal simplicity, but with a whole different world of meaning.

Father Kadir got shakily to his feet, looking down at them from what seemed an incredible height. "We have seen," he said softly. "We have seen and paid the price.

"Now we must continue to pay the price. For the only hope for Kensho is one that requires great sacrifice on the part of a few so that many may live. And even then, the outcome is not sure. So many possibilities," he muttered to himself, "So many possibilities."

"We must try," Josh croaked, his voice quivering with exhaustion. "We must try."

The Way-Farer nodded. "And who will carry the burden?"

Myali looked groggily up at him, her eyes, still brimming with tears, drooping with sudden fatigue. He was looking directly at her as he asked the question.

Suddenly she knew the answer, knew to the very depths of her being who would carry the burden of Kensho. And oddly, the knowing, rather than oppressing her, made her feel free for the first time in years. She understood how slim the chances for success were. And how slight the odds in favor of personal survival. But something of Mother Illa's iron will, perhaps the fragment she had managed to grasp as the rest had slipped away, sustained and strengthened her.

She held her head up proudly and said firmly, "I will, Father."

V

"Damn it," Admiral Yamada complained, "it just doesn't make sense!"

"I agree, Thomas, and that is precisely what worries me." Bishop Thwait was pacing back and forth along the table in the briefing room. "But you have seen the data and the close-up photos. That is a whole different type of civilization down there. One we do not even have a classification for. They obviously use metals, but only in limited quantities. They have a multiplicity of energy resources, yet do not even bother to exploit some of the most obvious ones. Industry is present, but scattered in basically inefficient units. Most astonishing of all, however, is the total lack of any form of long-distance communications network or transportation system." He shook his head. "It is a world of glaring contradictions, Thomas, and I do not like the feel of it."

Thomas slapped the table with his hand. "To hell with all that 'socioeconomic' crap! They can have all the contradictions they want in their stinking society.

What worries me is there's not one indication of any
military complex anywhere on the whole damn planet.
Nothing!''

He spun his chair around to glare at the pacing
bishop. ''Damn it, that's not natural, Andrew! Hell,
there aren't even any population complexes. They're
just spread out all over the place like a peaceful herd of
grazing cows or something. But they aren't cows, damn
it! They're people. And people fight and have armies
and military bases and . . . and . . . Shit! It just isn't
natural!''

Bishop Thwait stopped pacing and gazed thoughtfully at the seated man. ''It would make sense if all their
defensive and offensive systems were located off-
planet. If the systems were so powerful that their very
presence on the planet would endanger the lives of the
inhabitants.''

''Nice idea,'' Thomas replied sarcastically, ''but it
doesn't pan out. Most of the probes we sent around the
system have reported back by now and there's no sign
of anything.'' For a moment he paused, considering,
then slapped the table again and stood, his mind made
up. ''Andrew, contradictions or not, there's only one
obvious answer. The bastards are a Class Three or less.
We can go in and take over ourselves. No need to even
call in the fleet. I suggest we land a full company of
marines, secure a beachhead, and impose our rule,
soonest.''

Andrew looked pensive. ''Hmmmmm. That would
be a nice little feather in your cap, wouldn't it, Thomas?
Capturing a whole planet single-handedly? Excellent
for the record.'' He held up his hand to forestall the
other man's protest. ''But on the other hand, suppose
your little company of marines were to go planetside
and be wiped out? How would you respond? Fire on the

planet from space? Burn it? Call in the fleet and create another Quarnon?''

"Damn it,'' interrupted the admiral with an angry shout, "who in the hell do you think—''

"I think I am the representative of the Power aboard this scout, that is who I think I am!'' the bishop interrupted coldly. "And I will permit no unnecessary or potentially dangerous military action.''

"Dangerous? Tell me how in the hell a military action against an unarmed planet can be dangerous?''

"Because I do not believe for one moment that that planet is unarmed! Thomas, Nakamura was a military man, an admiral. Do you think he wouldn't have made some provisions for the defense of his colony? All right, I agree things look amazingly calm down there right now. But that could be the result of the fact that they feel secure because they have a very adequate defensive system we are not aware of yet.

"Now I know we have made a thorough search of every hiding place we can think of. But what we are looking for may just be hidden in some place we haven't thought of. And I would hate to discover that with a company of marines down-planet.

"Thomas, believe me, I want to bring this planet to the Power without having to resort to the fleet as much as you do. It certainly would not hurt my career any more than it would yours.

"But at the same time, attempting that is putting both our futures out on a limb unless we are damn sure we will succeed. I do not wish to have to call the fleet in here to rescue us.''

Somewhat mollified, the admiral sat back in his chair with a grunt. "Huh. So what are you proposing, then? It better be good. I'm getting bored waiting around for some action.''

Thwait sighed. "There will be action, Thomas. I can assure you of that. But it will be at our time and of our making. First, I propose we send a squad of your men and mine to the flagship to secure it. I do not like it sitting out there, dead or not. With our own crew aboard, we would control it and be rid of one more potential threat.

"Second, I think we should send a reconnaissance mission on-planet to gather more information and probe the enemy more thoroughly than is possible from out here. This should be an on-ground mission, not simply fly-overs. That way it would be both less conspicuous and less provocative."

Yamada eyed the bishop coldly. "Who did you intend to send down on this suicide mission? That's what it's likely to be, you know."

"I was thinking of a team of your men and mine, say three of each."

The admiral shook his head. "No. I won't risk any of my men that way. They'd have to be adjusted, I assume? That's what I thought. I have few enough effectives as it is. Can't afford to destroy any of them that way. Sorry, Andrew, you'll have to use up your own men."

The bishop swore silently. Thomas is such a fool, he cursed. The farthest he can see beyond the end of his nose is to the end of the muzzle of his gun. Of course the adjustment necessary for such a mission would destroy a few men's minds. But how many more might be destroyed, body as well as mind, if we make a false move and get engaged in a battle? Well, then, he thought, if Thomas refuses to cooperate, that fact will be noted in my reports. And if things turn out as I think they will, such obstinacy will reflect as poorly on him as my handling of it will reflect well on me. Thomas,

Thomas, you seal your own fate. Out loud he asked, "I take that as an official refusal?"

"Take it any way you want, damn it!" the other man said, his temper running short. "If you want to diddle around with a damn spy mission on a planet that obviously couldn't defend itself from a stinking shuttle, go right ahead! But let me tell you this for the record, too, Andrew. I'm getting a company of marines ready to go down-planet. And I'm giving you exactly one week standard to show me why I shouldn't send them down. If you can't make one hell of a good case, I'm going to take this planet myself and shed as much goddamn blood as I can while doing it!" Flinging his chair back to crash against the wall, he rose and stomped from the room without a backward glance.

As soon as he was sure the man was actually gone, Bishop Thwait moved swiftly to the comm-unit and punched in Chandra's code. As the man's face appeared and he bowed, Andrew asked, "Did you get all of that down?" Chandra nodded. "Everything, Worship." "Good, good," the bishop murmured, rubbing his thin hands together. "Now come up here right away. I will want your advice on planning the on-planet spy mission. No, on second thought, meet me in my quarters instead." He slapped the disconnect button without waiting for the other's response or bow.

Turning, he went to the door, palmed it open, and strode into the corridor. It was officially nighttime in this section of the ship, so the corridor lights were low and there was very little traffic. During the entire walk back to his own quarters, he saw only one other person, a crew member with a clipboard and a worried expression. He nodded at the man in response to his formal bow.

Chandra was waiting at his door when he got there.

Ah, Chandra, he thought. So efficient, so loyal. Thirteen years of service. In a way, though, that worried him a little. The man knew so much. Perhaps too much. Might it not be wise to replace him?

Thwait led the way into his quarters, motioning Chandra to a chair. "Would you care for some coffee?" he asked. "The real thing, not the ersatz. Of course, it is not from Earth. Became impossible to grow it there years ago. But this is a hybrid that seems to thrive on Barnard Two. Very like the original, I am told." While he talked, he moved to a console where he punched out his request. After a moment, a panel slid up, revealing two steaming cups of a brownish-black beverage. Thomas lifted them out and handed one to Chandra, taking the other over to his favorite chair and settling down.

After a few appreciative sips, he began. "Yes, well, to business. A spy mission to the planet. Have we three we can spare?"

"Worship, I honestly don't think so. Since suspending Dunn, we've had to do a lot of shifting of workloads. People are still acclimating and haven't made the adjustment yet. I fear pulling three more out would cause a major disruption."

"Hmmmmmmm. Yes. But your mention of Dunn gives me an idea. He is already wiped clean, so an adjustment would be easy on him. No loss at all, really. Let's see, we would have to give him an overlay of a spy profile. That would be easy enough.

"The problem, though, would be the rest of his personality. A profile is hardly adequate to create a functioning human being. And of course Dunn does not have a personality any longer. A conundrum, to be sure. We could always do a transfer with someone else, but that would take someone out of action for a good week. Hmmmmmmm.''

For several moments, Bishop Thwait sat quietly, his fingers gently stroking his lower face as he concentrated. Suddenly his eyes brightened and he sat upright. "Yes! That's it!" he cried. "Perfect! A bit unorthodox, but it solves several problems at once!"

He stood and began pacing about the room. "Chandra," he began, "this is ultra secret. No one aboard ship must know of this except you and me. I will leave the details to you, and they are considerable, including stealing a shuttle without anyone knowing about it. But I am sure you will manage.

"Now. I am going to send you and one other man of your choice down-planet. Wipe the other man when you get back, by the way. There you will kidnap a native, a young one about Dunn's age. Sex is immaterial. But do it so no one on the planet sees you. Pick some isolated area, some isolated individual. Bring them back here, again letting no one aboard ship see you or be aware of what is going on. We might use the placing of a crew on the flagship as a cover, by the way.

"So. Bring the kidnapped person to the Room. I will have Dunn ready. We will do a transfer there. That way Dunn will get a basic personality, one suited to the planet itself. And he will also get the language rather than having to hole up for a while on-planet to learn it.''

The bishop rubbed his hands together gleefully. "Neat. Yes, very neat. You see, Chandra, that way we even gain a subject to probe for information we could not get any other way! We can learn more from peeling off the layers of a native's mind than by all the sensor probes in the galaxy. Data! We will have some good, useful data. And it will be subjective, psychological information rather than a bunch of electromagnetic rubbish. We will find out how their minds work, Chandra. And once we know that, we will have the key to defeating them!''

He came back to his chair and sat down again with a sigh. ''A few details. The transmitter we implant in the spy must vary slightly from standard. I want a direct, leak-proof, coded channel paired to my personal receiver. All information will be sent to me first, for editing, before it is sent out on the general channel. Of course, no one is to know of this.

''Second, I want a mind scrambler implanted as well as the usual belly bomb. Hook them both up to the computer and my voice command. Cue word is to be, hmmmmm, let's see . . . ah, yes, 'Einstein.' Yes, very suitable for Dunn, I think.

''Is everything clear, Chandra? Yes? Good. Then get to it. I want the down-planet mission arranged and ready to go simultaneously with the flagship takeover mission. Say in ten standards.'' The bishop arose and escorted Chandra to the door. The man bowed and left.

Humming in a pleased way, Andrew Thwait walked slowly over to his bookcase and pulled down his copy of the Book. At random he opened it and began to read aloud:

> ''Yea, they knew more of the heart
> of the atom than they knew of the
> heart of themselves. They knew not
> themselves, nor the evil that lurked
> within them. Yet in their pride
> they thought they knew all.''

He paused, musing. Chandra, he thought. Perhaps it is time to be rid of the man and all he knows. Especially

if this whole affair goes well. Should some little acci-
dent happen to Chandra, there would be no one else to
take any credit at all. In fact, he calculated, the loss of
my closest lieutenant will make any victory much more
clearly mine. Against all sorts of odds. Hmmmmmm.
Yes. But not quite yet. No, Chandra is still too useful to
dispose of yet. Perhaps after the kidnapping and place-
ment of the spy.

Andrew chuckled to himself as he thought over his
plan once more. Perfect. And Chandra would be an
enthusiastic participant, he knew. Especially if the kidnapped native was a female! Or even a male, for that
matter. Chandra didn't seem to be particular, just lust-
ful. And brutal. In a way he pitied the poor captive. It
wouldn't be any fun being caught by Chandra. Oh, not
that any major or permanent damage would be done.
Except maybe to the ego or self-esteem. But that was
really all to the best, since a weakened ego made probing that much easier. Yes, yes, it all fit together quite
nicely.

In the admiral's quarters, Thomas Yamada was
ready to turn in when a call came over his comm-unit.
He was about to slap the copy button when he noticed
the call numbers. They were a special code, known
only to himself and one other person aboard the scout.
He hit the scramble key and sat down to receive the
man's report.

A few moments later, as he hit the wipe-and-clear
key, his mind was swirling. "So," he muttered, "you
bastard, you scheming bastard!" Getting up from the
comm-unit, he walked out into the front sitting room,
over to the bar, and poured himself a stiff whiskey. He
took a healthy gulp, then went and sat in his easy chair.
Sipping slowly, he began to think.

So Thwait's going to kidnap a native, eh? Then do a transfer to that heretic he'd wiped the other day and send the man down as a spy. Grudgingly, he had to admit the plan was clever. And the draining of the native afterward, plus the little trick with the double transmitter, was a beautiful twist. Just the kind of thing that would give the bishop the edge on information and allow him to control the plan for contact and subjugation of the planet. Damn, but Andrew's devious, he cursed.

A sudden idea hit him. Devious? God! What if . . .? He almost hesitated to think it. But what if his spy was really a double agent, working for the bishop? Oh, he knew the man worked for the bishop, had for thirteen years, but what if this whole thing was a ploy to feed him phony information? Shit! Thwait was capable of it, no doubt about it.

Come to that, what *had* motivated Chandra to seek him out and offer to be *his* double agent against the bishop? Did the man really desire a bishop's robes as much as he appeared to? Or was it all a front to sucker him in?

In a way, of course, it made sense. Thwait certainly isn't about to let Chandra move up in the hierarchy, he thought. Not with all that the man knows about him! So if Chandra ever wants to go any higher, it will have to be over Thwait's dead body. And apparently that's what he wants. Enough to come to me and offer his services. Knowing that if he is useful enough to me, I can pull enough strings to get him raised up to take Thwait's place.

Damn, he admitted, I'm just not up to all these twisted double- and triple-crosses. Give me a clean, straightforward battle any day!

Then he chuckled out loud. "But for an old soldier you did a pretty good job of acting today, my boy," he congratulated himself. He raised his glass in salute and took another slug of the whiskey. Yeh, he reminded himself, but it's easy for me to play the hotheaded soldier, champing at the bit, breathing fire and destruction. Shit, that's typecasting if such a thing ever existed!

But he'd fooled Andrew with it. Suckered him right in. Hell, he thought, I wouldn't send a goddamned company of marines down onto that stinking planet if you paid me! Goddamn deathtrap, that's what it probably is. Nobody, but nobody is ever that defenseless. Gotta be a trick. But nobody ever accused the Fighting Admiral of cowardice or lack of enthusiasm before. And after my little performance today, they sure won't in the future. Getting Andrew to overrule me that way. Ha! Took me off the hook and put him on it!

So now he's got his chance to look for whatever danger is lurking down there. If he finds any, well and good. I look brave, but not foolish. If he doesn't, well and better. Because then I prove right all along. Whatever happens, the key thing is to stay on top of it. Always be one step ahead of Andrew. Or at least keep up with him. That's why the Committee sent me, he remembered. They figured I was the only one up to taking on the formidable Bishop Thwait.

To embarrass or outdo Thwait was to embarrass or outdo the Power. And that was the purpose of the Committee. To chip away, bit by bit at the Power. To make it look bad. To weaken it. And then, at the right moment . . .

He drained his glass, rose, and carried the empty back to the bar. Placing it in the cleaning slot, he turned, stretched, and shuffled off to his bedroom, ready now to turn in. Got to be careful with Chandra, he decided. Check everything he says, weigh it against what really happens. Maybe he's telling the truth, maybe he isn't. But even false information can be useful if I know it's false.

He undressed slowly, whistling tunelessly the whole time, his mind idling and relaxed. Finally he lay down, pulled the sheet and blanket over himself, and turned out the light.

Just before dropping off to sleep he murmured, "Andrew, Andrew. You're not the only one who knows how to scheme."

VI

The mid-morning sky arched blueness from horizon to horizon without so much as a puff of white to mar it. Yesterday, with all its pains and doubts, had been washed into the past by a good night's sleep. Today Myali was meeting with the Way-Farer to prepare herself for the new pains and doubts that stretched off into tomorrow and tomorrow and tomorrow.

So far, the two of them had just sat on the top of the hill and let the beauty and peace of the morning slip softly through their minds. But now Myali felt the growing pressures of unanswered questions and knew she would have to speak. She quietly cleared her throat and saw by Father Kadir's minute nod that he was waiting for her to begin.

Although she had planned to be less direct, her first question came tumbling out in urgent starkness. "Father, Mother Illa died to save me. Why?"

The Way-Farer shrugged. "Perhaps because she saw even more clearly than I and knew you hold the future in you. Perhaps because she loved you. Perhaps because

she was tired of living and it was a beautiful day to die.
Perhaps because she knew of no other way to start the
fate of Kensho on its proper path.

"Myali, Mother Illa was a complex and wonderful
person—just like everyone else I've ever met. I cherish
her memory and know that her existence in the universe
has sent waves of meaning rippling off in all directions.
And perhaps her passing beyond our existence has set in
motion the biggest wave of all.

"You, my dear, have been chosen to ride the crest of
that wave."

"But why, Father? Why me? Of all the people I
know, I can't imagine anyone less suited for the task.
Josh, yes. He's calm and deep in the Way. Or a
thousand thousand others like him, men and woman
who have realized the dreams of Nakamura, Jerome,
Edwyr, and Yolan. The true Homo Kensho!"

Father Kadir cocked his head to one side and raised a
questioning eyebrow. "Are you not one of us, Myali?"

A look of deep anguish welled up in her eyes and she
was forced to drop her gaze from his face to the ground.
"I . . . I . . . don't know," she whispered, her voice
husky with confusion and pain. "I'm not sure."

"But you passed Judgement, my dear. And carry the
Mind Brothers. And, if I remember correctly, are a
Master in your own right in both the Way of the Fist and
the Soft Way."

"Yes," she acknowledged despondently. "Yes, of
course." She looked up, her gaze suddenly sharp, her
voice tight and tense. "But those are just . . . just
'things' I do, Father. I know genetically I'm Homo
Kensho. But . . . but . . . I . . .

"Father, I know all the words of the koans. I've
solved every one of them. I know the ideas of the Way,

the practices, the disciplines. I *know* them. But I don't *feel* them. Not here, not deep down inside me.

"Gods! At times I . . . I think I'm just an actor, a mime, going through the motions, faking it, mouthing words that have no real meaning for me. I find myself walking the Way like I would a path in the woods. To get from here to there. Not because I want to, but only because I know I'm supposed to.

"There's a part of me, Father, that always holds back, that never lets go. At times, that part takes over and I become so wrapped up in myself that I don't see the rest of the world. Sometimes not for days! I'll walk and look and not see or feel a thing. It's . . . it's like when I'm the most there within myself, when I feel my own existence most fully, the rest of the world becomes a painted backdrop, a thin, faded veil drawn across . . . across . . ." A panicked look filled her eyes. "Gods," she murmured, "Gods . . . across what?"

"Reality?" offered the Way-Farer.

"Reality?" she repeated, a sense of questioning wonder in her voice. "Reality? Father, I'm not even too sure what that means any longer. I know we say the Way leads to reality by showing us the real aspect. I understand what we mean when we say the Way is simply our everyday mind and that all things are the real aspect. But the Way and reality must be more than that. I can't bring myself to accept the idea that the word 'is' in both those ideas sets up some kind of equation, or balance, making one side the equivalent of the other. Because if the Way merely leads us to reality and reality merely contains and is all things, then what contains reality?

"Again and again, Father, I find myself driven back into myself because I can't find any stability or meaning

anywhere else. And that part of me that stands aside
mocks all my efforts and calls me constantly back and
in, in and down." Her voice fell to a strangled whisper.
"I fear it, Father. I fear that place inside me. It's dark
and quiet there. It has no end and no beginning. Nothing moves and nothing is."

She was silent for long moments as she fought both
the tears that clouded her eyes and the hard knot of
anguish that choked her and made it impossible to
speak. Finally she was able to croak, "So who am I to
stand for Kensho? To take the burden of the lives of all
on my back? To meet them and do whatever has to be
done?

"I'm the one who doesn't even know who or what
she is. I'm the one who might not even be worthy of the
name Kensho." A sense of bitterness entered her voice.
"I'm the one who might be a throwback, a freak actually closer in mind and spirit to *them* than I am to my
own people." With a sob, she buried her face in her
hands. "Who better . . . to sacrifice . . . than the one
. . . good for nothing else?"

The Way-Farer reached out and put his hands on
Myali's shoulders, drawing the young woman to him as
she sobbed. She came and settled in the curve of his
arms, her face turned into his shoulder. And let her
anguish flow.

After a while, when her sobs diminished, Father
Kadir began to speak in a soft voice. "Myali, Myali,
Josh told me doubt rode your mind, but I had no idea
how hard you've been ridden! You think and you think
about these things, twisting them round and round in
your mind, taking them apart and putting them back
together again endlessly.

"There is no end to such labors. The picture of

reality you create in your mind is a limited one, limited both by the boundaries of your perceptions and by the horizon of your understanding. At the most it is a model, a measuring rod for the sake of comparison. You're absolutely right in saying that the Way must be more than your everyday mind and that reality must be more than all things. For reality is simultaneously both fully itself and all things, and hence more than either.

"But, my dear, reality has no obligation to conform to our idea of it, no matter how complete or detailed that idea may be. That's looking at things the wrong way around! Reality is not something added to things when we perceive them 'correctly.' It is not like the sunlight that brings out the colors in things already having color but hidden in darkness. It simply is."

She sat back and shook her head. "But, Father, does the word even have any meaning then? If it simply is, then it seems forever beyond definition. I can't just point to this and that and say, 'This is reality and that is reality,' and then add them all up, including the whole itself, and point to it and say, 'All that, that's reality.' I just can't find any significance in that or any meaning in the word."

He smiled. "Think what a lot of trouble it saves us if the word indeed has no meaning. Then we don't have to spend so much time looking for it! No, my dear, you may be right. The word 'reality' may not have a meaning. But it has a use."

Continuing to smile, even more broadly, he cocked his head to one side and looked up at the sky. "Ah," he sighed hugely. "What a beautiful blue sky!"

Startled by the sudden shift in topics, Myali looked upward. The sky *was* incredibly blue, bluer than she could ever remember seeing it. The blueness of it soaked into her, filling her to her very fingertips. "Yes," she murmured, awed by the beauty of it. "Yes, so very blue."

"And how do you know it's blue?" asked the Way-Farer quietly.

Surprised, she looked at him. "Because . . . because . . . it *is* blue!"

"But what *is* blue?"

"The sky. And . . . and bluecups. And eyes. And, oh, lots of things."

"But those things aren't 'blue.' They're things that are colored blue. Where is this thing called 'blueness'? Point to it. Don't just add up things that are blue and tell me 'That is blue.' Point to blueness itself."

"I . . . I . . . can't."

"Then how do you know the sky is blue?"

"Because . . . because . . . that's what I learned to call it. That's how I was taught to use the word."

"Ah, and how were you taught to use the word 'reality'?"

Myali was silent. She could think of nothing to say.

The Way-Farer gave her another smile. "When Yolan came back from her Wandering, some people asked her what problem had driven her to Wander and if she had arrived at an answer. Her only reply was to smile and say, 'Explanation must end somewhere.' " He shifted his position slightly, leaning forward to look at her intently. "A great Master of Zen on the home world once advised that if someone asks who you are, tell him your name. But if he then asks you, 'No, I mean who are you really?' be silent.

"Eventually, Myali, we exhaust justification and explanation. Then we arrive at the bedrock of our language and can only say, 'Because this is what I do.'

There comes a time when the only answer is silence or an inarticulate sound.''

He settled back again and looked off into the distance. ''Meaning is not to be found in words alone. Remember that words, or even more importantly, languages, are learned. But they are not learned in isolation. Rather the process takes place within a context of interacting perceptions and experiences mediated by those perceptions. Thus the two both shape and are shaped by the learning. Can you really doubt that if our perceptions differed greatly from what they are, both our experience of reality and our language wouldn't differ equally greatly?

''The way we use language often places it on the borderline between the logical and the empirical. There meanings often flipflop back and forth, and words stand now as expressions of norms (or as ideal visions of how we expect the world to be), and now as expressions of our actual experience. Many of our problems and much of the nonsense we speak comes from our failure to recognize when we are doing which.

''And seeking final answers in terms of words is one of the most arrant pieces of nonsense that come from such a confusion. You can't find meaning in the word 'reality'? Why do you expect to? Perhaps because when you use language in its logical form, it seems so clean and clear-cut. Meanings are there, precise, measured in definitions that seem persuasive, easily understood, complete.

''But that is only appearance. Even that most logical and coherent form of language, mathematics, isn't really what it seems to be. Ask some of the Keepers who've studied the knowledge from the home world that lies in the flagship's computer. Have them tell you of Gödel. What you'll discover is that even arithmetic is incomplete in that no proof for its consistency is possible within the limits of the system of propositions that it is built from. To accomplish that, you always have to posit at least one extra proposition that isn't part of the original system and can't be proved within it.''

He chuckled. ''At times I wonder if anything that can be said clearly and distinctly, anything that can be definitely declared true or false, isn't simply trivial and irrelevant. Or if perhaps the only time we can achieve complete clarity is when we make the question we're answering disappear completely by ceasing to ask it anymore!''

Father Kadir gazed up at the sky for a few moments before continuing. ''So you see, Myali,'' he finally said, ''the question about the meaning of 'reality' must end somewhere, just as the question about 'blueness' did. It must end somewhere because language ends somewhere, somewhere short of reality, somewhere bound and limited by our learning and perception and experience. Where you chose to end it is up to you. But the Way teaches you to carry it on and on until you find yourself reduced to silence.''

''But doesn't silence have a meaning, too?'' she asked, half in jest.

The Way-Farer laughed appreciatively. ''If it does, my dear, you haven't gone far enough!''

''Is that what Nakamura's koan means, then, Father? Is the place where we dwelt before we were born the silence you speak of?''

He shrugged. ''Nakamura's koan means whatever you want it to mean. And I'd wager that in the history of Kensho it's meant just about everything possible to just about everybody possible.

''If you want my personal opinion, Nakamura's koan

is just so many words, subject to all the frailties of words. An inarticulate grunt or a loud 'Mu!' would be just as meaningful and probably a lot more effective. At most, it's a finger, pointing at something that can't really be put into words.

"If I can give you any piece of advice, Myali, I guess I'd just have to warn you that language is a labyrinth. You approach a place you know from one side and everything seems clear and as you expect. But if you approach the same place from a slightly different angle, you no longer know your way about and can wander hopelessly, lost and bewildered. Many are the bones of strayed wanderers that line the corridors of that maze.

"Ah," he sighed, "but that's just more words added to the pile I've already buried you beneath. If I were a good Master I'd just hit you with my staff and keep quiet!"

Myali bowed her head for a few moments and sat without responding. When she looked up again, there was a new calmness in her eyes. "Thank you, Father," she said in a soft voice. "'You've given me a lot to work through." She hesitated for a second, as if trying to decide whether to say something or not. "I . . . I . . . maybe I am the best one on Kensho for this task after all. Perhaps my very unsureness both of myself and of the Way will make me better able to deal with others who don't know a thing about it. And . . . and . . . just maybe . . . in facing *their* doubts I can resolve my own."

"I hope so, my dear. I really do." He looked at her with a measuring, appraising gaze. "In any case, you'll soon find out. As near as we can tell, They'll be coming down for you tonight."

Her head snapped up sharply. "Tonight? That soon? But I don't even know what our plan is! I don't know what's expected of me. I mean, what am I supposed to do?''

"Whatever seems right to you. There is no plan. All we're doing is starting the process we saw. And hoping that all the factors we saw interact in the right way to create the path that leads to the results we desire. Nothing more than that is possible.''

"But . . . but . . . how am I to communicate with you to let you know what's going on?''

"Oh, Josh will try to call you occasionally through the network. But I'm afraid we don't even know if it will work that far. My dear, I'm sorry, but I fear you're going to be pretty much on your own.''

She swallowed nervously. "And . . . and . . .'' she began, fear peeking through the tone of her voice, "how am I going to get back?''

"I don't know if you can come back,'' Father Kadir said sadly. "Josh seems to think he can work something out, but I have my doubts.''

The young woman tried to hide her emotions by forcing her face to go blank. Despite her efforts, the corners of her mouth trembled ever so slightly. "I understand,'' she whispered in a hoarse, emotion-laden breath.

"We know approximately where they'll land their shuttle, at least if the probability line we saw is the right one. Several teams are scattered about the area. When the ship is sighted, the team nearest it will snatch you there and send you off in the right direction to be captured.''

"I see,'' she murmured a reply.

"Now,'' said the Way-Farer suddenly standing, "Josh has been patiently waiting to talk to you for some time.'' He winked at her. "I think he needs comforting, my dear.'' With a final smile, he turned and waved to

Josh, who was standing at the foot of the hill, and then strode off in the opposite direction. Just before Josh arrived at her side, Father Kadir turned and looked back up at her and the sky. "A *very* blue sky," she heard him call.

"What the heck was that for?" Josh muttered.

Myali smiled. "A private joke, Josh."

"A joke? You? My, you *are* changing. First you volunteer for a suicide mission and now you're making jokes. What is the family coming to?

"Seriously, though, little sister, are you sure you want to go through with this? I mean, I'm sure I could persuade the Council to let me go—"

"Josh," she interrupted. "No. I'm going."

"But why?" he asked in obvious exasperation.

She shrugged. "Why not? Doesn't the humor of the situation appeal to you? Think of it as a joke: The person sent to represent an enlightened race is the least enlightened one. That ought to confuse them no end." She grinned maliciously at his discomfort. "Not laughing, big brother?"

"Damn it, Myali, it's not funny! You could die up there!"

"Josh . . ."

"No, don't 'Josh' me. Listen for a moment, you little bull-head. You always were the stubbornest damn kid! As soon as Mom or Dad said no, you were bound and determined to do it anyway. This isn't a game, Myali. It's the life or death of Kensho!"

She closed her eyes wearily. "And mine, too, Josh."

"I know. I just said that! That's why I want to at least know why. You must have a reason, a purpose, to risk your life."

"Josh," she said gently, "I don't have to have a

purpose to serve a purpose.''

He stared at her, speechless.

''Brother, I love you and I know you love me. So
why can't you just accept the idea that I might want to
do something important, really important, with my
life? Something better and more meaningful than just
Wandering around trying to find answers to questions I
can't even intelligently ask myself.

''Damn it, Josh, I've been miserable for a long time
now. Lost, unsure, confused, sick at heart and not too
damn stable in mind. Now I have a chance to resolve
everything, to find out who and what I really am.
Maybe even to answer my questions, or at least come to
understand what they are. If all I have to risk is dying,
it's well worth it to me. Because I've been dying slowly
for quite a while.

''Oh, I'm not doing this strictly for myself. Or even
for reasons I can explain. Part of it's tied up in my love
for you and Mom and Dad and Father Kadir and Mother
Illa and the whole planet of Kensho. Part of it's tied up
with something bigger than all that, something so big I
can't even think about it, much less name it.

''Let it be, Josh. I'm going to do it. Love me for it.''

He bowed his head. When he raised his eyes to hers
again, they were filled with tears. ''I do, little sister, I
do. Damn, you haven't got freckles any more. But
you're still the same kid!'' He laughed and shook his
whole body, shaking away the sadness like a dog
shakes away water.

With a conspiratorial grin he leaned toward her and
said in a stage whisper, ''Don't tell anybody, but I think
I know how to make the network reach that far. At least
once a day, in any case. And I'm experimenting on a
method of snatching that'll whisk you right back here at
the first sign of danger.''

"Good," she grinned back. "Can I come home for dinner now and then?"

Josh chuckled appreciatively, then was silent, shifting nervously from foot to foot. "Well. Guess maybe I ought to get back to work organizing the teams for sighting the shuttle. Most of them are in place, but there are still a few blank spots. So . . . guess you've got things to do to get ready. Well, think I'll go now." He started to turn away, then suddenly spun back around and grabbed her in his arms, hugging her fiercely. "You take care now, little sister. Do you hear? And come back." With a barely suppressed sob, he twisted away and ran down the hill.

Myali tried to watch him go, but the tears kept clouding her vision. When she couldn't see him anymore, she sat down and cried for a long time.

The sky was *very, very* blue.

PART TWO

We dance round in a ring and suppose,
But the Secret sits in the middle and knows.
—Robert Frost

VII

It felt like someone was in his head, kicking the backs of his eyeballs. He groaned and rolled over, burying his face in the folds of his sleeve.

This is only temporary, his conditioning whispered. It is the inevitable result of adjustment and overlay. So is initial confusion, until the new personality structure and the overlaid memories become a coherent whole.

Cautiously he turned over on his back again and opened his eyes just the tiniest bit. Strange moving shadows, dapplings of faraway light, hints of blue and brown and green. As the pain began to ebb, he opened his eyes wider. Tree, his memory supplied. In particular, a ko tree.

He raised himself on one elbow, gazing around dully at a blue-green riot of growing. Trees, bushes, all kinds of plants crowded his field of vision. Forest, his memory coached. Planetside, his conditioning warned. Planetside among the enemy.

With a grunt of pain, he came to a sitting position and leaned back against the trunk of the tree. No great

danger, his memory reassured once the swirl of pain
and nausea brought on by his movement had ebbed.
The forest is fairly safe. Be cautious, always be cautious, his conditioning countered. A spy must assume
every man is his enemy.

Vulnerable, he thought. In pain. Sitting, weak and
sick, against a tree trunk in the middle of a forest. Bad.
Dangerous. He tried to get to his feet, but the agony in
his head forced him to his knees.

He groaned. Something's wrong. Too much pain.
This is only temporary, his conditioning repeated. It is
the inevitable result of . . . Stuff it! he cried to himself.
Can it! Damn it, it hurts! Enough platitudes and reas-
surances. When the hell will the pain stop? I'm in
danger if I can't even stand up.

Not really, his memory soothed. There are a few
dangerous animals in the forest, but not many. It's such
a beautiful place. Just look around.

He did. The trees soared over his head to form a
canopy some forty feet or more above. Sunlight slipped
through here and there to splash against the trunks and
occasionally spatter itself across the undergrowth. Not
much of it reached the ground. The very air itself
seemed blue-green and thick with the presence of all the
leafy life that surrounded him.

He lurched up to a standing position. Something
about all this growing, all this fecund greenish-blueness
frightened him, stirring black things that lay deep,
deep, forgotten or repressed within him. Fear? Is it
fear? he wondered, looking around once more. Or is it
longing? Not a productive line of reasoning, his conditioning interrupted. It is time for personality integration
exercises.

He nodded and, with a sigh, leaned against the tree

trunk. Ko tree, he reminded himself. Ko pods are good to eat. Sort of a cross between fruit and nut. Very high in nutritional value. No weird proteins to mess up the human system.

Exercises. First, mission: to proceed from drop to the assigned destination, known planetside as First Touch. This seemed to be the most important objective available on this rather dispersed world. The Way-Farer was there and it appeared to be the governing center. Or at least the Council met there. No, that didn't seem right. His memory didn't indicate the Council really governed. Coordinate? Yes, that was a better word. But that made no sense. He felt the headache coming back with a vengeance and shifted his focus to another topic.

Mission: Proceed to First Touch. Gather information on state of preparedness of planetary defenses (*What defenses?* his memory wondered.) Evaluate extent and character of possible resistance to a landing. Identify key leaders, especially those whose removal might cause a disruption in the functioning of government. (*Government?* queried his memory. He told it to be quiet.) If, as preliminary analysis indicates, the Way-Farer is indeed head of planetary government, assassinate him. (*Kill Kadir?* His memory recoiled in horror at the thought.) Sudden pain throbbed through his head. He groaned and sagged against the tree trunk.

For several moments he hung there, breathing raggedly in agony. If the Way-Farer is that well loved, his conditioning coldly calculated, his death might have very satisfying negative effects on the enemy's morale. Move assassination from Three Priority to Two Priority, Tentative, subject to further evaluation.

It is now time to leave the clearing, the conditioning instructed, and begin . . .

His eyes snapped open. Hold it! he cried silently. Clearing? Ignoring the surge of pain, he concentrated hard. Clearing. I was landed in a clearing . . . but I'm in the middle of the forest. He looked around wildly, circling the tree trunk so that he could stare off in all directions. Thick forest stared back with dark, formless eyes. Clearing, where's the goddamn clearing?

Calm, his conditioning advised. Do not panic. Evaluate. He took several deep breaths and sat down once more, his back to the tree trunk. First, he began, my conditioning says I was landed in a clearing. Second, I'm not in a clearing and can't even see where one might be. Therefore, either I wasn't landed in a clearing or I was and I moved myself. The first alternative is possible. My conditioning was given before the landing. Perhaps some emergency came up and the drop spot had to be changed. But how could they have landed me here? Where would the drop vessel have found room to maneuver?

No. No, I couldn't have landed here. Which means I landed in a clearing and then moved here on my own. Damn. Don't remember a thing. But then, it's possible I was so confused by the hasty adjustment and overlay that I moved without realizing it.

Or somebody moved me.

That idea shook him to his very core. Someone moved me. Who? A drop vessel only contains one person, the drop. I'm the only one of my people planet-side. Who moved me?

And why?

The spy shuddered, then gasped as the pain lanced through his head, stabbing his eyeballs from behind. He felt a bitter panic rising in his throat. His tongue reached back into his mouth for the right top rear molar. Only in

case of emergency, his conditioning commanded. Fuck
you, he retorted, his fear welling up. Fuck you! He
pushed the tooth.

Command, came the immediate voice in his head.
Location fix, he subvocalized.
There was a pause, then an answer. *About twenty-
three kilometers southwest of drop. What the hell are
you doing? Objective was due north of drop.*
Uh, sorry. I seem to have walked in my sleep.
Don't get wise. Get moving.
Aye, aye. Over and out.
*And don't get lost again. Use your compass and the
recon map. And don't use this channel except in
emergency. They might be listening. Over and out.*

The spy grunted and shut his eyes against the throbbing. How long, he wondered, how long since drop?
Shit, I forgot to ask.
He took several deep breaths. The pain began to
recede a little. With the fingertips of each hand, he
gently massaged his forehead and temples. Better, he
thought. Not great, but better. He could feel the muscles in his shoulders and neck begin to relax. Contact
with Command, with his own people, had calmed him,
made him more sure of himself. Nobody moved me, he
decided. I moved myself. Nobody knows I'm here
except me and Command. Nobody's hiding out there in
all that green, watching, waiting . . .
He closed down his thoughts abruptly and stood.
Get walking, he told himself. Get moving. Fumbling in
the pocket of his robe, his fingers found the round disk
of his compass and the rectangle of the folded map. A
glance at the map and a quick compass reading were

enough to get him started. Got to get going, he thought
again. North northeast is good enough for now. I'll
figure out a more exact course later when my mind's a
little clearer. He picked up the pack that lay next to the
tree trunk and shrugged it on. With a last look around,
he set off.

Something's wrong.
?
*While we were moving him from the clearing where
They dumped him, I probed his mind.*
?
*He's not a unit. I mean, it's as if there are three in the
same mind. First, there's someone he knows as the spy.
Pretty simple, that one. Just a set of rules, commands, a
basic personality profile, decidedly on the paranoid
side. It really isn't enough to qualify as a true person.
More like an outline.*

*Second, there's a whole bunch of confused
memories, definitely Myali's. But they're strange. Lots
of gaps. It almost seems like she held back certain
things on purpose.*

*Finally, there's something else in that mind. It's
deep, way below the conscious level. Very basic.*

Interesting, Josh. What do you think we should do?

*Darned if I know. Just continue with the plan, I
suppose.*

Agreed. Stay with him.

*Right, Father. I'll call if anything interesting hap-
pens.*

Trees. Goddamn trees everywhere. And bushes. No
real landmarks anywhere. He looked down at the compass he held open in his palm. North northeast. That
should do it. Just keep on this heading.

He caught a movement out of the corner of his left eye. He spun to face that direction, his hand moving to his pocket and his weapon. Shit! Nothing. Or at least nothing now. Something *had* moved. He was sure of it.

Nervously looking over his shoulder, he began to walk again. Each time his feet touched the ground, a surge of pain swept through his head. Damn! Damn them and their quick and dirty integration job! Bastards. The nausea came again in a wave. Unable to control it, he stumbled to a tree and sagged there while he heaved up his stomach. Each spasm was matched by an agony behind his eyes.

Empty and weak, he slumped to the ground at the base of the tree. Shit. Oh, shit, I've got to pull myself together. Can't go on like this. Anybody catches me this way, I'm done. He glanced fearfully at the green walls that surrounded him. Could be any number of them out there. Watching. Waiting. He planted his back more firmly against the tree trunk, happy that at least one part of him was protected.

Got to get it together. Let's see. I'm a spy. Here on . . . Kensho, that's it . . . to gather information. Maybe to kill the . . . Way-Farer, yeh. He touched the laser wand in his pocket.

Good. Now my cover. I'm Wandering. Right. And my name is . . . is . . . He felt something deep inside his mind stir. My name is . . . It moved in the silence of utter darkness, locked and barred from all light. My name is . . . A serpent of memory, uncoiling and shifting, retreating into the dark. He yearned for it. Reached out to catch it before it disappeared. My name is . . . He stretched and grabbed and . . .

Dunn! An incredible flash of pain blinded him and left him gasping, just at the edge of consciousness. The darkness surged up and threatened to overwhelm him.

He fought back and slowly, slowly the blackness re-
ceded and the pain ebbed. He heard the name echoing,
echoing . . . DUNN . . . Dunn . . . dunn . . .

"Dunn," he said hoarsely, almost startled by the
sound of his own voice. "I'm Dunn." Yes, the name
felt right on his lips. And it seemed full of significance.
Behind it, trailing off into the blackness it had almost
escaped to, were threads of meaning. He shuddered.
The darkness frightened him and he turned away.

"All right," he muttered, "I'm Dunn. Whoever he
is. It sure as hell wasn't an easy name to come by, so I'll
keep it."

"Dunn," he said in a slightly louder voice, speaking
to the trees and bushes. "I'm Dunn, Forest. I shouldn't
be here. Sorry, But somehow I seem to have lost my
clearing. I . . ." His monologue trailed off to an
indistinct mumble. Stupid, he reprimanded himself.
Talking to the goddamn trees. Get it together!

Concentrating, he began to conduct the series of
integration exercises necessary to give his spy personality complete access to the memories they had transferred to his mind from the captured native. There was a
regular procedure to follow, one that would give him
control, one that would . . .

She watched the little lizard dart about the cage Josh
had built for it. It was a beautiful cage, woven from the
springy reeds that grew at the edge of the marsh to the
north of their home.

"Will it sing?" she asked.

"Huh? Sing? Yeh, sure, sis. It'll sing. Once it gets
used to being in the cage. Sure. It'll sing just like it did
before."

"Even in your room it'll sing?"

"Uh-huh. Even in my room. Every morning it'll

wake me up, chirping like they do just as the sun comes over the horizon. And it'll sing that long warbling note at high noon. At dusk, it'll make that hollow whistling sound they all make. Even in my room.''

"Why's it sing, Josh?"

"Why? Uh . . . . well, I heard one of the Keepers at the 'hood say it's the way they tell others to keep out of their territory. It's kind of a warning.''

"But why is it so happy in the morning and so sad at night? And why does it have to sing to warn other lizards? Why not just croak?''

Exasperated, Josh shook his head. "I don't know, sis. Why don't you ask a Keeper? Hey, I got things to do.'' And he walked away.

Myali stayed there, watching the lizard. After hopping all over the cage, looking for a way out, the creature climbed to one of the perches Josh had included in the structure, and sat, staring back at her. Its bright, unwavering gaze disturbed her for some unknowable reason. Finally, she turned her eyes aside and whispered, "Sing, little lizard, sing.''

The tiny gray-green creature made no response except to shift its weight and turn its head to follow the flight of an insect that was buzzing around the top of the cage.

Every day for a week, Myali went and sat by the cage for a couple of hours, just watching the lizard. It never sang. It was silent in the morning, at noon, and at dusk. All day long it jumped around the cage, catching any insect foolish enough to come within its reach and devouring it with relish. Occasionally it would sit still for a few moments returning her stare with its dark, shiny little eyes, head cocked to one side as if listening for something.

"It doesn't sing," she told Josh.

"It will," he replied. "Just give it time."

"But if it sings to warn the other lizards to stay out of its territory, it won't sing, 'cause it doesn't have a territory any more. It just has a cage."

"It'll sing. They all do. It's . . . it's . . . well, they're made to sing. They just do. Wait and see."

So she waited. One day, tired of waiting, she tried singing to the lizard. She tried the noon song, since it was that time of day. She wasn't very good at it, but the lizard sat quietly and listened to her. When she was finished, it turned its head and chased an insect. That evening, she tried the evening song with identical results.

From that day on, she sang to the little caged creature several times a day. Josh laughed at her and said maybe he should put her in the cage.

About a month after the caging of the lizard, Myali spent two nights at the home of one of her friends. She was still too young to enter the Sisterhood, but she had attended the pre-classes for youngsters that were held for a couple of weeks every fall. There she had met several girls her own age. One in particular had become her closest friend, and the two of them walked miles across the Plain to play with each other.

When Myali returned, Josh met her at the door with a big grin. "He's singing. Just like I said he would. Would've done it sooner if you hadn't bothered him so much. You did so much singing he never had a chance!"

Myali ran into her brother's room to see the little animal jumping and hopping around in its cage. She sat there for two hours until the sun was overhead. Then, sure enough, the creature sang. She listened carefully and her heart sank.

Unmoving, she stayed by the side of the cage until

sundown, waiting for the lizard to sing again. When the sun slid over the edge of the Plain to the west, the haunting whistle of evening song filled the air. When the creature had finished, she rose and left the room, tears in her eyes.

She found her dinner, cold, in the kitchen. Her father was there, cleaning some vegetables from the family garden. Myali sat at the counter next to where he was working, watching him and dispiritedly nibbling at her meal.

After a long silence, she finally asked him, "Dad, why do lizards, even lizards in cages, sing?"

"What kind of an answer do you want?" he said gently.

She stared blankly at him. " 'What kind' of answer? Are there different 'kinds' of answers?"

He nodded. "There are as many different kinds of answers as there are ways of looking at the world. An animal behaviorist might say lizards sing as a way of establishing their territory. A neurobiologist might say lizards sing when certain synapses in their brains open up or when certain neurotransmitters are emitted. A physicist might talk about sound waves. And a poet might claim they sing for joy or grief."

Myali shook her head impatiently. "But what's the *real* reason? What does it *mean* when they sing?"

"Ah," he replied with a slight smile, "you want to know the truth, eh?"

"Yes," she nodded vigorously to make it more emphatic.

"There are only two ways to know *that*." He paused. "The first is to eat your dinner with relish."

She looked down at the food and wrinkled her nose. "But it's all lumpy and cold," she complained. "What's the other way?"

"Become a lizard," he said and turned back to finish washing the vegetables. "Or at the very least," he added over his shoulder, "stop being Myali."

He awoke suddenly, jerked back to consciousness by a loud crashing in the undergrowth. Confused, he stared about in dismay for a second, wondering where the hell he was. Then it all clicked into place and his hand moved to his pocket, finding and taking out his laser wand.

The crashing continued, but seemed to be moving away from him. Myali's memory, now more accessible to his conscious mind as a result of the integration exercises, told him that the noise was most likely a creature known as a forest dragon. About the size of a pig, it foraged the forest floor for nuts and roots. Although frightening looking, it was basically a harmless beast, given to flight instead of fight. If cornered, it could turn nasty and dangerous. Probably rummaging around and bumped into me sitting here, he thought. Gave it one hell of a scare, from the sound of things.

Dunn listened until the crashing faded and the forest became still again. Then he rose, placing the wand back in his pocket.

Surprisingly, his head didn't hurt as abominally as before. Not exactly up to doing cartwheels, he judged, but certainly good enough to make it possible to get this expedition under control.

For the first time, he took stock of his appearance. He was wearing an ankle-length brown robe, with a hood and a large pocket in front. Otherwise, it was quite plain and unadorned. The material was coarse, but sturdy and tightly woven. The fit was loose and comfortable.

His feet were covered with what appeared to be a

kind of short boot. No, they were really more of a
moccasin, he decided. But they came up a good three
inches above the ankle. Like the robe, they were unadorned. He lifted one foot. No sole as such, but by
touch he could tell the bottom was a lot thicker than the
rest. He wiggled his toes. Comfort seemed the main
criterion for fashion on this world.

Kneeling down, he opened his pack to see what it
contained. Food packets, each one holding what appeared to be a mixture of dried meat, grains, some
crumbly gray stuff, and several completely unrecog-
nizable ingredients. Myali told him it was common fare
for a Wanderer. It could be eaten dry or dumped in a pot
with water and made into a stew. Naturally, there was a
small metal pot. And a bowl. Some slightly pointed
sticks about nine inches long. (For eating, Myali
coached.) Something that looked a lot like a carefully
folded waterproof poncho. Another robe. An extra pair
of boots. And several small containers filled with odds
and ends.

They certainly travel light around here, Dunn
thought as he repacked everything. And speaking of
traveling, maybe I'd best do a little planning while it's
still light and my head is clear. He sat back and took the
map from his pocket. Opening it up and flattening it out
on the ground, he placed the open compass on top and
aligned the two. The slice of territory shown was
bordered on the east by what was probably an ocean. To
the west were a series of hills and mountains. The area
between the water and the mountains ran in a north-
south direction and was bisected by a major river.
Where the river met the ocean, and extending up it on
both sides (but mostly to the south), was an extensive
swamp. Along the eastern edge of the mountains

closest to the ocean a smaller river ran in a northeasterly direction. It joined the swamp at a point where the mountains narrowed the land to a mere corridor.

His landing position was marked with a small black X to the south of the swamp. The smaller river lay west of him, but if he continued due north, he would have to cross it at the point where the strip of land narrowed, or venture into the swamp. He ran his finger northward until he found the spot marked "First Touch," his goal. It actually was dead north of his drop. But clearly, he'd have to detour to the west to get around the swamp.

Then he remembered he'd already made a detour. His hand shaking just slightly, he estimated a new starting point to the southwest of the original X. Nearer the river, nearer the mountains. Farther from his goal. How? Why? Best not to think about it too much, he decided as he felt his headache returning. He slipped the map back into his pocket, stood, and lifted the pack to his back. Checking the compass, he began to walk.

The forest stretched off in all directions. Any way he looked, it appeared the same. Not that the vistas didn't change with disconcerting rapidity. But the changes were basically meaningless to him. Alien. Hidden. And as it began to grow dark, the whole thing took on an ominous overtone that made the hair on the back of his neck rise.

He tried to rationalize the feelings away. He was armed. Better armed, perhaps, than any other person on this planet. Furthermore, Myali assured him there weren't that many dangerous creatures in the forest. So there was no reason for his sense of anxiety. No reason at all.

Yet the forest watched him. It peered out from deep green places and stared at his soul. The forest held its

breath and watched. He could occasionally catch it
looking, out of the corner of his eyes. Just a flicker, but
he knew. It watched. And waited.

As the dark crouched down between the trees,
Dunn's fear grew. I've got to stop, he told himself. Stop
and make a camp. I need fire and light and food.

Scurrying along, throwing ever-more-worried
glances over his shoulders as he went, Dunn suddenly
came to a vast tree. So huge and dense was it that the
ground around its trunk was clear of underbrush for a
good thirty feet in every direction. With a cry of relief,
the spy scuttled across the open ground to the huge
trunk. A ko, Myali said. He sank down and leaned back
against the reassuring solidity of the tree. After a
moment's pause, he began to rummage through his
pack, looking for something to start a fire. He found a
box of matches. Dunn almost laughed. Matches! How
prosaic. How comforting.

A quick circuit of the edge of his clearing yielded a
fair amount of firewood. He'd just make a small one, he
decided. Just to give a little light. That way, the wood
should last until dawn.

Hurrying back, oppressed by the growing weight of
the dark, he quickly built his fire. As the flames leapt
up, cutting a bright hole in the night, he sighed with
relief and leaned against the tree trunk, closing his eyes
wearily. Ah, he thought, that's more like it.

He sat quiet and relaxed for several moments, enjoying the brightness he sensed beyond his eyelids. As
long as he didn't open them, he could almost pretend
the glow was daylight. But it isn't day, came the uneasy
thought. It's night. And sitting here with my eyes
closed is like being blind.

There's nothing to worry about, he reassured himself. Nothing. Besides, even if I open my eyes there's nothing to see but what the firelight shows, maybe a patch some ten feet across. So why open them? Relax. Enjoy a moment of peace and quiet. And control your silly fear of the dark.

But the uneasiness grew. And was joined by a sickening sureness that there *was* something out there in the night. Something moving. Coming toward him. Closer. Closer.

Fear finally gained the upper hand and his eyes snapped open, wide and staring. There, just beyond the flickering glow, sensed more than seen, was a darkness within the darkness.

VIII

Moving carefully and slowly, Dunn reached out and added two more sticks to his little fire. The flames rose just far enough to give the darkness form.

Much to Dunn's immediate relief, the figure that appeared seemed to be human. Or at least the head was. The body was hidden by the folds of a dead black robe and little could be said of it other than that it was generally of the size and shape acceptable as human.

That first flash of relief passed quickly, though, as the spy took a closer look. The other's face was utterly still and calm in a way that spoke of alienness that went soul deep. There was no flicker of warmth or human emotion in the eyes. Not even a glimmer of fellow recognition lit them. They merely stared, flat, detached, with an almost disembodied sense of concentration. The mouth was firm, thin, unmoving. Above it reared an arrogant beaklike nose. Hair as dark as the robe hung straight and roughly cropped to the shoulders. From the look of him, Dunn's visitor appeared to be kneeling, sitting back on his haunches. Two white hands rested on top of what must be thighs. Peeking from a fold of midnight cloth on the left side was the hilt of a sword.

Raising his glance once more to the other's eyes, Dunn cleared his throat by way of starting. "Ummmm. I . . . uh . . . I'm Dunn."

The man in black didn't answer for several moments. When he finally did speak it was in a murmur, almost as if talking to himself. "This one confuses Totality," he hissed. "This one is strange. Totality searches for this one's essence, but cannot find it." He nodded to himself and muttered a few unintelligible comments. The creature's whole demeanor, the way he ignored Dunn's presence as a living, responding being, the manner in which he spoke to himself (or was it to someone else, someone invisible?), chilled him to his very core. Human form or not, this visitor out of the night was alien.

"Yes. This one is not one. This one is three. But how can one be three if there is no Totality? One is deep in darkness, yes, deep, deep. Yes. One is not whole, a skeleton, a husk, a shape without solidity. The last is shadow, a presence of other, not here, not now, yes, mere memory." The visitor's lips barely moved. His face was equally still and dead in its masklike immobility. And the flat, unblinking stare of the eyes . . .

Dunn shivered and made a decision. This was not a friend. It probably wasn't even human. In any case, the creature on the other side of the fire quite possibly was dangerous. Moving as surreptitiously as he could, Dunn slowly moved his right hand toward the pocket which held his laser wand. Gently his fingers found the opening and entered, reaching for the cool firmness of the weapon. He almost had it. He . . .

With a sudden swirl of black, the figure before him moved. In one fluid sweep, almost faster than Dunn could follow, the visitor's sword was out and stretching across the fire, aiming directly at his throat. So swift was the motion, that the spy did not even have time to react. Ever so lightly the point of the blade, glinting redly in the firelight, touched his Adam's apple. He stared down at it, too surprised and fascinated to so much as move.

A hiss of laughter brought his eyes back up to the dark visitor. "Yes. Yes, Triple One. There is no self for the Mind Brothers to grasp and bring the Madness to. Oh, no. There is no one. But still Totality sees your mind and knows it as soon as you do. Leave the little death stick in your pocket. Touch it and all three of you die."

Slowly Dunn removed his hand from his robe pocket. His eyes riveted to the sword blade, he held both hands out, palm forward, to show they were empty. "What . . . what do you want?" he finally managed to croak out.

The black-clad creature laughed its wheezing cackle again. "Want? What does this unit want? This unit wants nothing because Totality wants nothing. Totality wants nothing because you have nothing to give, Triple One. You seem to be, but are not. Perhaps you are becoming. But until you are, you have nothing to offer. No, you are not even worth the feeding." As suddenly as it had appeared, the sword disappeared, back into its sheath. The figure stood. "Becoming, yes. Perhaps becoming. For the one lost in darkness may yet be found. And then . . ."

For a brief moment, the swordsman seemed to be holding an inner dialogue. Then he nodded, as if reaching an agreement. "We will follow this one to see if he becomes. Then we will decide what we want. Yes." With an unexpected swirl of black robes, the creature simply disappeared into the night.

Dunn took several deep breaths, trying to calm his thudding heart. His hands were shaking so badly he sat on them. What the hell was that, he wondered. He blinked and shook his head as if to knock loose the recent experience. Lifting the fingers of his right hand to his throat, he felt the area carefully. When he looked at his fingertips, there was no blood. Was it real? Did it happen?

He called on Myali. Yes, it was real. A Ronin. Dangerous, but not insanely deadly as in the old days. The creature was human, or at least mostly human. The mind of a Ronin was somewhat outside the pale of humanity since it had developed for generations under the direct influence of the . . . the . . . Dunn drew a sudden blank. He thought harder, demanding access to the memory. Under the direct influence of the . . . It wouldn't come. It wasn't there. Only a hole, an emptiness, a sense of vague menace. Why? Why was the memory faulty? How much of the rest of his memory was faulty?

The thought shook him. If the memories he had been given were not complete, what did it mean? Myali couldn't have held anything back from the machine. Or could she? Impossible! Yet . . .

His mind raced on. If she had withheld information, she must have done it for some definite reason. My God, he thought, stunned by the idea. The only reason she could have had was if she'd known what was going on. And if Myali had known, that meant others here on the planet knew!

In an unexpected change of direction, his thoughts

turned back to the Ronin. Something the creature had said bothered him. No, it wasn't any one specific thing. It was the general tenor of his remarks, the way the things had talked about his mind as if he could see it, the way it had known what he was about to . . .

"Oh, my God!" Dunn groaned out loud in sudden realization. "The damn thing can read minds. And if it can read minds, then it knows . . ."

In a fit of sudden panic, the spy stood and glared out at the darkness pressing in on his tiny fire. They know! They're out there, waiting, watching. They'd sent in their mind reader to make sure, but now they were certain, drawing the net tighter and tighter. They were the ones who'd moved him. It was all just an elaborate trap, a game they were playing for their own twisted amusement. He could hear them now, hear them in the dark, coming closer and closer, getting ready to leap out of the night and . . .

Damn it, get hold of yourself, bellowed the spy in his mind. Panting and gasping. Dunn sat down and wrapped his arms around his body, trying to control the shudders that were surging through him in waves. "Control," he whispered huskily to himself. "In the face of the enemy, control above all else."

The sound of his own voice in the midst of the stillness of the forest appalled him. Stillness? But just a moment ago he had heard them coming for him, crashing through the underbrush. He listened again now, carefully, critically. There were noises, yes. Creakings and groanings from the trees as a high, light breeze stirred them. Rustlings as little things scurried to and fro on nameless night errands. An occassional squeal or grunt of pain or surprise. But no crashings, no comings or goings of spy-seeking hordes.

Calmer, his shaking stilled and his thudding heart

slowing to normal, Dunn sank back against the trunk of
the tree. As his head touched the rough bark, he realized
that his headache had returned. Not as bad as before,
but damn irritating anyway. Between the surges of
pain, he worked at convincing himself there was
nothing out there in the dark after all. It's all right here,
here in my damned, throbbing head. Damn lousy integration job, he cursed silently. Sloppy hurried-up,
fuck-up! Should have checked this all out before they
landed me. Grimly he gritted his teeth against the growing agony. Got to sort it all out. Got to get control.
There must be more info in Myali's memory, things
I've got to know before I make some really serious
mistake. Got to get on top of this before I take one more
step toward First Touch!

With angry determination, he began to clear his mind
for a second run at the integration exercises. The first
try had given him access to some of Myali's memories.
But the access was strangely limited and far from complete. It had been more like waking up a second mind in
his own, a mind that had been very willing to share, but
had stayed separate instead of becoming integrated. It
was pleasant, almost like having a very good friend he
could talk to and share with. But it was not integration
and would never do.

As he worked his way carefully down into his mind,
his body calmed and he slumped slightly, physically
relaxed for the first time in hours. Time passed and the
flames of his little fire died down to a few glowing
embers. The dark crept in and in, until finally it
smothered even the last few glimmerings of light.
Blackness lay like a soft blanket, covering everything.

She blinked back the tears and tried hard to concen-

trate on the drifting clouds. Lying there, looking up,
she knew that Karl was watching her from the corner of
his eye even though he pretended to be staring at the
ground while he talked. She was only half listening to
him now. His first few words had thrown her into such
confusion that she had instantly fled inward in an attempt to regain her equilibrium.

Myali shot a quick glance at him when she thought he
wasn't looking. She knew that profile well. A strange
combination of stern and soft. The lips were full, the
nose slightly turned up at the end. A forehead, corru-
gated now with concern, soared like a cliff over heavy
brows that scowled in concentration. On the other end
of the face, a bold chin thrust forward.

The thing that fascinated her most, though, were his
eyelashes. She had noticed them the first time she had
seen him. They were long, thick, and wonderful. For
some reason, every time she looked at them a shiver
went down her spine and her stomach felt warm.

The rest of his body she knew equally well. They had
been lovers for over a year. She pictured the curve of his
back beneath his robe, the way that curve met and
flowed into his buttocks, then swept down to his muscular legs. She resisted a powerful urge to reach out and
trace that line with her fingers.

Her eyes drifted back up to the clouds again. Many
curves there. But none so beautiful as those on . . .
The tears came back and she couldn't see.

Because Karl was leaving. Not just for a while.
Forever.

Karl was two years older than Myali and had finished
his training in the 'hood last year. Since then, he'd
worked with his father, a talented artisan, who was
designing a new type of wind turbine to be used on the

Southern Continent where the winds were weaker and
more erratic than here in the north.

But now he was leaving. Going to the Southern
Continent to settle in the Far Out. And he was going
alone.

Oh, he'd said something about coming back to see
her once he got things under control. Even something
about seeing then if she wanted to come down herself.
But she knew it was just to make her feel good, to make
the break easier.

That's exactly what it was, a break. He was leaving.
Taking his eyelashes, the curve of his back, his strong
legs, all of it, about as far away as someone could go on
Kensho.

Suddenly she couldn't stand the apologetic droning
of his voice. She felt an overpowering urge to say
something, anything, to break the flow of his words, to
stop the way he was draining the life and joy from her
through his mouth.

"I won't go south. I'll never go south," she muttered.

He fell silent, turning his head to look at her. She
refused to meet his eyes. The silence between them
stretched on and on until it was so thin she could barely
stand waiting for it to snap.

Karl sighed. "No. No, I guess you won't. I guess
your Way lies someplace else. I've thought so for some
time now."

In surprise, she looked at him. Tears had wet his
cheeks.

"Myali, Myali," he said in a choked voice. "I've
known for months that there's no real place for me in
your life. It took a long time, but I've finally learned to
accept the fact that no one else can walk your Way with

you, that you travel alone. I . . . I tried to tag along. But . . . but . . .''

She started to shake her head in denial, but he started again. "Yes," he insisted, "yes. It's true. You're going someplace, maybe you don't even know where yourself, but you're going and going and going. All the time."

"Even," she whispered hoarsely, "even when we make love?"

He sucked in his breath sharply, as if struck in the stomach. For a moment he held it, then let it all out in a sigh. Several times he tried speaking, but failed. Finally, though, he managed to murmur, "Yes. Yes, even then." His voice picked up strength. "Myali, something's driving you, and it's more than just a hunger for love. I . . . I don't mean you don't want love. Of course you do. Everybody does. And when we're together I can feel your need and I try my best to . . .

"But no matter how far I reach out, there's part of you I just can't touch. Part of you that's not there, as if . . . as if it was always somewhere else, searching.

"I don't understand your need. It's deeper and more basic than anything I can deal with. It scares me because I know I can't satisfy it and I know it's capable of consuming me if I keep trying."

"So you're going south." Her voice was brittle with control.

He nodded. "I'm going south."

"Because you think I don't love you."

Karl dropped his eyes, as if looking in the grass for words he couldn't find anywhere else. "You still don't understand. It's not because you don't love me, Myali. It's because you can't."

Can't. The word beat at her mind. Can't let go.
Can't just be. Can't love. No! she cried silently. No, it
isn't true! I can! I just need time and understanding
~and. . . .

Can't, came the quiet voice in her mind. Look yourself and see. You know how. Look and see.

For a moment she hesitated, afraid to even try. Then
with a mental shout of defiance, she plunged into her
own mind. Down through the cerebral cortex she dove,
down through the neopallium, deep into the archipal-
lium. There, amid the thalamic, subthalamic, and limbic portions of her brain, in a place so ancient it had
crawled through the slime of primeval swamps and
bellowed up through the mists at a huge, glowing moon
that still hung hot and close to its mate, she searched for
the roots of *can't.*

She found her desire for Karl. The hot seething that
rose up in waves when he touched her and they lay,
moving together toward climax, washed over her and
left her gasping in its wake. Passion, yes. Love?

She looked farther and found the joy they had shared.
That warmth at sitting together and listening to the song
of a lizard in the evening. That bubbling, light feeling
when she played a trick on him and he laughed. Friendship. Deep friendship. Love?

Growing more frantic, she cast about trying to find
something, anything, that answered that quiet little
question. If these things aren't love, she cried, what is?

What is? echoed back. She turned toward the echo
and sensed something, a vagueness, a dimness. Without thinking, she rushed toward it demanding, What is?
What is? What is?

The darkness grew and surrounded her as she moved.
Suddenly, she felt fear and tried to slow down or turn

away. But it was too late. Looming in front of her was a curtain of such black intensity, she dreaded to touch it. With a cry of terror she hurtled straight at it and burst through to . . .

Chaos. Hatred. Aversion. Anger. Cancerous frustration. All, all aimed at Karl. He was a millstone around her neck, dragging her down, tying her to earth when she was meant to soar. To be rid of him and his suffocating demands for love and attention would mean freedom. Good riddance!

No! she cried, horrified at the dark maelstrom. No! That's not me! That's not how I feel! The darkness is a lie!

Yet she knew that it was true. The darkness and the hatred were as much her as the light and the passion.

But darkness was no more the source of the *can't* than light had been. It lay deeper yet. And now, unable to escape the vortex of the retreating question she chased, she tumbled helplessly inward to the place where all began.

She found herself in a vast stillness. Nothing moved, nothing stirred, no sound or vibration penetrated. It was a waiting, a brooding, an indifference so vast she shrank from it with greater fear and revulsion than she had felt for the darkness. Here was true limbo, uncaring, un-becoming, a vast nothingness, an absence of spirit and of meaning. This was the abyss within, the ultimate *can't*. And it filled the universe.

This can't be, she wailed. This mustn't be!

This Is, came the reply. This is the root of the *can't*. Here is where the foundation lacks, where the building falters and all tumbles into ruin. This is why you do not, can not, love.

Screaming despair into the infinite silence, she fled.

With one fluid motion, she was on her feet and moving across the Plain, westward toward the sun. She heard Karl call out, even heard the pain in his voice, but there was nothing she could say that wouldn't increase it, so she didn't turn back. She walked and walked and walked.

Toward the sun. She knew she could never reach it, but she stretched out her legs to try. The farther the sun slid toward the horizon in front of her, the closer the dark crept up behind. Soon she was running, fleeing as well as pursuing things that couldn't be fled or pursued.

A swarm of darters flashed away from her, dipped and rolled. The Plain heaved and shuddered. Beneath, in dark caverns, something stirred. Dunn-un-un-un echoed from the earth itself.

He stumbled and fell but never hit the ground because it dissolved and he tumbled into things that weren't there down, down, down seeking a something, a memory, a past, a laugh, pain, ripping at his mind and flinging it down, down, down he floated in fear, lashing at the shreds of childhood ripping at fading youth, dissolving manhood, who, what, where, was anything, something stirring, something he reached for, wanted, oh please let me touch, hold, be, please . . . he reached, stretched, strained, missed as it withdrew, retreated before his desire, desperate he drove after, flinging himself into the dark, the hole in his soul, too late he saw the blackness, churning, smothering, oh HELP HELP HELP . . .

It was dark. Huge shapes pressed in on him from all sides. Eyes, ears, mouths, tongues, lips. Hungry, the black pressed on him. He opened his mouth to scream and heard it, that cry in the night from his own throat.

Panting he pressed against the tree trunk, clinging to
its solidity in the vagueness. Light! Must have light! In
panic he dropped on all fours next to the little pile of
ashes. He blew on it. A red glow. Light! Hope! He blew
again, adding a few dry leaves, a twig. Oh, light, light,
catch on, he prayed. A flame licked up along the edge
of the leaf, a whole galaxy of bright stars splitting the
heavens with their glory. Light, light! Trembling, he
fed it, coaxing it, pleading with it to live, to grow, to fill
the world.

Finally he sat back, his eyes smarting, his face
streaming sweat. He stared at the little fire, terrified to
look up at the darkness. Light. Light to keep away the
darkness at the center of his being. God, how it repelled
and drew him!

What am I? he moaned silently. Why do I feel like
I'm not, and yet fear to be what I might be? A spy? How
could anyone be something so . . . so . . . partial?
Myali? No, I'm not Myali and yet her memories are
more real than I am.

No! I'm real! He bit his finger, hard. Real! I feel
pain. Or do I just dream I feel pain? Am I a dream? Or a
dream of a dream?

He wrapped his arms around himself and rocked
back and forth, moaning softly. I am a spy. I have a
mission. I am not a spy. I do not have a mission.

Can't go to sleep. Can't ever go to sleep. It's all there
waiting if I sleep. Control. Must take control. He fum-
bled in his pack for a moment and drew out a small box.
Snapping it open, he gazed at the tiny round forms that
filled it. Take one, he commanded himself. Take one.
Stimulant. Keep you on top, in control. Take one.

He did.

Waiting for it to take effect, he dared a quick glance

out at the night forest. He whimpered in fear at the depth of the darkness. It falls forever. Oh, God. Something's wrong. Something's so damn wrong.

Myali's memory. Wrong. Shouldn't be that way. Should be simple, surface things, general information. Not. That. Deep. Not something that clutched and sucked and twisted, plucking and pulling at sanity and being. Remembering the darkness, he shuddered.

But the memory recalled something else, the thing he had sensed and desired and pursued. A warm wave of yearning washed over him. What was it? Why had it retreated? Where had it gone? I've got to know!

Beads of cold sweat broke out on his forehead. Knowing. Instinctively he realized this was treacherous ground. *Can* I know? And what would it *mean* if I did know? Would knowing reveal something good? Or evil? Or nothing . . .

He hesitated, his heart and mind skipping a beat. Nothing. Is that the key? What if I peel back the layers of my being, strip off one denial after another . . . not a spy, not Myali, perhaps not even Dunn . . . Will I find anything at the core? Or does nothing lie at the end of knowing?

Is there no me?

There's a complication.

?

A Ronin found him and is trailing him. It seems to be intrigued by his mental mess.

And you?

Mystified. I've been trying to follow his thinking. It's chaotic. There are definitely three "personalities," or whatever, in his mind. I'd recognize Myali anywhere. The other one, the one who seems to be in charge, is the spy. Doesn't seem to be a real person, just some sort of set of instructions.

And the third one?

That's the fascinating part. It's very deep and very basic and almost impossible to get hold of. Every time you reach out, it pulls away. He almost caught it once, when he found his name. But it escaped at the last moment. He wants it, though, whatever it is. Even when he's not consciously thinking about it, I can feel his mind searching, hunting, seeking. Father, I don't know why, but somehow it seems familiar.

So. Three.

Yes. And the question is, which is the real one?

No, Josh. That's not the question.

He looked up, ready to add another stick to the fire, then checked himself. Uh, I can see the bushes over there. Couldn't half an hour ago. He blinked and gazed skyward. A definite lightening. Dawn coming.

With a sigh of relief, he leaned back and closed his eyes. Dawn coming. Night going. Good. The forest was bad enough. But the forest *and* the night . . .

He opened his eyes and watched the growing light creep warily through the brush as if uncertain the forest was a safe place to be. Slowly, the gloom beneath the canopy of leaves changed from black to dark blue-green to light blue-green.

The long vigil had taken its toll. He felt tired again. Without thinking, he reached into his pack and pulled out the box with its pills. He opened it, then hesitated. Too much of this stuff is dangerous, he remembered.

A slight flicker among the trees to his left caught his attention. Something (living? dangerous?) moving there. The image of the Ronin from last night came to his fatigued mind. The tension tightened another notch. His hands shaking with weariness and dull fear, he quickly gulped a pill down.

He allowed his head to slump forward while he waited for the drugs to take effect. Gradually he felt alertness return, felt a rising flow of energy fill his body. But there was a metallic aftertaste of exhaustion clinging to it, a taste that only increased his nervousness. I'm winding the spring tighter and tighter, he thought. When does one more turn break it?

Finishing a quick meal he rose, brushed the crumbs from his robe. He took the compass from his pocket and picked the direction he had to travel this morning. Last, he leaned down, broke the fire up with an unburned stick, stamped on the few remaining embers, and then shrugged into his pack. With a cursory glance around, he started off.

As he walked along, the mere presence of the sun, even if mostly screened by the forest, made his spirits rise. A memory flashed across his mind of Myali striding through different woods, not quite as thick, on her way to meet someone she loved very much. He tasted the delicious anticipation she felt and it almost made the forest into a friendly, sheltering place. Myali was not afraid of the forest. On the contrary, she felt very much at home in it even though she'd been born on the Plain. It was living, and she was part of life. How could she not feel the kinship?

A sudden flood of light brought him snapping back into the present. A clearing. No, not quite. A sudden ending of the forest. And a hill. It appeared perfectly circular, perhaps twenty feet high and three hundred or more in diameter. No trees grew on it. A few bushes huddled near its crown. The rest was covered by a short bluish-green grasslike growth.

Myali told him this was something relatively rare, but nothing to get excited about. There were hundreds just like it scattered all over the face of Kensho. It was at their bases that one could occasionally find smoothstones. If one was very, very lucky.

Dunn scrutinized the ground closely, wandering slowly to the left around the base of the hill. There! He pounced on it as though the smoothstone was a living creature likely to scamper away.

Squatting, he gazed down at the thing in his hand. It looked like a stone, all right, but it was smoother and more regular than any stone he'd ever seen. About two inches in length, it was a slightly elongated ovoid in shape, a matte white in color. He ran his finger along its surface. Soft, it felt soft. And warm. He squeezed it. No, it wasn't soft. It just felt soft. Actually, now that he thought about it, it looked more like a skinny ceramic egg than a stone. Queer. Well, Myali has one. Now I do, too.

He was about to stand when a motion to his right, just at the point where the curve of the hill cut off vision, caught the corner of his eye. He hunched down farther, making himself as small as possible against the blue-green grass.

The black-clad Ronin stepped from the forest and began to climb the hill, heading in the north-northeast direction Dunn had originally been following. In a few moments he disappeared over the crest of the hill, descending the opposite side without so much as a look in any direction but the one in which he was going.

Dunn sat down with a grunt. Shit. The damn thing's probably been on my trail all morning. Damn. Said he was going to follow. Guess he meant it. Can I lose him?

His thumb absently rubbing the smoothstone he held in his right fingers, Dunn decided a slight detour farther

to the west, before turning north northeast again, might
be the best way to shake his follower.

Well, he thought, soon enough he'll realize I'm not
up ahead of him any more. Then he'll double back and
see if he can pick up my trail. But since I was tending
east, a sharp move west might throw him.

Worth trying, he decided, remembering the sword
and the speed of the creature from the night before. It
would mean more time spent in the goddamned
forest—but the trees were better than the Ronin any
day. Or night.

He stood and checked his compass. Just before he
plunged back into the woods again, he looked down at
the little white stone he still held in his right hand.
Thanks, stone, he thought at it. Looks like you did me a
good turn. If I hadn't looked for you, I'd still be heading
north with that Ronin on my tail.

The greenness swallowed him.

IX

Dunn trudged westward for about two hours. The land grew more and more rugged as he went, until he found himself scrambling up and down a series of ever steeper ridges. Judging from the fact that they ran north and south, directly across his path, he decided he must be approaching the foothills of the mountains shown on his map.

Finally, after a long and exhausting climb up a particularly difficult slope, he came to an open place at the crest. Several trees had been torn from the thin, rocky soil by a storm and now lay in a jumble, creating a view toward the afternoon sun. Clambering over the fallen trunks, he reached a clear spot in the middle and stopped to catch his breath. To the west he could see the forest rising in rolling waves that finally broke against a ragged line of distant blue mountains.

This is far enough, he decided, Ronin or no Ronin. Every muscle in his body ached and his legs were quivering with weariness. He wiped the sweat from his forehead. Damn pill must be wearing off, he realized.

He'd have to rest or take another one pretty soon. Either alternative worried him. He wasn't too sure how long he could continue to take the drugs without doing himself real damage. And if he rested . . .

He cut the thought short with a shake of his head. "Let's see now," he said out loud to help focus his attention and keep his mind from wandering to that other thing. "Time to turn north again. Make that northeast. Best get out the old compass and check." His voice dropped to a mumble as he rummaged about in his pocket for the compass. At the same time, he turned to his right to be facing as nearly north as possible.

From the corner of his right eye he caught just the slightest flicker of movement among the trees at the edge of the little clearing. Whirling to face the spot, he forgot the compass and grabbed for his laser wand. His eyes were faster than his hands. He saw the Face among the leaves. But by the time he had the weapon out and pointed, the Face was gone.

For several endless moments he stood frozen in place, laser wand thrust out, eyes staring. Nothing moved within the darkness under the trees. With a sob, he sank against one of the fallen trunks. Oh, God, he moaned. Now what?

The quick glimpse Dunn had caught of the thing in the shadows wasn't very reassuring. The Face's features were certainly within the range of what was considered human. But then, he remembered, the Ronin's had appeared that way at first glance, too. The Face was square, strong, solid, with a firm, straight nose and a mouth permanently set in a line of stubborn determination. It had been too far away to determine the color of the eyes, but the hair had been short, curly, and reddish blond. Certainly nothing out of the ordinary there.

The problem was that he couldn't remember seeing anything *but* a face. There had been no body, human or otherwise, in evidence. When the thing had moved, it had gone instantly, soundlessly. Hardly the way a creature with a body would have moved. A face without a body. Lurking in the shadows at the edge of a clearing. Myali, he asked, have you any idea what it could be? The question found no answer. There was nothing in her memory to match it, nothing to help him find a way to deal with it. He'd have to handle this one completely on his own.

He waited for a while, crouched behind the fallen trunk, to see if it would return. When it didn't, he began to feel better. Maybe, he told himself, it wasn't there at all. Maybe I'm so damn tired that I'm starting to see things.

Eventually he put away the laser wand and took out the compass and the map. He estimated a new course and set off, picking his way carefully along the crest of the ridge.

It was more than an hour later, just after he'd finally managed to convince himself that the Face had been nothing more than the random twitch of an exhausted mind, that he saw it again. This time it was ahead and slightly to his left, peering out from the depths of a clump of bushes. He stopped, rooted to the spot, unable to move or talk or even think. He just stared at it, his mind as blank as its gaze.

As suddenly as before, it disappeared. He almost fell in a heap. His mind was gibbering with fear and his body was shaking so hard he could barely stand. The drain on his system was too much and he could sense a great wave of utter weariness about to break over him. Frantically, he pulled off his pack and ripped it open. With trembling hands he dug around until his fingers found the firm roundness of the pill box. Twisting it open, he grabbed two of them and, ignoring the stern warning his conditioning and his common sense cried out, he shoved both into his mouth. He had no saliva. The pills made a bitter double lump in his throat and he had to swallow several painful times before he finally managed to force them down in spite of his gagging.

Shivering with fear and swaying with fatigue, he stood there, waiting for the drugs to take effect. Can't do this much longer, he told himself. These pills will kill me if I keep this up. Too hard on the body. Too hard on the mind. He could feel the sense of warmth and well-being the drugs brought gradually spreading through his body. It's a lie, he reminded himself. A lie and a trap. It'll kill me as sure as the Ronin will.

Nevertheless, his confidence returned as the pills took effect. He was ready to set out again, to carry out his mission, to go to First Touch, to find and kill the Way-Farer. (When had he decided that? he wondered. And who had decided it?)

Repacking his pack and shrugging it back into place, he checked the compass and began walking once more. His stride was firmer and surer than before, but his head kept swiveling to and fro, and his eyes tried to pierce the interior of every bush both to the right and left of his path. He was looking for the Face and he knew it.

This gets stranger by the hour.

?

About noon he managed to give the Ronin the slip. But some of the swordsman's Mushin found him and now they're hovering around the edges of his mind.

Whatever for? There's nothing for them to feed on, is there?

Oh, there's something there, but I don't think they can get at it. Too hidden. He doesn't really have access to it himself. No, I'd say he's safe from the Madness at least.

Then why are the Mind Brothers bothering? Odd. Very odd.

If you think that's odd, wait, I haven't finished yet. A little while ago he stopped for a rest and something completely new showed up.

?

Well, it's hard to explain. If I call it another mind, that's too much. It doesn't seem all that coherent. More like bits and pieces stuck together. Scraps of a mind, maybe. No, that's not right either. It's whole, but limited. Father, I really can't be any clearer than that. I've never encountered anything like this in my life.

Could the Mushin have anything to do with it?

Hmmmmmmmmm. Never thought of that. It did happen shortly after they showed up. Worth looking into. Thanks.

Uh, by the way, Father, I estimate two more days minimum before we make it to First Touch. Provided he doesn't completely disintegrate before then.

Help him if you must, Josh. Don't let him fall apart.

Yeah, I understand. But, uh, you know what he intends to do. I was just wondering if you have any plans I should know about in advance. I mean, I could . . .

We will follow the flow, Josh. We will follow the flow even through those areas where the shadow is too deep for us to see the outcome. Get him here, Josh, alive and functioning, at least minimally. He is an important part of the plan.

But he intends to kill—

*Alive and functioning, Josh. You must do your part
so that he can do his part so that I can do my part so that
. . . round and round, back and forth until the pattern
is woven. Remember how much Myali is giving, Josh.
Would you have us do any less?*

No, Father. And yet . . .

The root snared his foot and he tumbled down the last
few feet of the slope. Dazed, he lay sprawled at the
bottom of the ravine for several moments, trying to
regain his wits and his breath. He sat up slowly, groaning and cursing as he took stock of his condition. Bad
bruises on his shoulder, back, and knee. Cuts on his
face and neck where the brush he crashed through had
torn at his flesh. Lacerations and scrapes on his hands,
especially the palms, which he'd used to break his fall.
Gingerly he stood and continued to assess the damage.
His left ankle hurt like crazy, but would carry his
weight. Not sprained, thank God. He reached into his
pocket and pulled out the compass and laser wand. Both
were all right. The smoothstone was still there, too. His
pack hadn't opened, and there wasn't anything break-
able in it anyway.

All in all, he decided, not bad. Lucky. But watch it.
Because next time your luck might run out.

He looked up and saw the Face staring at him from
the branches of a small tree. Anger rapidly followed his
first twinge of fear. The damn thing was following him!
Peeping at him everywhere he went. He'd tried and
tried to ignore it, but everywhere he looked, there it
was.

Dunn took a couple of deep breaths to get his anger
under control. He glared back at the Face and made a
decision.

"Why are you following me?" he demanded.

"I'm not following you," the Face denied flatly.

"You're following me. Every time I try to get away, you come after me."

"That's ridiculous. I'm a Wanderer going to First Touch."

"So *you* say. *I* think you're chasing me."

"Good God! This is stupid. Look, I'm not . . . oh, what the hell. You're imaginary. I'm just imagining all this."

"Perhaps. But if so, you're crazy."

Dunn considered for a moment. "No, I don't think so. Exhausted, confused, mentally fucked-up, yes. But not crazy."

"Ergo," the Face responded triumphantly, "I'm real and not imaginary."

"Not necessarily. You could still be imaginary without being the product of a sick mind."

"Huh," the Face snorted. "You mean I'm just a mental sniffle, not a case of double pneumonia. Not very complimentary."

"I think you're some kind of side effect of these damn drugs. Myali's never heard of anything like you before, so I doubt if you're something native. And there's nothing in my own experience—"

"Your experience," the Face interrupted with a sneer. "You don't have any experience."

Dunn glared at the Face, his whole body suddenly tense. "What do you mean by that?"

"I mean you don't have any experience. Or any memory. Or any anything. You're a cipher, a nonentity, a blank. Hell, if either of us is imaginary, you're the most likely candidate!"

A fist clenched Dunn's stomach and the feet started

kicking the backs of his eyeballs again. He felt sweat break out all over his body even though he shivered as a chill passed up and down his spine. "I'm . . . I'm . . . not . . . a . . . blank. . . . I'm . . . Dunn," he gritted out between tightly clenched teeth.

"Dunn," the Face snickered nastily. "Oh, sure. Likely story. Dunn."

He drew himself up angrily. "Yes, damn it, Dunn! What's so funny about that? I'm Dunn."

"Ha! You claim Dunn's name. But what else of Dunn is there about you? Do you have Dunn's personality? His dreams? His memories? Any of the things that were his and his alone?"

The spy's mind was in such a turmoil of anger, confusion, and fear that he could scarcely think. He fought to stem a rising sense of panic. "No," he growled. "No. I'm Dunn. See!" He held up his left hand and pointed to it with his right. His voice rose toward hysteria as he spoke. "Me! That's me! Dunn! I'm Dunn! Me!"

Coldly, the Face replied.

"Shouting a name and pointing at a hand doesn't make you Dunn. Dunn is more than four little letters or a hand. Change the letters around and what have you? Nnud. Unnd. Ndnu. Meaningless without a reference. Just as Dunn is. And the reference you offer, a hand, what is that? Every cell in that hand changes constantly, like the water flowing in a river. Point again, right this instant, and it's not the same hand. No, Dunn must go beyond such transient things as shifting letters and flowing hands."

"It does!" cried the man, "It does! I know . . . I know . . ."

"You know!" laughed the Face with evil glee. "Your mind tells you! Ha! Listen carefully to your

mind, fool. Is it steady? Is there a beat of Dunn-ness
that keeps a measured pace, an unchanging rhythm of
self-awareness? Or is there nothing but a ceaseless swirl
of changing?

"And where is the Dunn of yesterday?"

The spy panted in terror, his eyes wide and staring as
he sank to his knees. "No," he whimpered. "No. I'm
Dunn. I'm me."

"You're you," the Face mocked triumphantly.
"And a spy and a girl of this planet. Three, three, not
one! Is Dunn the spy? Has Dunn always been the spy?
Did Dunn pick yellow eyes on the Plain or listen to a
caged lizard sing its despair? Where is the Dunn-ness
you cling to? Where does it come from and what does it
mean?"

"I KNOW!" the spy screamed as he jumped to his
feet. "I KNOW!" he shrieked, his mouth twisted and
flecked with foam. "I KNOW!" he bellowed as he
whipped the laser wand from his pocket and slashed
madly at the tree with its intense blade of light. "I
KNOW! I KNOW! I KNOW!"

Suddenly alone, standing in front of the smoldering
ruins of the tree, he collapsed in a heap. The pain pulsed
through his head in swelling waves. Myali, oh God,
Myali. Help me. Take me away from here.

The staff swept toward her ankles. She leapt into the
air to avoid the bone-shattering blow. But rather than
jump back or straight up, she flew forward, twisting to
the right and snapping out a side kick with her right
foot.

Her opponent saw it coming and shifted his weight
backward at the last moment. The kick caught him on
the upper part of his right arm, but his movement
absorbed most of the force. He staggered, caught his

balance, and aimed another attack at her head as she
landed. It came slashing down from left to right across
his body. Since she was already halfway turned, with
her right side facing the enemy, she continued her spin
to the left and thrust a left back kick up under the
whizzing staff.

The man's movement made the blow go wide, just
grazing his left hip. As she twisted fully around to face
him once more, he jabbed at her face with the tip of the
staff. She easily blocked upward and drove in with a
front kick to the stomach. He swung his left hip back
and the blow missed by inches. The other end of the
staff came rushing from her left as he drove it with his
right hand for the ribs. She barely managed to step back
and found herself off balance. Before she had time to
regain it, her opponent thrust the right end of the staff
between her legs and pushed hard and suddenly on the
left end, catching her right leg just behind the knee and
knocking her on her back. As she fell, she saw the end
of the staff rushing toward her face. She knew it would
hit right between the eyes and smash her forebrain.

The staff touched her lightly and the Master stepped
back, watching her solemnly as she rose and dusted off
the practice robe. When she was finished, he motioned
to her to join him and walked across the sunlit practice
yard toward a band of shade at its eastern edge. It was
only mid-morning, even though she'd been practicing
for two hours.

Following the Master's example, she sat in full lotus
and composed herself, calming her breathing and slowing the pounding of her heart. The moment she had
regained a suitable degree of serenity, he began.

"Not bad. Though you would have died."

"How can that be 'not bad'?"

"You learn. Two months ago you would have died a lot sooner."

"I don't understand what's wrong, Father. At the 'hood I was the best in both the Way of the Fist and the Soft Way. But here . . ."

He shrugged. "A tree lizard looks big to a water lizard. But to a Strider, neither is worth the effort of opening its mouth."

She blushed. "I'm . . . I'm just a tree lizard?"

"You are what you are."

"But my technique . . . Is my technique good?"

"Excellent. The best I've ever seen."

"Then why do you always beat me so easily?"

He gazed at her silently for several moments. Then he began to speak in a quiet voice. "Once a man asked a great artist for a picture of a cat and gave him a large amount of money in advance to draw it. After a month or so, the man returned to the artist and asked if the picture was ready. The artist said no and sent him away. A few months later, the man returned and again the artist sent him away, angrily declaring he would deliver the picture when it was finished. For a full year, the man waited and waited, hoping his picture would be done at last. Finally, losing all patience, he stormed into the artist's studio and demanded his painting. The artist nodded and calmly took out a sheet of his best paper, lifted his favorite brush from where it lay, and in an instant dashed off a painting of a cat. Without even looking at it, he handed it to the man.

"Gazing at the picture, the man was stunned. It was the most beautiful, most incredible painting he had ever seen. It was perfection. Line, proportion, design— everything, perfection.

"With sudden exasperation, he turned to the artist

and demanded to know why, if the artist could do something this magnificent in a few moments, hadn't he given him the picture sooner?

"The artist said nothing. He merely reached out and opened the door of an immense cabinet that stood in his studio. From it tumbled thousands of paintings of cats."

The Master fell silent and sat looking at her expectantly, awaiting her reaction.

Myali was puzzled. "I . . . I guess," she began, "the point is that it took the artist that long to master the technique of drawing the cat?"

He shrugged. "That's part of the meaning, surely. But it's more than that. Mastering technique does not make you a Master. Knowing brushwork, understanding the nature of various paper types, studying the characteristics of different inks will not allow you to create a great painting.

"The artist in the story went beyond merely mastering his techniques. Remember, he dashed off his final masterpiece almost carelessly. He had arrived at the point where he had so assimilated the technique that he had forgotten it. It was no longer something conscious to be thought of. It merely was. Thus the technique had vanished or become transparent so that only the subject of the technique showed through. That is why genius is impossible to copy. It is totally transparent and leaves no trace of how it is done."

She nodded. "I see. So that's the meaning of the story."

The Master smiled. "No, that's still only part of the meaning, Myali. In fact, that's the smallest, most insignificant part." She looked blank and he laughed.

"The real purpose of technique is not to produce anything at all. The artist's real purpose in mastering the brush is not to paint. Nor is fighting the real purpose behind a Seeker's mastering the side kick.

"Technique is really a form of knowing, or of coming to know. It's a way of opening up the thing to be known, a revealing that brings forth and makes present the thing as it is. The artist uses his technique to become entirely at home with the thing he paints. Eventually, when he comes to know the thing thoroughly, when its being is revealed fully to him, his technique is no longer necessary because he is truly in and of the thing itself. If it is a cat, he is totally immersed in its catness and its itness. There are no longer any barriers between the thing and him. It stands naked and open to his view."

Myali sat quietly musing for a few moments. "I . . . I think I understand," she began hesitantly. "The thing we study in the Way of the Fist is ourselves. The techniques we use—the kicks, punches, blocks, everything—put us in contact with our own bodies. And the mental discipline brings our minds into it, too. We sort of 'learn' ourselves, I guess."

The Master nodded. "Yes. The techniques of Way give us a method for bringing forth our own being. And in revealing it, we, like the artist, also open a view to something greater yet—being itself."

She gave a sad little laugh. "I'm afraid that's beyond me. I'm still trying to catch a glimpse of my *own* being. Oh, I understand what you're saying. It's just that I've never experienced it. I don't seem to be able to . . ." A sudden surge of longing swelled up within her, choking off her voice for an instant. As quickly as it came, it drained away, leaving behind only a bitter residue of empty despair. Confused and frightened, she tried to find something, anything, to say to fill the echoing emptiness before . . .

"But . . . but . . ." she blurted, achieving a slight sense of security by clutching at things she knew, "that doesn't explain why you beat me so easily. I mean, if my techniques are so good I should do better."

"I can beat you so easily because you're trying so hard to beat me. You're using the techniques as techniques rather than as a way of knowing. You see my staff coming toward your head and you block. Then you see it coming toward your ribs and you block again. Each time you fix your attention on my staff and follow it hither and yon in attempts to block or counter. In so doing, you shift your mind to one spot and leave a different one open for attack. Eventually, I draw you so far in one direction, you can't return in time to another, and I win. Only when you are truly immovable, when you are anchored firmly in your being, rather than leaping wildly here and there fixing on all manner of things, only then can you be everywhere by being no one-where.

"The way to achieve such an anchoring in your being is to use technique as a way of knowing instead of merely a way of doing. The artist's painting of the cat was not great because his technique was polished and perfect; it was great because he understood his own true being and that of the cat. And therefore his next painting and every one after will be equally as great.

"This is the deepest lesson to be learned, Myali. Technique is a way of knowing that reveals the thing studied and makes it present in its true being. But the very act of opening the being of a thing to knowing opens our own being to knowing as well. And that, in turn, opens being itself. This is the point we seek to reach. It is only here where we can find a place so firm we cannot be moved."

Myali looked down at the hard-packed dirt of the

practice-yard floor. "Then the real goal of what I'm doing is being?"

"Yes. You search for being."

"And if I search and search and find nothing?"

"Ah, but *nothing* is one of the most important things you can find. Jerome gave us the Way so that we could cut through the commonplace reality constructed by our senses and preconceptions and come face to face with the nothingness of the abyss. When we find it there, yawning bottomlessly just beneath the surface of our everyday existence, we are forced at last to recognize what we have always known but feared to admit: The anxiety which has ever haunted us, the unfocused fear which is so much a part of the human condition, is nothing less than an unconscious awareness of the abyss. As long as it remains unconscious, and unrecognized, it produces nothing but a vague discontent, a muffled anguish that casts a continual shadow over our lives. But confronted and known for what it is, this anxiety is the very force that impels us on our search for being."

Myali shuddered involuntarily. "I've known the nothing. I've stood at the brink of the abyss and seen all meaning fall forever into darkness. I've felt the anguish, sharp and clear, and known it as central to my existence. And I've found myself thrown back into the world to seek out that very being the nothing denies and I feel *must* exist.

"But, Father, I can't find it! I search and search and always, just when I think I can reach out and touch it, it retreats and moves away and I'm left grasping nothing. I . . . I . . . . At times when things seem most dark, I wonder if what I seek isn't mere illusion. And if the abyss isn't true reality after all." She bowed her head and gazed silently at the ground.

A look of soft compassion flashed across the Master's face and he half reached out his hand to touch her. "Being, my daughter, always withdraws from us when we actively seek it and try to give it a form that matches our understanding. In its withdrawal, however, it pulls us along behind, and, like a compass needle in a magnetic field, we become a sign that points to it even in the midst of its concealedness.

"We are signs pointing to being. We cannot read ourselves, because it is only being that gives us meaning, and we do not yet understand being. The most we can do is let ourselves be drawn along and hope that eventually the withdrawal will arrive at a place or a time when the being we seek unfolds in unconcealedness and we recognize what we have been looking at all along."

The young woman gazed up into the old man's face. Tears were welling in her eyes, making her vision fuzzy and blurred. "But, Father," she murmured, "what if the withdrawal always seems to lead back to the abyss? What if the path always leads into the endless night?"

His response was instant. "Then leap into the void and build firm foundations in the nothing."

Dunn opened his eyes on blackness. Nothing. He fought back a sudden surge of fear, using the breathing and concentration techniques he'd picked up from Myali. It's not the abyss, he reassured himself. Merely night. I've spent hours in this particular memory and now it's night.

He was lying on his back, his pack on the ground next to him. Sitting up, he pulled it to him, opened the flap, and began to dig for the matches. Have to grope around to find some wood, he thought. Must still be at the bottom of the ravine I fell into.

Suddenly he stopped, utterly still, a sense of awe dawning in his mind. "My God," he whispered out loud. "It's night, I'm completely surrounded by the dark and the forest, and I'm not terrified." Surprised, he tried to feel the state of near panic that had been his constant companion every since landing on Kensho. It was gone.

With a woof of amazement, he flopped on his back again, his hands behind his head. If he looked hard enough, he realized, he could see the dark patterns the leaves overhead made against the lighter background of the sky. Here and there a star slipped quickly between the gently stirring leaves.

He felt a thrill run through his body. I can deal with it. I can handle the night and the darkness and the forest. Oh, he admitted, as a rustling in the brush startled him, I'm still a little bit anxious. But not afraid anymore.

How about the darkness within? Can I handle that, too?

Cautiously, he reached in to find it.

Still there. But somehow, some way, it didn't seem as menacing. Hardly friendly, he granted as he pulled back toward the surface of his mind. But not as threatening as before.

He shivered with pleasure. I . . . I *feel* different. Wonderful. Like a huge weight's been lifted off my back. How did it happen? he wondered. God, when I was talking to the Face, just before the Master came, I was nearly off the deep end.

The Master! Of course. That had to be it. Something he'd said must have made the difference.

Carefully he reviewed the old man's words. Two things struck him as most significant. First, the Master claimed that being withdrew when you sought it. Second, that the darkness of the nothing pervaded everyone and everything. Or at least that seemed to be what he was saying when he declared that the abyss lay just beneath the surface of everyday existence.

If being retreats to concealedness when you look for it, he thought, it's no wonder I have such a hard time grasping the thing I pursue through my mind. And if the darkness is part of the order of things, if it isn't just something peculiar to me, then the fact I find it at my core is no cause for alarm.

The Master's last command suddenly shone brightly in his mind. "Then leap into the void and build firm foundations in the nothing." Could he do that? Could he chase the thing he sought right to the edge of the abyss and then leap, soaring through the darkness after it? Would he drop, lost and alone, forever? Or would he somehow be able to build a firm foundation in the void itself?

What would he build on? He had no memory, no detailed sense of self. But was one necessary? Sure, he didn't have access to Dunn's experiences. He couldn't feel Dunn's past joys and sorrows. Yet still, he *knew* beyond any shadow of doubt, that he *was* Dunn, that he did exist.

How could he prove it? Well, for himself, it was enough that his body hurt like hell. He chuckled. And if nobody else would accept that proof, how about a good smack on the head from his imaginary fist? The idea pleased him immensely and he laughed out loud.

He sat up again and picked up the pack from where he'd dropped it. Don't need the matches, he decided. Just a little bit of food. Then maybe I can get some sleep. First Touch is still a long way off.

He ate in calm silence. Finishing, he lay back and

once more began to think about what the Master had told him. Again and again he went over it, trying to wring the last shred of meaning from every word.

It wasn't until he was just dropping off to sleep that he realized he'd never talked to the Master, never met him, never even seen him. His final thoughts, full of warmth and gratitude, were of Myali.

X

The next morning, the spy prodded Dunn's mind to wake him. "We are falling behind schedule, Dunn. Our ETA for First Touch is late tomorrow. But if you don't get up and get moving, we won't make it."

Dunn just rolled over. Huh, he thought blearily, seems so real. Like he was outside instead of just in my head. Like that damn Face. Like . . .

"Damn it, on your feet!" The spy squeezed Dunn's mind slightly and the groggy man sat up with a yelp.

"Okay, okay. You don't have to get nasty about it!"

"Just do as you are told, Dunn. Review briefing. Mission."

Mechanically, he responded. "Proceed to First Touch. Gather information on state of preparedness of planetary defenses. Evaluate extent and character of possible resistance to a landing. Identify key leaders, especially those whose removal might cause disruption in the functioning of government. In particular, assassinate the Way-Farer."

"Good."

"Good?" Myali asked. "How can killing Kadir be considered good?"

"Evaluation indicates his removal will have a disorientating effect on the population and lessen resistance to landing. While he is not a commanding officer in the usual sense, the Way-Farer appears to be an important symbolic figure. His death will weaken enemy morale. Full evaluation and advancement of this objective to First Priority status awaits final confirmation based on actual contact." The spy sounded smug and Dunn felt like hitting him.

Myali just laughed. "The life or death of the Way-Farer won't have any effect on Kensho's will to resist. If anything it'll stiffen our resolve, since the act of assassination will reveal the true character of our enemy."

"The Way-Farer is the primary leadership symbol on this planet," the spy insisted stubbornly. "He is an authority figure, a—"

"Nonsense," Myali interrupted. "Father Kadir leads no one. Where would he lead us? Each must walk his own Way and walk it alone. The only thing Kadir can do is offer encouragement and help us when we stumble. But lead? Nonsense."

"In any military-political system, the leadership is the critical nexus of the structure. Destroy the leadership and the rest of the organization collapses and loses its will to continue fighting. The same is true of complex socioeconomic systems, though of course the character of the leaders changes. It is clear—"

"But Kensho isn't a military-political-socio-economic system!"

The spy hesitated for a fraction of a second. "It must be," came the tight conclusion. "Evaluation indicates—"

"Evaluation is wrong."

"That is not possible. Evaluation indicates—"

"Hey," Dunn interjected, "cut it out, will you?" He rubbed his temples with his fingertips, his face twisted in pain. "This argument may be great fun for you two, but it's taking place in *my* head and it hurts. Jeez," he muttered, "it all seems so real, so . . . so outside my head. Maybe I'm going nuts, huh?"

"This is an aberration," the spy declared stiffly. "The pain is a reminder that you should not indulge in aberrations."

Myali's sympathy flowed through his mind, soothing him. "Sorry, Dunn. I guess he's hurting you if you don't behave?"

"Yeh. He hurts me. Must have been what all those early headaches were about." Dunn laughed grimly. "Guess I was an aberration from the very first."

"Is there any way to avoid the pain?"

He shrugged. "Do what I'm told. You know, conform to the conditioning. I guess the pain must be built in as a self-correcting device."

She was silent for a moment. "Do you suppose he could use that pain to force you to do something you didn't want to do?"

"Like what?"

"Like kill Kadir?"

Dunn considered. "Don't know," he finally admitted. "But I've got a feeling he's very strong. Hell, there's more of him, or of you for that matter, than there is of me. I'm the junior member of this team."

"But what if you tried—"

"This discussion is counterproductive and interferes with the mission. There has been entirely too much of this sort of deviation in the past. It has been tolerated because there was still hope you would achieve integration and conduct yourself properly. We are now too close to the culmination of the mission to allow such aberrations to continue. They must cease at once.''

Dunn felt sudden twisting pressure in his head and crushed his eyes closed against it. ''Uhhhhh,'' he grunted in pain. ''He's . . . damn . . . strong . . . Myali,'' he gasped out.

The agony grew in a swift, towering wave that broke over him, tumbling down, down into darkness. But just before he blacked out, he heard her whisper, ''Can't beat him at his own game. Have to switch the rules.''

When he opened his eyes for the second time that morning, he was still sitting in the forest at the bottom of the ravine he had fallen into last night. It was a dreary day and a light rain was trickling down through the forest canopy. Gingerly, he tested his mind to see if the others were still there. ''Myali?'' he asked tentatively.

''I'm here,'' came the muffled reply. But the spy cut in short with another squeeze.

Dunn buried his head in his hands as the pain struck. When it passed he looked up, his face contorted with anger. ''Damn it,'' he shouted. ''Stop that, you bastard! That hurts!''

''As long as you perform your designated function, it will not be necessary. But nothing can be allowed to interfere with the mission.''

''How the hell can talking to Myali interfere?''

''There is no Myali,'' came the curt reply.

''No Myali? But I . . .''

''You have failed to properly integrate the memory patterns transferred to you from the captured native. Because of this failure—''

''Nuts. It's more than a memory pattern. Myali's a

person. I know her. I . . . I . . ."

"The captured native is currently undergoing inter-rogation on board ship. There is no Myali."

Like a man wandering out of a fog, Dunn began to recognize the outlines of what had happened. "Ship," he muttered. "Interrogation. Yeh." He was quiet for several moments, a look of deep sadness filling his eyes. "Yeh," he finally mumbled. "Yeh. Just a mem-ory pattern . . . in my head."

Listlessly, he opened his pack and took out some food. Without speaking, he ate. Still silent, he repacked his gear and rose to leave. A quick look at the compass set him on the right course.

For several hours he trudged north northeast through the gradually increasing rain. By noon, when he stopped to eat, it was pouring.

"Maybe I should hole up someplace until this eases off a little," he said to the air.

"No," the spy answered instantly. "We are behind schedule as it is. There must be no further delay."

"But he's soaked," protested Myali.

"That does not affect his ability to perform his func-tion to any appreciable degree."

"It will if he gets sick."

"Sickness and wetness do not equate."

"No, of course not. But when he's wet, the water conducts away his body heat more rapidly than the air, and he'll definitely get chilled, which in turn may lower his resistance to disease."

"No negative effects would transpire within the time limit set for the accomplishment of the mis-sion."

"Oh, swell," grumbled Dunn. "Terrific. I might catch my death of foolishness. But not until after the mission, so it doesn't matter."

"Correct," the spy confirmed. "The fate of the agent upon the completion of the mission is irrelevant."

"You meant you don't care?" Myali asked.

"Correct."

The Face objected from a thicket. "That's a hell of an attitude."

"It is the only possible attitude."

"But—" the Face began, only to have Dunn interrupt.

"Stop it, please!" His voice shook with something between fear and anger. "Shit," he muttered, bringing himself back under control, "it all seems so damn real. Like you're all here. No me any more. Just you. Or mostly you. So damn real." He held his head for several minutes, calming his breathing, relaxing his tight muscles. "Better," he finally said, lifting his head. "Okay, spy, I won't hole up. But it's kind of hard walking in this rain. Cuts down my visibility. You got anything against my slowing the pace a little?"

"Only a little," the spy grudgingly granted.

Dunn rose. "You might put on the rain poncho in your pack," Myali offered. He shook his head. "Why bother? I'm already soaked. At least in the pack it helps keep my other gear dry."

He started off in the direction of the thicket from which the Face peered. "Still think you're Dunn, huh?" it asked as he approached.

He hesitated before answering. "This morning's sort of shaken my confidence a little. Maybe I'm losing my grip and that's why you and Myali and the spy seem so real. Maybe I'm going crazy. Maybe there really is no me. But . . ." he hesitated again, feeling momentarily confused. "But, damn it, I still *feel* like Dunn!"

"Hmmmmmm," the Face mulled over this statement from a clump of fernlike plants. "I assume you're using the word 'feel' here loosely to mean something like 'perceive internally'?"

Annoyance restored some of Dunn's confidence. "Huh! There you go again. You already did the whole 'perception' and 'continuity' bit with me yesterday. Look, Face, I'll grant you there are all kinds of discontinuities in existence. Even in my immediate perceptions. Even when perceiving myself. So what? All that proves is that there are discontinuities. It doesn't *disprove* that there *are* continuities! Hey. I close my eyes, the world goes away. I open them, it's back. Proof of discontinuity or of continuity? Take your pick. Is the glass half empty or half full? A pretty little problem, but since I'm thirsty and have to live with whatever is *in* the glass, who cares?

"Listen, Face. Somebody's obviously been messing with my mind. These aren't my memories. I'm not the one in control. But there's something here, something conscious of not being something else. And although that something can doubt *your* existence even while talking with you, it can't doubt its *own*."

"Why?"

Dunn laughed harshly. "Because it's sopping wet, its feet hurt, and it's got one hell of a headache."

The Face smiled condescendingly. "Cogito ergo sum."

"Don't believe I've met her," Dunn replied drily.

"I mean, what you're saying sounds very much like the old idea of 'I think, therefore I am.'"

"Not quite. It's 'I feel' instead of 'I think.' And the 'therefore' isn't necessary."

"I feel I am," murmured Myali thoughtfully. Dunn sensed the warmth of her approval glowing in his mind. For a moment he experienced such intense happiness that it seemed as if his chest would burst. He could think of nothing else to do, so he started to whistle.

The black-robed figure stopped dead in its tracks. Leaning slightly forward, it cupped a hand to its ear, listening intently to catch a new sound amidst the drip, drip, drip of the rain. A whistling, something like a lizard's but more complex. Puzzled, he continued standing there, tense and alert. Could the Triple One be whistling? In this rain? Knowing he was pursued? It seemed the height of foolishness, but there also seemed to be no other explanation.

The sound came from ahead and to his right, farther to the east. How had he failed to notice the trail? He had to have crossed it, since he'd been coming from the east in search of the creature that had given him the slip once already.

He began to move, swiftly, silently, in the direction of the strange being he pursued. Ah! Ah! Yes! There, the subtle, confused aura of the Triple One's mind. Yes. A thrill of anticipation ran through him. Ready! Almost ready! The Triple One was becoming, and rapidly! The Mind Brothers could sense the change. They were hungry and eager!

Suddenly he paused again. What was that? He probed ahead. Another mind? And Mind Brothers already there? Not feeding? Dismayed, he shook his head back and forth for several moments in indecision.

Finally he decided and began moving again. Three minds or four, it made no difference. The Mind Brothers were hungry. His sword was sharp and swift. There would be feeding, interesting feeding. And soon.

The Ronin's picked him up again, Father. I'm paralleling them both about fifty yards to the west.

Is the Black Robe dangerous or only curious?
He's deadly.
Dunn must not die before he reaches me, Josh.
I know, Father. But I can't help wishing . . .
Don't wish. Act. The Ronin must be stopped.
Yes, Father.

The brown-robed figure stepped unexpectedly from behind the tree, directly into the path of the Ronin. With a hissing intake of breath, the black-clad creature stopped short.

They stood facing each other without moving. Their bodies appeared relaxed and at ease, their eyes locked tightly in mutual appraisal. For several moments the motionless tableau continued while the rain fell between them.

Then with a cry and a swirl of black, the Ronin sprang forward, his sword leaping from its sheath in an overhead cut. His opponent was simply not there when the blade descended. At the last possible instant he spun out of the way to the right. Now his own sword was out, held firmly in front in on-guard position, the point aiming directly at the Ronin's throat.

The killer attacked again with a flurry of blows directed at Josh's head and neck and wrists. All were parried effortlessly and no attempt was made to counter.

Seeing that the brown-robed man didn't attack, the Ronin paused and stepped back a pace, out of striking range. ''This unit carries Mind Brothers,'' he hissed. ''This unit wants something. What is it?''

''Hunt other game. The Triple One must not be harmed.''

The Ronin snorted. ''The Triple One is Totality's.

This unit has followed him for many miles waiting for him to become. Now he is almost ready. The Mind Brothers are anxious. Step from my path.''

Josh did not move.

The Ronin shrugged. ''Then die,'' he said and flung himself at Josh again. Two slashes at the head were followed by a sweeping cut for the chest which actually sliced the material of the brown robe. Josh parried and countered in earnest now, realizing this fight was to the death. Ronin were capable of reason, but only up to a point. Push beyond that point and there was nothing left but to kill them. Or be killed.

The Black Robe was a seasoned fighter. Josh had fought men this good before and triumphed, though he bore the scars of one of those battles. He blocked a head cut and countered with a slash at the killer's neck. The Ronin parried and thrust for his throat. Josh knocked the blade aside and lunged forward, aiming for the wrists.

Disengaging, the man in black began to circle his brown-robed adversary warily, looking for an opening. Josh's sword followed him smoothly. As he turned, however, the tip of his blade dipped down ever so slightly. Instantly the opponent was leaping in, slashing for the head. Without a moment to spare, Josh met the attack and returned it with a cut at the Ronin's head. The swordsman simply stepped back again, out of range.

So, Josh thought, he wants an opening and likes head attacks. And is good at them, he added, remembering the man's speed. A plan formed in his mind. Give him the opening by lowering the sword tip. Then when he comes for it, step in and thrust for his throat. A good plan, if only the man wasn't so fast. His speed, though, made it risky.

A few more passes and Josh decided it was time to finish the whole thing. He could feel his own growing exhaustion and the ground was becoming slippery and churned up with their maneuvering. Soon it would become too sloppy for sure footing and chance might decide the whole thing.

Suiting action to thought, he lowered the tip of his sword as he stepped. The Ronin was in like a flash, sword sweeping down for Josh's head. But rather than blocking, the young man moved forward, his sword thrusting out as he straightened his arms, heading for the exposed throat of his enemy.

At the last moment, his rear foot slipped in the mud and the blade hit low, striking the Ronin in the right shoulder. Halfway through his own attack, the killer saw what was happening and threw himself backward in a frantic attempt to escape. As a result, his own blow went awry and sliced downward short of its objective and off to the right side.

With a sickening thunk, the blade smashed into Josh's upper arm. As he went down, driven by both the blow and his own loss of balance, the young man ripped his blade out of his opponent's shoulder. Hitting the ground with a soggy thud, he looked up to see the Ronin's blade raised for another, final stroke. Without thinking, he thrust upward, catching the man in the lower stomach with the tip of the blade and ripping him open until the tip stopped, wedged in his sternum. The Ronin's guts cascaded out, spewing across Josh, as the man crumpled, lifelessly following them to the ground.

Stopped him, was all Josh managed to send before he blacked out.

The spy twisted his mind again and Dunn collapsed into the mud with a grunt of pain. His head was reeling, his vision blurred and distorted.

"Get up, Dunn," Myali urged. Trying to respond, he surged groggily to his feet. "Don't think I can beat 'im," he muttered. "No way to protect myself. No way to fight back. He's inside. Can't touch 'im."

"Try, Dunn," she coaxed. "You've got a chance. And now that you're beginning to understand, it's more important than ever for you to fight. You can't let him win or it will all be for nothing."

"Gotta try. Yeh." He stood, swaying gently with exhaustion. The fight with the spy was finally in the open. Dunn had refused to continue on toward First Touch, refused to complete the mission. The spy had struck and struck hard, slamming at his mind with a force even Dunn, who had already felt his power before, had not expected. But even though he'd known he had nothing to equal the strength of the spy, he'd fought anyway. And been knocked down once, twice, three times.

His body ached in a hundred places. His mind felt like it was on fire. Pain dulled his senses and made him stagger with every step. Fight, he ordered himself. Fight what? he asked. My own mind? How?

The spy sneered. "You have no hope, Dunn. You cannot beat me. Even with the help of these mental constructs you have created, you are no match for me. I am your conditioning, the core that was placed in an empty mind to give it shape. You will conform to your conditioning and complete the Mission."

"No, not the core," Dunn mumbled. "Not core. I'm core. Dunn."

"There is no core. There is only me. These continual aberrations will cease once and for all. This time I intend to stamp them out permanently. We will arrive at our target late this afternoon and you will be in complete compliance by that time.''

Dunn spread his legs to steady himself. ''I'm the core. You're wrong. Maybe I can't beat you, but I'll try. Tired of being pushed around. Time to push back.''

The spy laughed. ''With what? You have no weapon but the laser wand, and that will not work against me. Unless you intend to perform brain surgery on yourself! You are helpless, Dunn. Helpless and hopeless. You can only fight me with your mind. And I control your mind. You will comply with your programming.'' He began to squeeze again, slowly applying the pressure. ''You will comply.''

Gasping in pain, Dunn went to his knees. ''Hold on,'' Myali urged, her voice fading in his agony. ''Uh-uh,'' he grunted. ''Spy's right. Can't fight.'' The pressure mounted. ''Too strong. But I'm the core. The core . . . must . . . endure . . .''

With a final twitch of blinding anguish, Dunn fell forward and smashed into the ground.

Father Kadir watched silently as the lone, mud-spattered figure slowly climbed through the late afternoon sun to where he sat at the top of the mound. Even from a distance, he could see how the man's shoulders drooped wearily, how his steps dragged in exhaustion. A wave of sorrow swept over him. So this is how our fathers use their fellow men, he thought. The wave swept on and he watched and waited.

''Analysis indicates that is the Way-Farer, Dunn. Obtain positive identification before commencing action. Hate him. He is evil, a danger to our race. The Way-Farer seeks to destroy you and all like you. He is the greatest threat the Power and Earth have ever known. He must be killed. Hate him.''

"I hate," Dunn mumbled in reply.

The spy squeezed his mind. "You hate *him*."

"Uhhhh. I hate him.''

"Kill him, Dunn. Kill him.''

Now he could see the man's face distinctly. It was suffused with fatigue and pain. The eyes were hollow and glassy, the mouth constantly alternating between slackness and a grimace of anguish. He was breathing heavily, sucking in great gulps of air, even though the climb wasn't long or steep. Occasionally the man's whole body would shake or twitch as if struggling against some invisible bonds.

Closer yet. He could see the sweat pouring off the man's brow. His fingers were like claws. Father Kadir sensed an aura of intense suffering flowing from the approaching figure. Here, he thought in wonder, is a struggle that makes ours fade into insignificance. For the battle being waged in that man's soul is the Final Fight, the Ragnarok of being. And he fights it totally alone.

Or is he alone? Where has Myali gone? And the other one Josh spoke of?

The sitting figure rose calmly as Dunn shuffled up. "Father Kadir?" he managed to croak out. The man nodded.

"Kill him! Kill! Kill!" screamed the spy.

Dunn reached into the front pocket of his robe. His fingers closed over the smooth shape of the laser wand. He began to pull it out, flicking the activate switch.

Father Kadir smiled at him warmly. "Welcome home, Seeker," he greeted softly. "Welcome home.''

"Now, Dunn!!!''

PART THREE

The most difficult learning is to come to know actually and to the very foundations what we already know.

—Martin Heidegger

XI

Bishop Thwait looked up from the brain-scan read-outs that lay spread across the table in front of him. The young woman in the chair was stirring. Coming back to consciousness already? He checked the clock on the wall. A good twenty minutes too early.

Her eyes snapped open and he found himself caught in her stare. No confusion of an awakening mind here, he judged. No disorientation. No worry. No fear.

With an effort he pulled his eyes away from hers and began to study the readouts once more, purposely ignoring her. Even as he did it, he knew he'd made a mistake and given her a victory. Damn it, he silently cursed. I'm letting her throw me off balance. Stubbornly refusing to let her know he recognized her tiny triumph, he continued to peruse the charts spread across his table.

Fascinating. The girl's brain was well within the human norm as far as size and general structure were concerned. Yes, he decided, well within. Except for a few structural oddities. He traced one with his finger. There to there. A group of neurons that led from the association areas of the frontal and temporal lobes in both hemispheres to the limbic system. A whole bundle of neurons, actually. Enough to be considered a separate structure, a corpus, or perhaps even a lobe. "Corpus Thwait" he tentatively named it.

The other anomalies were scattered, seemingly at random, across the cerebral cortex. They consisted of groups of neurons attached to each other in what seemed to be a closed feedback loop. Only one cell in each group had a dendrite that connected outside the loop to other neurons.

Is the girl unique? he wondered. Or are these strange structures typical of the people of this planet? And if they're typical, what are their functions? Do they even have functions? Could they merely be random mutations caused by the higher than earth-normal level of radiation their sun puts out? Was it possible that . . .

"Anything interesting?" the girl asked. Thwait looked up. He'd almost forgotten her in his fascination with the data. Once again her eyes caught his and held them. Again, more slowly and distinctly, she said, "Anything interesting?"

"I understood you the first time," he answered in an irritated tone. "Your accent is strange. Long vowels, clipped consonants, but the speech is still Basic even after eight hundred years. Surprisingly pure, actually. I would have expected far more drift, given the isolation in which your culture has developed." He stopped and frowned. The calmness of the prisoner bothered him. It wasn't right. She should be totally confused and disoriented. She'd been unexpectedly snatched from her home planet, probably raped by Chandra, knocked out with sedatives, and undergone transfer. The subsonics alone should have her at the edge of hysteria. Yet there she sat, strapped into the chair in the Room, calm and collected, acting for all the world like she was right at home.

He pushed his chair back and stood up abruptly. The woman annoyed him. It was time to take command of the situation and begin the oral interrogation. He leaned forward on the table, his fingertips touching its surface, and demanded harshly, "Who are you?"

"Myali Wang," she responded mildly.

"What is the name of your planet?"

"Kensho."

"Does the name have any significance?"

"It refers to one of the stages of Enlightenment."

"Ah, a Zenist term."

"I assume so. Admiral Nakamura gave it the name and he was a Zen Master."

"You know of Admiral Nakamura?"

"Of course."

So, the Bishop thought, they haven't lost their history. Which means there was no major break in their culture—and that they've had eight hundred years to develop it! Keeping our presence hidden might have been the correct tactic after all. And Thomas's headstrong desire to go in with his guns blazing could well have led to exactly the kind of disaster I feared. Eight hundred years!

Since the girl was being so cooperative, Thwait decided to soften his tone. It was possible he'd learn more by being friendly.

"Ah, my child," he began, "I imagine you're wondering what all this is about."

"Yes."

"To be walking through familiar countryside one moment, and the next to wake up, strapped into a chair in a strange room with an unknown man asking you questions, all that must make you wonder.''

"Yes.''

"Well . . .'' He paused, unsure of how to continue. Her reaction was not what he had hoped for or expected. She seemed too calm, too sure of herself. For a moment he wondered if she really had been unconscious the whole time. Then the thought struck him that perhaps she already knew exactly where she was and what was going on. But both ideas were so preposterous that he immediately rejected them, disgusted with himself for even thinking them. Data, Andrew, he reminded himself. Data, not fantasies.

"Well,'' he repeated, "I am Bishop Andrew Thwait of the Power. And you are on a scout ship of the imperial fleet. We are here to re-establish contact between this colony and Earth.''

She nodded. "So. Yes. I understand. That explains why *you* are here. But it hardly explains why *I* am here.'' She looked down at the bonds that held her to the chair, then back up at him with a slight smile.

"The bonds are a precaution,'' he said stiffly.

"Against me?''

"Against unexpected occurrences.''

"Have any arisen?''

"No.''

"Then?'' she raised an eyebrow in question, once again looking down at the straps that held her to the chair.

"Ah. Just part of procedure, my child. They will be removed when the questioning is completed.''

"I see. Questioning.'' Myali gave the bishop a cool, appraising look, a slightly mocking smile playing about her lips. She appeared relaxed, completely in command of both herself and the situation.

Behind the facade of external calm, however, her mind raced furiously. More "questioning." What would it be like this time, she wondered. The last time had taught her that these people had unexpectedly powerful resources at their command when it came to dealing with the mind. Thinking back, she remembered the "questioning" she had undergone immediately following her arrival on the ship.

She'd still been feigning unconsciousness, so they'd strapped her to a gurney and hurried her through dim corridors to a small room. There they'd hooked her up to a strange machine unlike anything she'd ever seen before. Not knowing quite what to expect, she'd been astonished to discover that the machine could enter her mind.

Her first impulse had been to resist. She'd quickly realized the futility of that, however. The machine had vastly more power than she did, and simply pushed her aside when she tried to stand in its way. Playing it cautious, she'd backed off and watched passively for a while as it bumbled about, stirring up memories, copying them, and then relaying them out of her mind. For the life of her, she couldn't figure out the purpose behind the machine's actions. It didn't seem to have any particular sense of discrimination or ability to evaluate the relative importance of the material it copied. It just grabbed whatever came to hand and then moved on in an apparently random pattern.

Moving very gently, she'd tried an experiment. Rather than attempting to stop the machine, she'd tried deflecting it. The principle was simple, basic physics. The amount of force needed to shift the power of the machine a few molecules left or right was significantly less than that required to meet it head on. In a very short time she'd found she could steer it, giving it access to certain memories, keeping it away from others.

The problem was, she still didn't know what the machine's purpose was in copying her memories. And until she knew, it was impossible to know which information would be harmless to yield and which critical to withhold.

There was only one way to find out. Carefully pushing the machine into what she remembered of arithmetic, she'd gone exploring, probing back into the machine itself. It wasn't particularly difficult. The machine used organic neurotransmitters in its circuits instead of electrons, so moving along them was much like moving through her own mind. The circuitry was relatively simple and not very interesting. But what she discovered at the other end of the machine was both fascinating and frightening.

It was what was left of a human mind. An utter shambles, it had been twisted, torn, turned inside out, scrambled, and emptied of most of its contents. Still, it was a mind, and enough remained of the man who had once inhabited it to give her a fairly accurate reading of his general character. She'd even stumbled across his name, half buried amid the detritus scattered along his neural pathways. Dunn.

She'd paused for a moment, wondering what to do. It was plain the machine was feeding the information gleaned from her own mind into Dunn's. There had to be a purpose behind the transfer, though she couldn't imagine what it could be. Nevertheless, she was fairly certain that whatever the reason, it was meant to be used against Kensho. She couldn't stop it from happening, that much was clear. But just possibly she might be able to turn it to advantage. Dunn appeared to be a decent sort, even if he was one of *them*. And there was more than a hint, both in what was left of his mind and in the fact that someone had tried to destroy it, that suggested the man did not get along well with his own people. Perhaps, just perhaps, there was a chance that . . .

She decided. Working feverishly, she assembled the bits and pieces of Dunn that were still left. Then she retreated back into her own mind and carefully fed Dunn the information she thought might help him reconstruct his sense of self. Exhausted by her efforts, she'd barely been able to keep pace with the machine. When it finally withdrew, she'd collapsed.

Even then, she'd come back to consciousness long before the bishop realized. Myali had awoken to find herself strapped into a sort of chair. The air was filled with a very low, almost imperceptible humming sound that grated on her nerves. She'd listened for a moment to familiarize herself with the sound in order to make it perceptually neutral.

For perhaps a quarter of an hour she'd watched the man seated behind the table in front of her. Through eyes barely open she was able to scrutinize his face and observe his every move as he pored over some sheets of paper spread across the top of his table.

His character wasn't hard to read. Intelligence virtually shone from his eyes. The strength of his will was equally evident. Here was a man who knew what he wanted and how to get it. And did get it. That was also plain. A sense of power radiated from his every move, the way he held his head, the firm motions of his hands. When this man gave an order, it was followed, immediately and without question. Myali shuddered inwardly. Despite his small size and gray hair, this one was dangerous.

But there were weaknesses as well. He was incredibly proud and egotistical. The set of his mouth betrayed a stubborn arrogance that knew no bounds. And the light in his eyes came from more than just intelligence. There was a gleam of fanaticism there and perhaps even a glimmer of madness.

One more thing completed her picture of him. At Josh's insistence, she had carried Mind Brothers with her in hopes of being able to use them to communicate with home. It seemed a slim hope, but now the creatures proved valuable in another, unexpected way. They were highly sensitive to the darker side of human nature and, attracted by something they detected in the man she was studying, they began to stir. Carefully she loosened her hold on them, allowing them to reach out and touch his mind.

The result was instant and shocking. A vast, seething turmoil broke over her: Hatred. Deep, violent disgust and aversion toward almost everyone and everything in the universe. This was not the tiny kernel of blackness that all men carried at their center, this was a darkness as wide and deep as the mind it filled almost to overflowing. She gasped and grabbed her Mind Brothers, struggling to hold them back.

He despises everyone he's ever met, she realized, and is predisposed to despise anyone he ever will meet! People are less than nothing to him, pathetic creatures to be used and destroyed as he sees fit. He keeps these secret feelings under tight constraint, but I sense that they leak through constantly, and control his conscious mind almost as much as his conscious mind controls them. That was why the Mind Brothers had been able to detect them so easily.

The force of his hatred momentarily stunned and confused her. The man was obviously a leader. Yet how could he be if he despised everyone, including his followers? A leader should love his people. Why else would they follow?

Fear. As soon as she asked the question, the answer streaked across her consciousness. They followed out of fear, fear of the power the leader wielded. Although together they were far stronger than the leader could ever be, the fear divided them against each other, isolated them, made them weak. His power came from their fear and their fear came from his power. It was a vicious circle and once started it would be difficult indeed to break out of it.

A great sadness welled up in her, bringing a lump to her throat. How unhappy these mighty men of Earth must be! How dreadful and bleak their lives! And this one, this gray-haired little man seated at the table in front of her was the most pitiful of all. In the midst of all his power, all his intelligence, all his pride, was an emptiness that made everything futile and worthless.

The sadness passed and she saw him clearly again for what he was . . . the enemy of herself, her people, and her planet. And she knew how to deal with him. Without waiting any longer, she'd stirred and "woken up."

Myali watched him now as he rose from the table and came toward her. It was about to begin. Oh, Gods, she wondered, am I really strong enough? A momentary sense of panic was replaced by a vision of Father Kadir's kind face, then by the strong, determined lines of Mother Illa's. Whatever I am, she realized, weak or strong, I am the one, and I can only try.

The bishop stopped and spoke to the air. "Equipment." The small column rose from the floor, carrying its load of syringes. Thwait picked one up and held it out so the bound young woman could see it clearly. "Do you know what this is, my child?"

"It's a syringe, used to inject liquids subcutaneously."

He nodded. Her answer was one more proof that there had been no collapse of culture on this planet. Yet if that was true, came the nagging question, why was there no evidence of an industrial-technical civilization? It was a critical piece of information he had to find out.

He replaced the syringe on the column top. She didn't appear to be afraid of it. Perhaps he would save the threat of using it until later when she had learned to fear him.

"I wonder what else you know. Does 'laser' mean anything to you?" She nodded. "Quantum mechanics?" Another nod. "Sarfatti-Aspect drive?" And another.

Musing, the bishop walked back and forth in front of his prisoner. "Hmmmmmm. Indeed. You seem remarkably well informed. Do your people have any lasers? No? Yet you know of them. Most strange. Most contradictory.

"How about weapons, my child? Surely you have weapons."

"Yes, we have weapons."

"Ah?" He gave her a questioning look, encouraging her to continue.

"The sword, of course, The staff. Spears. The bladed staff Jerome created. Knives. Most recently, the bow for ritual practice and meditation."

His eyebrows rose. "And?"

"That's all, aside from our hands and feet."

"No firearms?"

"None."

"No lasers?"

"None."

"Surely you don't expect me to believe you, my child?"

She shrugged as best she could in the restraining straps. "What you choose to believe is your business. I merely answer your questions to the best of my ability."

Thwait controlled his anger and stalked over to a panel of instruments on the left wall. When he reached it, he grabbed a dial and turned it all the way up. The subsonics were on full blast now, to the point where even he, with all his training, began to feel their effects. He turned back to watch their effect on the girl.

She was smiling. "It doesn't bother me anywhere near as badly as it does you. For your own comfort, you really should lower the volume."

Disregarding her comment, he walked back to the chair and stood glaring down at her. "You are clever. But you are lying." He waved his hand to indicate the room and the instruments within it. "I can tear your mind apart. I can strip you of every memory, every idea, every emotion. I can turn you into a drained, empty shell. And then, at my leisure, I can poke and probe into what I have ripped out until I get my answers."

"Like you did to Dunn," she declared softly.

Thwait was stunned to silence. His mouth opened several times before he could form his words. "Dunn?" he finally managed to say. "How in the name of Kuvaz do you know about Dunn?"

"I gave him my memories, or had you forgotten?"

The bishop spun around and walked back to the table. He sat down and stared at Myali for several moments. "Who the hell are you?" he finally asked, his voice heavy with menace.

"Myali Wang," came the calm reply.

"Who are you *really*?" came the demand.

She smiled and was silent.

"I can tear it out of you!" he screamed, jumping to his feet and knocking the chair backward to crash on the floor.

"I think you should turn that dial down again. The low tones are disturbing you."

"Damn you, I can force you to tell me who you really are!"

"I doubt that," she responded almost wistfully, "since I don't know the answer to that question myself. And I've been seeking the answer for a long time."

Thwait was about to yell at her again when he got control of himself. He looked down and saw that his hands were shaking. What's wrong with me? he wondered. I'm letting this little slip of a woman affect me more strongly than anyone ever has in my life! He turned to look at the panel to his left. The dial was all the way to the right. The subsonics. That must be it. The level is absurdly high. It must be affecting my judgement. He walked over and shut it off completely.

There. That was better. It was like suddenly releasing a pressure that had been building inside his mind. Yes, it had to be the subsonics.

Picking up the chair, he sat down behind the table again and stared at the young woman. No, he admitted, it isn't entirely the subsonics. It is at least partially this . . . this creature. She annoyed him more completely than any person he had ever met. Why? Was she doing it on purpose?

Andrew considered the data he'd gathered up to this point. In review, there was a surprising amount. And a great deal of it was totally unexpected. First, she answered any question he asked her. He glanced over at the readouts on the machines that monitored her through the chair. So far she had told the truth or at least had not lied. Second, she wasn't afraid. Her calm was as real as it was unnatural. The readouts showed that, too. Third, she was immune to the subsonics and somehow knew about Dunn. Impossible. Yet there it was.

And the answers about weapons! He shook his head. Something was very wrong here, very wrong. The data didn't correlate.

Reaching a decision, he rose slowly and walked over to look down at Myali once more. His face wore a brooding expression as he searched her for even the slightest signs of weakness or fear.

"I am afraid, my child, I have underestimated you and your people. There is more here than meets the eye. Much more. Dangerously much more. Hmmmmmm. Indeed. I have been using the wrong techniques. My own penchant for personal, oral questioning has led me in the wrong direction with you." He sighed. "It is a much, much kinder technique since it leaves the mind intact. But in your case, I fear it will be inadequate."

The bishop smiled and nodded. "Yes, in your case I must use a more thorough method. Harsher, more destructive, but undoubtedly more effective." He turned and picked one of the syringes from the column top. "This, now," he said, gazing in fond fascination at the orangish liquid in the tube, "is a very potent drug developed by the Power during the Readjustment. It is shockingly hard on the system, but it opens the mind up to the machine like a blossoming flower. Some say the holy Kuvaz himself created it. It was only used on the most stubborn and difficult of cases. Like the Zenists."

He moved behind her chair. "It must be injected in a very painful spot—just at the top of the spinal chord where it meets the lower part of the brain. That, you see, is the reason the needle is so long." With one hand

he grabbed her hair and jerked her head forward, exposing the curve of the back of her neck. Slightly licking
his upper lip, his eyes hard with concentration, he
slowly slid the needle home and emptied its contents.
Pulling it out, he moved quickly around in front of
Myali to catch the look on her face. She appeared calm,
detached, unreachable.

Disappointed, he turned and replaced the syringe.
"Helmet," he commanded the air. It lowered smoothly
from the ceiling to fit neatly over Myali's head. Working swiftly, Thwait attached the wires to the young
woman's body, all the while stealing glances at her face
and trying to pierce behind the unreadable surface of
her expression. Gradually, he saw her face go slack and
her eyes dull.

Finishing, he stepped back. He rubbed his hands
together as he returned to the table and sat down.
"Isolation," he ordered. The same shimmering circle
of light that had surrounded Dunn sprang up, making
Myali almost invisible. "Begin," the bishop said.

For several minutes, Andrew Thwait sat staring at
the vague form twisting and straining against the straps
that held it firmly in the chair. Then, bored, he got up
and left the Room. "Inform me when the process is
complete," he said just before the door closed.

"Nothing?" Thomas asked the blank screen. "Nothing at all?"

"Nothing that makes any sense," came the answer.

"Ha. Maybe Andrew's bitten off more than he can
chew, eh?"

"He's turned the interrogation over to the machine."

"Really? Bit of a defeat for him, I'd say. Good.
Well, he'll rip it out of her this way. Let me know
what's discovered when the machine's through with

her. Should be interesting. Swords and bows, indeed! Ha!''

The screen went dead. Admiral Yamada sat for some time, nursing his Scotch and thinking over what he'd just learned. Of course there was always the chance that Chandra was lying—he had to allow for that. But if not, one of two things had to be true: First, the planet was indeed helpless and he could blast them into easy submission. Or second, those Kenshites were the most devious and dangerous enemies since Quarnon.

He couldn't decide which would suit him better. Or which would make it easier to destroy Andrew.

XII

She was flung back, gasping and reeling at the violence of the attack. This was no random probing for memory like the first time, but an all-out assault bent on battering and utterly subjugating her. It came continually and from every direction with vicious, overwhelming strength.

There was no question of standing and fighting. Perhaps Father Kadir or Josh might have been able to, but she doubted even they would last for long against power such as this. Twisting and dodging, she began to retreat. She had to save something, some little part of herself, or the bishop would triumph. And Kensho would lose.

But how? How could she escape? There was no place to go but farther into her own mind. Even as she fled, deeper and deeper, she knew that the destroyer, the ravisher, was right on her heels. She remembered Dunn's mind. What the machine had done to him, it was doing to her. Desperation gave her strength and calmed her growing sense of panic. Cautiously and coolly, she began to fight the machine as she had been taught to fight. But she knew it was only a delaying tactic and that ultimately she would lose.

Yamada watched carefully as the bishop questioned the young technician in the brown robe. The man was clearly nervous and uncomfortable. He was just as obviously telling the truth.

"No, Worship. Not on any frequencies known to us. Or any others. We did a complete scan."

"What about moonlets, asteroids, and wandering junk?"

"Checked out by the probes, Worship. Thoroughly. Nothing larger than a few yards across could possibly have escaped our search."

Andrew stared gloomily at the man for a few seconds, then curtly dismissed him with a wave of his hand. As the door closed behind him, Thomas chuckled. "Not even a blessing, Andrew? My, aren't you a bit hard on the poor child? After all, he's just reporting what the data shows."

The overtones of malicious glee and hostility were easily detectable in the admiral's voice. Thwait looked sharply at him. He's up to something, he calculated. Ordinarily he's very careful to disguise his feelings of hatred and contempt for me and the Power. What could have happened to make him so sure of himself that he either forgets or feels he can afford to let his true emotions show? It can't merely be that the sensors and probes are proving him to be right in his estimate that the system is defenseless. No, that isn't enough, since that fact would redound as much to my credit as to his. It's something else. Could he know about the girl?

If he does know about Myali then he might very well force the issue and demand access to her, he calculated.

Which would ruin my advantage in having a source of data he is lacking. I can't allow that. Or can I? What if I actually turn the girl over to him? After I've gotten what I want from her, of course. There wouldn't be much left to turn over, but what difference would that make? It all depends upon how soon I can destroy her defenses and gain access to her data. If necessary, I must use the full majesty and strength of the Power on the poor child. So be it.

"The data shows what it shows, Admiral. It is what it does not show that concerns me. We have a mission on-planet at this very moment. I stick to my original demand that we wait until the data is in from that mission before we take any action."

"And I accept your demand, Andrew. But as of now I'm putting you on notice that upon completion of that mission, some forty-eight standards from now I believe, I require that you turn over all collected data to me for official fleet usage. *All* of it, Andrew."

The bishop looked at him in stony silence. Finally he spoke in a tight voice. "Are you invoking fleet privilege, Admiral?"

Yamada nodded. "Officially. I am declaring this a Triple Red Emergency, Class One."

"You know the consequences if you are wrong?"

The admiral nodded again, his face grim. "As well as you know the consequences if I'm right, Andrew."

Chandra watched the dimly visible form inside the shield. Incredible. The young woman was still struggling, still fighting. He could see her body twitching weakly, straining feebly against the straps. By now she should be limp as a rag doll. He wondered.

He thought back to the kidnapping. He'd disobeyed orders. Rather than knocking her out with an anesthesia

dart, he'd jumped out from behind a tree and grabbed
her. He'd intended to beat her up a little and rape her.
And he'd looked forward to the terror and anguish he'd
known her eyes would show as he did it.

But it hadn't worked out that way. The look she'd
given him was far from one of terror. Instead, her eyes
were full of cold contempt. The glance had stopped him
in his tracks. Then, before he could even work up his
anger to the point of assaulting her, she'd simply
fainted and crumpled to the ground, slipping through
his numbed fingers.

Confused, he'd slung her over his shoulder and run
back to the ship with her. She was still unconscious and
unmolested when he'd delivered her to Thwait.

The whole incident filled him with a resentful fury.
Damn the little bitch! How had she cheated him of his
fun? With just a look? Impossible! He wanted revenge.
Long-drawn-out, brutal revenge. Simple rape wasn't
enough. He wanted to degrade her, to destroy her so
thoroughly that she'd be ashamed of even being human.
No, he wanted to destroy even her humanity. He pictured her whimpering and cringing in the corner of his
cabin, violated in every conceivable way again and
again and again.

A warm excitement began to glow in the pit of his
stomach. He licked his lips and his eyes became
feverish as he stared at her form there behind the shield.
He imagined again some of the things he would do to
her and he became stiff and hard.

He was panting now, the sweat beginning to stand
out on his upper lip. His hands were clawlike and
trembling. If only, he thought, she wasn't behind that
damn shield, I'd start right now. I'd rape her and choke
her at the same time. Hurt her. Bite her till she bled.
I'd . . .

Overpowered by a passion he'd never experienced before, he made a decision. The bishop wouldn't be back for a long time. Hoarsely, he croaked out, "Shield down." Trembling as much from fear over the audacity of what he was doing as from his sexual excitement, he watched the form of Myali appear as the shield disappeared. "Helmet up," he whispered, his tongue almost too thick to let the words by.

As the helmet rose, he leapt to the chair and began to pull off the wires. His hands were trembling so badly he could scarcely undo the straps. There! Only two more to go. Damn! If only she was conscious so he could see her eyes when she realized what he was going to do . . . The horror in their eyes was the most exciting part!

The last strap fell away and he grabbed her slumped form. Supporting her with his right hand he gripped her robe with his left and ripped it down the front, exposing her body. With a strangled cry he flung her to the floor and crouched to spring down on her.

Chandra froze in that position as the voice cut through his haze of excitement. Befuddled he looked up to his right. The bishop was standing there, a laser wand in his hand.

"Chandra, Chandra, your enthusiasm does you credit," Thwait said coldly, "but you carry it too far when you countermand my orders to the machine. Luckily, I left it instructions to inform me when it had completed its task. When you interrupted the process, it contacted me with the completion message. Little did I think what form that completion had taken."

He walked closer, the wand still pointed firmly at Chandra's midsection. "I had no idea you had formed such a strong attachment to our prisoner. Could it be a case of lust at first sight? Surely you satisfied yourself during the capture. No? Truly amazing. The young lady is even more interesting than I thought.''

The bishop's voice lost its slightly bantering edge and became hard and vicious. ''Chandra, this is rank insubordination. You will be punished.'' To the air he said, ''Guards.''

For several moments the two of them stood there silently staring at each other. Then the door opened and four of the bishop's special security force came into the Room, laser guns drawn. One of them placed his weapon against Chandra's head from the right, another jabbed him in the back. The third quickly searched the former chief of security, discovering a surprising assortment of weapons in unsuspected places. The fourth guard stood back several paces, covering everyone.

The search completed, the officer in charge turned to the bishop for orders.

''Sedate him thoroughly and put him in solitary confinement until I decide what to do with him. Double guard.'' He motioned them to leave.

As Chandra reached the door he paused for a moment. ''Thirteen years,'' he said softly.

''That is what I do not understand, my child. And I have always found that if I cannot understand a man, the best thing is to destroy him. Goodbye, Chandra.''

Without warning, and beyond all hope, the attack ceased. Myali didn't even have time to be thankful or to wonder at it. Utterly exhausted, she simply collapsed into deep unconsciousness. Her Mind Brothers, separated during the battle with the machine, left Chandra as his emotions slammed to a sudden halt, and nestled back down into Myali's mind, sated by their little meal.

Bishop Thwait looked from the monitor readouts to

the girl, once more strapped into the chair, and back to
the readouts. He didn't like it. It wasn't anything definite, he admitted. The readouts seemed to indicate
things had gone as they should. But there were disturbing anomalies. Like this flurry of activity here long
after anything but a totally flat response should have
been observed. Or this strange spike here. Or the long,
slow decline in the overall response curve. Too long,
too slow.

Damn Chandra! What in the hell could have pos-
sessed the man? Thirteen years of cold, controlled
sexual sadism, and suddenly he becomes so excited he
can't contain himself. Unnatural. And worse yet, unpredictable. If the fool hadn't broken into the process
when he had, it would have gone to completion. But as
it is, there's no way to be absolutely sure how successful the operation was. What do all those anomalous
spikes in the readout mean? Damn it all!

The visual displays weren't detailed enough. Hardcopy printout would give more precise and complete
information. He tapped a code into the control panel
and stepped back to watch the printout feed swiftly into
a bin over to his left. In just a few moments, the task
was finished and he walked over, scooped it up, and
returned to sit at his table. He liked the feel of the
hardcopy, the heft, the weight, the solidity. It reminded
him of his books. Somehow visual displays were never
satisfying to him. Even though he admitted they were
more versatile and practical, they lacked the substance
of hardcopy. And data, he believed should always have
substance.

Carefully he went through the readouts. He paused
occasionally, musing, his gaze resting abstractedly on
the empty air, his fingers drumming a vague beat on the

table top. Then he plunged back into his study, more intent than ever.

When he was finally finished, and his eyes rose a last time from the information spread out on the table, he gazed long and silently at Myali, a puzzled expression softening his usually stern countenance. I wonder what you really are? he thought. And what really took place between you and the machine? The data revealed many anomalies, but there was no pattern to be found. The oddities were there, but seemed random and meaningless.

Random, meaningless? He found that hard to accept. The machine had hit the girl and hit her hard. She hadn't responded the way most humans responded. But on the other hand, her response wasn't totally unique either. In general, it had been quite as expected. And right now, for all he knew, her information was totally accessible. Yet there were those little differences, those odd spikes where curves should have been flat and flatness where there should have been spikes.

He got up from behind the table and began to pace back and forth in front of Myali, thinking, chances are, she's been battered so thoroughly by the machine that I can get anything I want from her. I'll have to operate on that premise until I have reason to believe otherwise. Therefore, I should have her moved to a recovery room, let her rest while she regains consciousness, and then question her in the usual manner. If anything seems incorrect at that point, I can always put her under the machine again and see to it that the process goes all the way to completion.

Yes, he decided, stopping to stare down at her still form, that's the course I'll take. The only danger is that if I have to put you under the machine again, I'll have wasted many precious hours. How long, he wondered, until Thomas finds out about you, my child? I *must* get what I need before he does. I *must* because I need it to maintain control of this mission.

"You are a problem, my child," he muttered out loud. "An unexpected problem. Rather than being the asset I thought you would be, you have complicated the situation. You were to be a source of data, an answerer of questions, a solver of mysteries. Instead, you have turned out to be as much a mystery as the rest of your damnable planet."

He turned away from her and paced back behind the table. Placing his open palms on the table top, he leaned forward and glared at her. "Yes, you have turned out to be a problem rather than a solution. You and your planet. A problem that cannot be allowed to remain unsolved. Thomas would like simply to smash you, the way he did Quarnon. But that would not solve the problem; it would simply remove it. No, the Power cannot allow that. For if this anomaly has appeared once, it may appear again. Therefore, we must be prepared to deal with it, to discover the origins and meanings of it, so we can wipe it out at its source.

"You and your entire people are a misworen patch in the fabric the Power is creating from mankind. We must pluck you apart, thread by thread, and then reweave you to make you merge with the whole. Ripping you out, destroying you, is not acceptable to the Power. You must be made to blend, to conform."

The bishop stood upright, clasping his hands behind his back. "I was right, you know; my hunch was correct. When I read the records of this Pilgrimage I immediately sensed a problem. Nakamura. The man was a Zenist and a scientist, and those two groups were the bitterest enemies the Power fought when it saved mankind."

He laughed shortly and began to pace again. "Ha! Thomas, that shortsighted fool, thinks you helpless and harmless merely because you lack a technological civilization and advanced weaponry. But I know the real danger you represent and it has nothing to do with science and technology.

"Yes. Yes. They all think the Power saved mankind from science, that we rescued them from the destruction of the home planet, from the fouling of its skies and water, from the rape of its natural resources. And they are right. We did. The Power stopped science dead in its tracks. Oh, yes. We took the knowledge away from the scientists who had so badly misused it. Now the Power, and only the Power, has access to it.

"But science was not the true enemy. No, science was only a manifestation of the actual demon we chained to save mankind."

He spun around and glared at her unconscious figure once again. "Not science, my child. No, not science. Freedom. Freedom was the beast we slew."

In triumphant silence he paced briskly back and forth for several minutes. "Ha! It surprises you! But that is only because you do not understand.

"Mankind as a whole cannot handle freedom. It sets people adrift, lost in a vast sea of insecurity. Freedom gives them the duty of making their own decisions, but denies them any guidelines. Freedom demands they take responsibility for their own fates, but fails to provide the power necessary to accomplish it. Freedom promises them the universe, but neglects to put even a crust of bread in their mouths. Freedom isolates men, pitting them one against another in a bitter struggle for survival, a war of all against all.

"Here and there, of course, there are a few men who prosper under freedom. They are strong enough, smart enough, vicious enough to grab the world by the throat and make it yield what they demand. They rob the weak, taking for their own use what has been wrested from nature by the sweat of others. They grow rich and powerful.

"Is it any wonder that the others, the mass of humanity, throng to these mighty ones, throwing down the freedom they cannot bear, pleading to be allowed to serve? After all, the powerful can provide the very things freedom cannot . . . warmth, wealth, a full stomach, and a level of security unattainable by the lone individual. Frightened, hungry, insecure, confused, men cast aside the freedom that has become an eternal damnation to them and seek salvation by bending their knee to someone or something greater and more powerful than themselves.

"But this partial yielding of freedom by the many to the few is not enough. The rule of the mighty ones does not bring on a Golden Age of peace and prosperity. Instead, it intensifies the struggle. Now the war of all against all that freedom makes inevitable takes place between organized groups of men. The random pilferings and occasional murders of the past are replaced with violence on a grand scale. Armies sweep through the land and whole populations are pillaged and slaughtered.

"Thus it had been for centuries on the home world before the holy Kuvaz spoke the Word. All was chaos. The mighty, with their herds of followers, were locked in a grim death struggle. Scientists battled politicans, environmentalists fought corporations, one nation attacked another. Race war, class war, religious war raged uncontrollably. On and on it went, a mindless cycle of death and destruction.

"Like many of the wisest, the holy Kuvaz saw the

inevitable end approaching. But unlike the rest, who simply threw up their hands in anguish and despair, he saw the solution.

" 'Take the burden of freedom from men's shoulders,' he declared. 'Give them bread to satisfy their bodies, authority to satisfy their minds, and miracles to satisfy their spirits. Make them all, even the mighty, once more like children so they may laugh and play in innocent happiness.'

"But the holy Kuvaz knew mankind and realized that the mere wisdom and truth of his ideas were not enough to guarantee their success. He understood that no matter how much men hated and feared freedom, they still desired it. How else could they feel? For generations they had been told freedom was the most wonderful thing in the world, the ultimate goal of humankind. Wanting it had become like second nature to them.

"No. The simple truth could not defeat a lie of this magnitude. Another, greater lie was necessary. One that would conceal the true goal, yet achieve it nonetheless. Thus was born the crusade against science.

"Science was the perfect scapegoat. Those who followed its myriad disciplines were some of the purest and strongest proponents of freedom. By defeating them, a tremendous blow would be struck at the very heart of the archenemy.

"And for all its incredible power, science was weak. Each scientist valued his own freedom to pursue his own research above all else. Hence they stayed aloof from the rest of the society, jealously guarding their independence. Even among themselves they generally remained isolated, organizing only occasionally to meet some invasion of their privacy and freedom to learn.

"Even more telling, though, was the fact that science had done a great deal of evil as well as a great deal of good. The good, naturally, was taken for granted. But the evil, ah, the evil was never forgotten nor forgiven. It was everywhere. In the thick and stench-filled air. In the dead and polluted water. In the ruined and barren land.

"So science became the enemy against which the holy Kuvaz rallied mankind. And none but the innermost members of the Power ever realized it was nothing but a surrogate through which we struck at the real enemy.

"It was not an easy fight. Science was stronger than anticipated. There were some who seemed instinctively to understand what the holy Kuvaz was doing, and, unlikely as it might seem, became allies of science. The Zenists were the strongest and most dangerous of the lot.

"But in the end, the Power triumphed. Science was shattered. The Zenists and the other allies, smashed. The knowledge came under the sole control of the Power and with the strength it gave us, we were able to destroy the last feeble bastions of freedom.

"Thus the holy Kuvaz saved the human race. Peace, rigorously enforced by the Power, spread across the Earth. Except for occasional actions to root out recalcitrants, all was quiet. Production increased because men no longer had to choose what to produce. The Power told them. There was bread for all. At the same time that men's bodies were satisfied, their minds were put at ease. The total authority of the Power told them what was right and what wrong, what to think and what not. Difficult decisions no longer tortured their days and nights. Nor was there any lack of miracles to satisfy their spirits. By keeping the knowledge to itself and

surrounding it with mystery, the Power made even the
simplest feats of science seem wondrous.''

The bishop paced back and forth for several moments. His face glowed with pride in the achievements
of the Power. He rubbed his long, slender hands together in barely suppressed pleasure. ''Ah, yes, ah,
yes,'' he muttered several times. Suddenly he stopped
dead and whirled on Myali, his arm thrusting out, his
finger pointing directly at her face like a laser wand.
''Yet still,'' he hissed intensely, ''there was danger!
The Power was not totally secure! Freedom was dead
on the home world, oh, yes. But out there,'' he gestured
grandly with his arms, ''out there in the rest of the
galaxy where the Pilgrimage had scattered the seed of
humanity, freedom still lurked. Who knew,'' his voice
dropped almost to a whisper, ''when it would return?

''Consider. The Pilgrimage had taken place before
the holy Kuvaz had spoken the Word and initiated the
Readjustment to save mankind. Many of its leaders,
men like Nakamura, had been the worst sort of heretics.
Those who followed them were equally dangerous
since they had been so infected by the poison of freedom as to leave the home world to seek it in far-off
places. The archfiend could only flourish in such a
hotbed of iniquity.

''It was not enough that the Power control only
Earth. Or even just the solar system. If we were to
achieve the goal of the Word and totally transform
mankind and the universe, we had to control every
man, woman, and child in existence.'' His eyes bright,
the bishop raised his hands in the Sign of the Circle.
''We believe in reality because we have faith in our
perceptions and we have faith in our perceptions because we believe in reality,'' he intoned with ritual

solemnity. "In the name of reality, in the name of humanity, so be it and so it shall be."

For a few moments he stood silently, looking up at the circle made by his fingers, his face transformed by a look of near ecstasy. Finally he spoke reverentially in a soft voice. "This is the central core of the holy Kuvaz's vision. This is why freedom had to be defeated and forever denied. We create reality and reality creates us. There is no place for freedom. We must grasp mankind and mold it to our ends. Thus we create reality. And in turn, reality will reinforce what we create. Around and around it will go, perfecting and improving with each feedback loop. We will become the ultimate masters of the universe because we will create it in our own image at the same time it creates us in its.

"So you see, my child," he said, lowering his arms and walking over once more to stand directly in front of the unconscious young woman, "you and your planet must be made to conform. You must be stripped of your freedom and blended into the whole we are creating. That is why, unlike Thomas, it is not your technology or weapons I fear—it is your ideas. I must crush them."

He returned slowly to the table, his head down, musing. Sitting, he leaned forward, his elbows on the table top, his chin in his palms. "First," he murmured, "I must find out exactly what the machine has done to you. There may be no problem at all." He hesitated. "And yet, I wonder. There is something strange here. Something I cannot quite put my finger on." He gazed briefly down at the readouts.

"Ah, well," he sighed as he sat back, "there is nothing for it now but to put you in a recovery room until you come to and then question you. Guards," he ordered. The door opened after a few moments and two men entered the room, their security-force uniforms soothing to his state of mind. Ah, the strength of the Power is evident on every hand, he thought complacently. "Take her," he ordered, "to C-forty-eight for recovery. Double guard. Call me immediately if she becomes conscious. Otherwise I will begin questioning at 0-six hundred hours."

The two guards unstrapped Myali from the chair, lifted her limp form to a gurney, and then wheeled her quickly away. When the door closed behind them, the bishop sat for a long time, staring off into space, a slight frown creasing his forehead.

The admiral cursed. Damn that fucking son-of-a-bitch Chandra! What a stupid-ass thing to do! Now my source of information is gone.

"Shit! I don't have time to corrupt another one of Andrew's people. I'll have to play my hand and demand access to the girl. It was a lot better when he didn't know I knew. Got all the info I needed without him one bit the wiser. Fucking, stupid asshole! If Andrew doesn't kill that cocksucker, I will.

XIII

It took Myali a long time to return to full consciousness. First she had to counteract the effects of the drug the bishop had injected at the base of her skull. It had immediately gone to her mid-brain, attacking the synapses in her amygdala and hypothalamus. There, in the cleft between the pre- and post-synaptic membranes, it had somehow decreased the absolute refractory period while acting as a highly efficient transmitter substance. The result was an almost continuous firing of the neurons, which sent massive waves of rage and fear surging through her mind. Without her training and the mutations in brain structure which gave her conscious control of her limbic system, Myali would probably have been driven insane. Instead, she was able to clamp down on the whole region, isolating it until the drug wore off.

The second half of the recovery was the part that worried her most. Exactly how much of her mind had the machine destroyed? It had felt like a lot while it was happening. Now, slowly and carefully, she checked through her mind to assess the full impact of the damage.

The result was more encouraging than she had hoped. A great many areas were badly battered and scrambled, others had been knocked about, but were still reasonably well intact. Nothing, she was pleased to discover, was entirely destroyed. It was all still there—just rather jumbled and confused.

She set to work putting things back in order. The job took considerably longer than isolating the drug had taken. Nevertheless, within two hours the task was pretty well completed. She opened her eyes and looked around.

The room she found herself in was rectangular, about twenty feet by fifteen. There was only one door, directly opposite where she lay strapped to the gurney, on the other long wall of the room. Next to the door, on the right, were a screen and some dials. The rest of the room was totally bare. Everything—walls, ceiling, floor, door—was the same dull gray color. Not a very inviting place to spend a weekend, she decided.

Finishing her investigation of the room, she took detailed stock of her situation. Physically and mentally, she was in unexpectedly good condition. Not great, mind you. There were plenty of bruises and strains in both mind and body. And here and there an actual wound. But, even though she admitted she was weaker than before, there was no question in her mind she was strong enough to carry on.

In compensation for being a little weaker, she was a lot smarter. Now she knew the enemy and how to fight it. And although she hadn't been able to beat the machine, she had been able to avoid being beaten by it. At least this time.

Her previous experience with the memory probe had proved very useful. Although this assault had been vastly more vicious and powerful than the first, the machine's method of attack had been similar. It moved in straight lines, smashing anything in its path by sheer brute force. She couldn't steer it this time; it was just too strong. But the technique she had used against the probe, combined with what she had learned from the Master of the Soft Way, had given her a method for defending herself.

"Always meet a rectilinear attack with a circular defense," the Master had explained. "Never try to stop it dead in its tracks or thrust it aside with a perpendicular force. Both may work on occasion, but sooner or later you're going to be too slow, too weak, or both. Instead, create a sphere of invulnerability around yourself. Allow each of your enemy's blows to touch that sphere only as a tangential line. Then use the energy he creates as he touches your sphere to spin, deflecting and redirecting his force by your motion. Thus he will miss his target and his own force will serve to give you the power to defeat him."

It sounded so simple. She almost smiled in remembrance. So simple. Yet she had spent years sweating in the hot sun of the practice yard trying to perfect the technique. "Softer," the Master had corrected her again and again. "Softer. Direct all your force to creating and maintaining the sphere. Don't reach out with your strength to grab the opponent. Let him come to you, graze your sphere, and impart his power so that it becomes yours. Softly, softly. Pull in your power. Absorb his. Thus. So."

Eventually it had come. And she became a Master in her own right. Never quite good enough to defeat her own Master; she lacked something deep inside to accomplish that. But good enough, good enough.

She had fought the machine that way—pulled herself into a tight ball of selfness against its battering strength.

The hardest choice, of course, had been picking which parts of her being to draw into the sphere and which to leave outside, helpless and vulnerable to the smashing power of the machine. She knew very well the fate that awaited anything left outside. The experience of Dunn's mind had been a useful warning.

Things had gone satisfactorily at first. But the machine wasn't like a human opponent. It never tired and it never made foolish mistakes. It wasn't possible to turn its power back on it, to throw it off balance and bring it helpless to the ground. Every time she managed to twist and spin away from the machine's awesome might, she took another step back. And slowly but surely the battle had turned into a gradual but inevitable retreat for her. A retreat that pushed her closer and closer to the one place she feared more than any other . . . the abyss within.

The abyss, the void, the nothing, the endless dark that fell through all eternity! It was worse than death itself. No, it was death itself, death at its most horrible. Death of the self, of meaning, of being; the ultimate disintegration, the final despair.

She knew the abyss. Every path she'd ever followed had eventually led there. Time and time again, just when she'd thought she'd finally caught up with that elusive thing she pursued, she'd found the void yawning hungrily at her very feet. And trembling in horror, she'd stumbled back away from it, defeated and despairing.

The Master had told her it was the thing she sought, that she should throw herself into the bottomless, Stygian depths and fall, fall, fall. The very thought took away her strength and left her quivering and helpless. To fall eternally. To disintegrate. To . . . No.

What was the abyss? It was the place all who followed the Way came to sooner or later. The Way showed the Seeker that the sense of reality so carefully constructed to make being-in-the-world possible was nothing but a tissue of transitory, limited, fallible sense perceptions. When examined closely, solidity disappeared, time halted, and even the self splintered into a thousand unconnected fragments. The world, the universe, simply evaporated like a wisp of morning fog.

This was the point of gravest danger for the Seeker. For while it freed one from the Mushin by ridding one of desires, it also set one adrift in a directionless void. If the whole world-view derived from the experience of being-in-the-world was nothing but the delusion of a limited and fallible sensual apparatus, if there was no true correlation between everyday reality and ultimate reality, if even the self was but a trick played by consciousness—where was purpose in the universe? How could one act in a world without form? And why? Was there any value to struggle and striving if ultimately only entropy and chaos ruled?

Jerome had found the answer for himself. Many others had found it since then. Myali could not. She only saw the void, the ceaseless flowing, the loss of all place to stand and be.

It wasn't that she hadn't tried. The Gods knew she'd tried! Again, again, until the search had all but consumed her energy and her life. Eventually she'd given up everything, family, career, friends, everything, to become a Wanderer and devote all her time to finding . . . That was as close as she'd ever gotten. For the darkness always loomed in the background. And all she ever found for sure was despair.

Luckily, the machine had been turned off before

she'd reached the abyss. Luckily, because she didn't know what to do if it pushed her to the edge.

No. She knew. And that was the final horror of all. She only had two choices: Give up and let the bishop have his way with her mind—which meant death for Josh and Father Kadir and Dunn and . . . Kensho. Or leap off into the dark—which meant the thing that was worse than death for her.

The bishop dismissed the guards as he entered the room. Myali lay quietly on the gurney, against the far wall. He watched from the door for several moments. The girl's breathing was regular, smooth, slow. The drug had worn off and she was undoubtedly sleeping.

He walked over and stood looking down at her. Heavy straps held her body securely in place, arms tight against her sides. The machine hadn't quite finished with its work, but it should have done enough to make it a simple matter to get the information he needed. It was time to wake her.

Before he could move, Myali's eyes snapped open and stared full into his. With a shock of surprise and confusion, he stepped back. Her head turned to follow his motion.

An inarticulate curse escaped his lips. "You . . . you're . . ."

"I'm fine, thank you," she said, a mocking smile curving her lips. "I've been better, of course, but everything considered, I'm fine."

"It can't be," he muttered, shaking his head in disbelief. "It can't be. An hour and a half at least under the machine. It's not possible. Those little anomalies, they . . ." He paused and gazed silently at her for a long time. His mind was racing, trying to understand it. The machine couldn't fail! *Couldn't!*

Without a warning, the door burst open and the admiral stood there, flanked by two marines with drawn lasers. Throwing a swift, cold glance at the bishop, he strode over to the gurney and looked down at Myali. The girl looked back without flinching. "Somehow," she said drily, "I don't think this is the cavalry to the rescue."

Thomas's face was quick to show his surprise, but equally quick to show his appreciation of her humor. He smiled and laughed quickly. "Ha! I see his Worship hasn't made a dent in you. Good. That means he's learned nothing." He turned to Thwait, his smile turning vicious. "So now anything *we* learn will be shared equally by both the Power and the military."

Andrew sighed in an admission of defeat. "All right, Thomas. I intended to share the information with you anyway."

"No doubt, no doubt. After you'd already used the most interesting part for your own ends."

The bishop shrugged. "Irrelevant now. How did you know about her?"

Admiral Yamada looked smug. "Guess. Surely the devious Bishop Thwait can figure out the simple plots of a mere Admiral of the Fleet."

"Hmmmmmm. Yes. There is really only one way, unlikely as it might seem at first glance. Yes, I should have gotten rid of Chandra earlier."

Thomas gave an admiring nod. "Direct hit on the first salvo. Damn! How'd it get past you at all?"

He shrugged again. "The obvious is always the most difficult to see clearly. After thirteen years, I had come to accept his loyalty as a basic assumption rather than as a hypothesis."

Yamada nodded and turned his head toward Myali. "Let's not ignore the obvious this time."

"Meaning?"

"You've failed, Andrew. Miserably. You've had her for two days now and been unable to break her, machines or not."

"Any suggestions?"

"Nothing as refined or sophisticated as the Power has to offer. But perhaps a bit more effective in this case."

The bishop bowed his head slightly. "Pray proceed. I am all attention."

Thomas snorted. "Huh. I'm the direct type. To hell with the needles and all that crap. Trouble with this little lady is she's too damn cocky. I know the type. Thinks she's tougher and smarter than us." He walked over and looked down at Myali again. "Need to knock a little bit of the spunk out of her. Physically. Teach her she's just another piece of meat. Too proud, my dear," he said softly to her, "too proud by a parsec. Got to humble you, drag you down through the shit and rub your face in it. Hurt you, make you cry and whimper. Then, when you've realized your real place in the scheme of things, why, you'll open up to us like a little bird and sing and sing and sing."

"Torture? Physical torture?" the bishop asked, distaste strong in his voice.

Yamada looked back over his shoulder at him. "Yes and no. I think the little lady might be able to handle straight torture. Make her feel noble and all that. I have in mind thorough, brutal degradation. Something that will smash and destroy her spirit and self-esteem."

He turned and walked back to face the bishop. "I'm thinking of a nice, vicious gang rape."

Andrew couldn't help the look of disgust that flitted across his face. "Gang rape?"

"Yes." The admiral's grin was positively feral. He

was clearly enjoying the bishop's discomfort. "I was
thinking of locking her in a room, this one would do,
with Chandra and three very nasty marines of mine,
with instructions to do anything they liked to her. Short
of killing her, of course. 'Take your time, boys,' I'd tell
'em. 'Enjoy yourselves. Anything goes.' Might take a
few hours. But in the end, I'd be willing to bet we'll
have ourselves a very cooperative little lady.''

"Chandra," the bishop mused.

"Right. We both know what he's like. Besides, he
might as well be useful to both of us one last time, eh?"

Andrew turned and walked to the door. For a moment, the marines held their ground, then stepped back
to let him pass. Halfway through, he turned and spoke.
"Do what you wish. I will have no part in anything so
barbaric. Call me when it is over. If it fails, Thomas,
you will have destroyed a valuable source of information. Just remember that.''

One marine unstrapped her while the other kept his
laser aimed at her head. Once she was loose, she sat up
on the edge of the gurney, flexing her body carefully to
make sure everything was in working order. Then she
stood and stretched a little, getting the blood flowing
again.

At that moment, she heard a faint voice in her head.
Myali? it called.

Josh? she responded.

Hey, yeh! I finally reached you. Knew we could do it!

Are you okay, Josh? How's Dunn?

I'm fine. Dunn's a mess. How are you?

*Oh, I'm getting along. This link is very weak, Josh. I
can barely hear you.*

Concentrate harder.

Can't right now, big brother. Got other things to do.

Think you could call back in, oh, an hour?

Guess so. It's night down here. Let me check with the others in the network. Yeh, okay. About an hour. Sis, are you all right?

Ask me in an hour.

If I'm still alive, she added silently.

Chandra swaggered in, a leer spread carelessly across his face. Despite his bravado, Myali could sense an underlying tension. His face was pale and drawn and his eyes had a tight, hunted look about them. His shoulders were slightly hunched and the muscles in his neck were tense. There's fear just beneath the surface of his mind, she thought. Myali felt a stirring among the Mind Brothers she carried. Yes, fear. And they sense it, too.

Thoughtfully, Myali evaluated Chandra as a fighter. Big, strong, he looked fast the way he walked slightly up on his toes. Dangerous. His hands were large and his fists would be enormous. She guessed, given his size and weight, he would be the type to close quickly and grapple. Once in his grip, she imagined most opponents wouldn't have much of a chance.

Three more men came into the room at that moment, dressed in marine fatigues. All looked like nasty customers. One was tall and slender, with a narrow face, thin lips that he constantly licked, a hook nose, and small, furtive eyes. The other two were rather nondescript. Medium height, a little overweight, with pasty, uninteresting faces. The only thing unusual about them was the burning, hungry look in their eyes as they gazed at her. The tall one, she decided, is dangerous. The other two are just brutal fools.

The admiral called the four men over to him and whispered his instructions. She looked straight ahead, out the door, at the two marines who stood there with their lasers still drawn. A third stood halfway between the gurney where she sat and the door, his weapon trained on her chest. There was no escape short of instant death. She decided against it.

A snicker and a throaty laugh came from the group around the admiral. A few more whispered instructions and he stepped back with a hearty, "All right, boys. To work. Duty calls!" The four chuckled appreciatively and turned to stare at Myali. Emotionlessly, she returned their stare.

Yamada walked to the door, motioning the one guard left in the room out ahead of him. Stepping across the threshold, he turned and looked at Myali. "Soon, my dear, you'll be telling us everything we want to know. Oh, yes, soon. Men, we'll lock the door from the outside. When you've had your fun, and don't hurry, just use the intercom and we'll open up for you. Enjoy yourselves, lads!" he slid the door shut and they all heard the lock click.

"The room," Chandra said softly, "is soundproof. You can scream as much as you like and no one will hear. Not that there's anyone about to help you anyway." He began to move toward her. The other three followed, the tall one's tongue out, furiously licking his lips. Myali stood and slowly backed to the far wall. In all too few steps, she felt its cool firmness behind her.

There was no more room for retreat.

Bishop Thwait searched the face of the man standing in front of him. Kohlsky. Second in command of his security force. Now, with Chandra's dismissal, first in command. Andrew had already perused the man's records. Excellent. A very competent servant of the Power. His only character weakness seemed to be a penchant for young boys. But it had never gotten in the way of his job, so Andrew saw no reason to be concerned. Besides, the current situation hardly had anything to do with young boys!

"Kohlsky," the bishop said gently, "Chandra made several serious errors. I hope his fate will serve as an object lesson for you."

"Yes, Worship," came the instant reply. "But, Worship, I need no lessons. My loyalty is unquestioned. I—"

Thwait shook his head. "My child, no one's loyalty is unquestioned." He sighed. "That was my mistake with Chandra. I ceased doubting his loyalty. Which made it extremely easy for him to be disloyal. No, my child, from now on, no one's loyalty is unquestioned. It is better that way."

"Yes, Worship."

"Now we must plan against the problem that faces us. I fear the admiral has serious intentions of seizing total control of this mission and forcing contact with the planet in his own manner. This cannot be allowed. Control must remain with the Power. Do you understand?"

"Condition Kuvaz, Worship?"

"Yes, Kohlsky. Condition Kuvaz. All forces to all strategic positions. All secretly armed. All alert and ready until further notice. Issue drugs as necessary. I will prepare the shunt into the ship's intercom from the Room so we can flood every compartment, every passageway with subsonics. Also see that an override is rigged on the external comm channels. I do not want any unauthorized messages leaving this ship once we strike. It must be swift and flawless. If we do it right, great credit will redound to the entire staff. If we do not

. . . well, I do not like failure and neither does the hierarchy.''

"There will be no failure, Worship.''

"Good, my child. Just remember Chandra.''

The four men closed in on her. Chandra was slightly in the lead, about three steps in front of the others. The tall one was on the far left, about four feet from the wall opposite the door. The other two were bunched together on the right.

Chandra lunged at her, his arms wide to grab no matter which way she darted. Myali didn't run. Instead she snapped a quick, vicious kick with her left foot up into Chandra's groin, moving forward to bring her weight onto her kicking foot as it came smashing down onto the man's right toes. Her hand, stiff as a spear blade, slammed into Chandra's throat just at the point where the chin meets the neck at the same instant that her descending foot crushed his. Unable to even scream through his ruined windpipe, Chandra simply collapsed in a heap.

Without missing a beat, Myali spun to her left, deflecting the tall man's reaching arms by striking his elbow lightly with her right hand, palm open. Then she grabbed the arm just above the elbow, slipped her left hand on the other side of his arm near the wrist and jerked quickly in opposite directions, breaking the arm neatly at the elbow. At the same time her right foot slashed out and downward, striking his left leg at the knee, dislocating or breaking it instantly. The man twisted sideways and crashed against the wall.

Myali turned her head just in time to see one of the two remaining men leap at her, fear and hatred twisting his face into a fury. The second was frozen in place, a

stunned look in his eyes. She threw her Mind Brothers
at him and concentrated on the one who was attacking.

Having no time to turn, she dropped forward, placing
her hands on the floor. From that position, like a mule,
she kicked back and up, her heel slamming into the
man's groin. He staggered back, merely stunned, since
the kick had not hit dead center. Myali sprang to her feet
and attacked. A swift roundhouse kick smashed into her
opponent's left temple, followed by a solid punch which
shattered his nose and sprayed blood all over his face.
Stepping right up to his body, she thrust her elbow into
his solar plexis and swept his left foot out from under
him. He hit the floor with a thud, his head making a
sound like a melon breaking open when dropped from a
height.

The fourth man was no problem. He was writhing in
his final death throes, driven into the Madness by the
Mind Brothers. She could sense them feeding joyously
as the last gurgle of terror escaped the twisting body.

Suddenly it was silent in the room. The only sound
was her own breathing. She went to check each of the
men. The Mind Brothers had done their job well. Dead.
She retrieved them. The other one had died when his
head had hit the floor. In three steps she was standing
over the tall one. He lay in a heap, his head at an odd,
unnatural angle. Neck broken. Must have happened
when he slammed into the wall, she guessed.

She turned and examined Chandra. Dead. His throat
was crushed. He had strangled, unable to make a
sound. Carefully she straightened out his body. Then
she pulled the others over beside Chandra and
straightened them out, too. Four bodies. Menacing in
life, rather foolish-looking in death.

Finished, Myali went back to the gurney, got up on it

and arranged herself in a cross-legged meditation posture. Slowly, she calmed her breathing and her mind. Four dead, she thought. How many more to go? She waited, unaware of time, for Josh to call.

XIV

"No, sir. Not a sound." The marine's voice was crisply military.

"Hmmmmmm," responded Admiral Yamada thoughtfully. "Been three hours now. Shit, doing the job right is one thing, but those boys are taking too much time. Stay here. I'm on my way down. Time to break it up." He cut the connection even as the marine was saluting.

A small worry lurked around the edges of his mind. Three fucking hours. Could anything have gone wrong? What the hell *could* go wrong? Andrew. Did that bastard have some secret access to the room? Had he already taken away the girl to get the information from her? Damn! That'd be just like the son-of-a-bitch. He picked up his pace, forcing the marine guard in front to trot to hold his position. He heard the one behind puffing to keep up.

As he approached the corridor that led to the room where he had left Myali with the four men, he saw the bishop with three of his security-force guards hurrying toward him. They met at the mouth of the corridor. The bishop was blunt. "Something is wrong. I grew concerned when I realized three hours had passed. I tried to raise them on the intercom. No reply."

"Shit," Thomas said and began to run toward the room. The others pounded down the corridor after him. Two marines were standing about fifty feet from the door, their weapons drawn. As the admiral came up, they came to attention and saluted. "All's quiet, sir," the senior one said.

"Still nothing, eh?" asked the admiral.

"Not a peep."

"Open the door," demanded the bishop. "Something is wrong, I tell you."

"You bet your sweet ass something's wrong," Thomas snarled. "That girl damn well better be in there, Andrew, or the shit's going to start flying." He gestured with his left fingers and suddenly all the marines' weapons were drawn and ready. The security-force men were an instant too slow and stood looking foolishly at the lasers pointed at them. "Not a sound, Andrew. Not one fucking sound. Not a move or a twitch. Dead still, dead silent, or dead. You," he gestured to one of Andrew's men, "go open the door. Slide it back quick and then hit the floor to give my men a clear field of fire." He indicated two of his own men. "You and you watch this scum. If they move, fry 'em all." He turned to the other two marines as he drew his own laser pistol. "Come on." Together, the three moved toward the door, following the security guard.

Arriving at the door, the three armed men placed themselves in a semicircle so each could fire into the room without the danger of all being hit with a single blast from inside. The guard reached out, fingered the lock open, and slammed the door back with a swift jerk.

He hit the floor with a thud, twisting to get out of the way.

For a moment, there was a dead, stunned silence. Then the admiral said softly, "Holy shit," and walked to the door. Andrew hurried down the hall, the others following in his train.

He reached the door and looked in, discovering what had so amazed the admiral. There seated on the gurney was Myali, unharmed and calmly meditating. On the floor, near the left wall of the room, lay four bodies.

Admiral Yamada had just finished examining the last of the four. He looked up at Andrew. "Dead," he said tersely. "All four of 'em." A thunderous scowl on his face, he rose and stared at the bishop. His laser pistol came up and pointed directly at Andrew's heart. "This has to be your doing, you bastard!"

"Don't be a fool," the bishop said. "How in the name of Kuvaz would I have done it? You had two guards in this corridor the whole time!"

"Must be a fucking secret passage." The admiral swung his head around as if expecting to find one still open.

"Then search the room, if you really believe something so melodramatic."

"I damn well will!"

"No need to," Myali interrupted lightly. "I killed the four of them. The bishop really had nothing to do with it." She unfolded her legs and let them hang over the edge of the gurney. "They attacked, so I killed them. I'm sorry. I had no choice."

Both the admiral and the bishop stared at her in utter surprise. Yamada was the first to respond. "Holy shit," he said breathlessly.

Thwait rounded on him. "This," he gestured to the

dead bodies, ''is the result of your meddling with my
attempts to obtain information from the prisoner. Fool!
Four men killed. And from the looks of things, they
have been dead too long to be of use in the organ banks.
A total waste.''

"Torture! That's the only way. Break the little
bitch!''

"No,'' the bishop shouted. ''No! I let you have your
way once and I will not allow it a second time. In the
name of the Power I claim this prisoner, and any who
stand in my way are eternally damned!'' He glared
around at the four marines who had crowded into the
room. ''Is that clear?''

Yamada made a mighty effort and brought himself
under control. ''Worship, I yield the prisoner to you.
But I demand access—equal access, to all information
gathered.'' The bishop nodded curtly. ''What do you
intend to do with her?'' Thomas asked.

"The machine. This time to completion.''

"I'll watch. Just to make sure.'' Reluctantly, the
bishop nodded his acquiescence.

"Take her,'' he gestured to his men, ''to the
Room.'' Without waiting for the order to be carried out,
he turned and swept out.

For a second time, Myali was wheeled into the Room
and strapped into the chair. This time, though, she was
completely conscious of what was happening. And
aware of what she faced. Fear of it struck deep into her
heart. She had fought as long and hard as she could. The
end was near. Soon she knew she would face the ultimate, impossible choice: yield or leap into the void.

The bishop turned from calibrating the machine to
check one more time on the positioning of the wires and
tightness of the straps. Yamada paced back and forth,
watching the whole procedure with a scowl on his face.

Finally everything was ready and Thwait stepped back in satisfaction, looking triumphantly at Myali. "Soon," he said happily, "you will tell me everything I want to know. I have turned the power up higher than I have ever set it. It will be brutal but swift, my child. And then I shall know at last."

"Know what?" Myali asked innocently.

"Know what I want to know," the bishop responded testily.

"And precisely what do you want to know? I've answered every question you've ever put to me. And I've told the truth, too. What more do you want to know?"

Yamada turned and watched as the bishop began to pace up and down in front of the girl. The little man's voice was angry and agitated as he spoke. "I do not want to know any one specific thing. You do not understand. The Power does not need to know any particular thing. I collect data. All the data I can gather. When I have enough information, the truth emerges automatically. The only thing that ever stands in the way of understanding is a lack of data. Once we have all the information, we know everything.

"Therefore, my child, I want everything. I want all your memories, all your thoughts, all your ideas and hopes. Everything. Once they are accessible, I will have all the data I need to learn everything I need to know."

"But again, then, why not just ask me? I'll answer any question truthfully."

The bishop smiled cynically. "Ah, yes. But you see, there are two obvious problems with that. First, you place the burden upon the questioner. He must pose the correct question, or the answer, even if true, means nothing. To pose the correct question, he must know exactly what he wishes to know. That is not the way of the Power, for the Power wishes to know everything.

"Second," he continued, "You say you will answer truthfully. 'Truthfully' by whose standards? And do you even really know the 'truth' I seek? I doubt it, my child.

"So the way of the Power is the best way. The machine will make all the data in your mind accessible to me. I will record, correlate, analyze, and finally discover everything I wish to know." He finished with a smug smile.

"But even granting all that," Myali protested, "wouldn't knowing what you were looking for ahead of time make looking a lot faster and easier? All that recording and correlating and analyzing takes time and sounds pretty complex. Errors could creep in. I mean, if you're worried about our defense capabilities, why not just hunt in my mind for those memories?"

"That is not the way of the Power," the bishop responded in an annoyed tone.

"So," Myali smiled in understanding, "I see. Your machine isn't capable of distinguishing between thoughts. All it can do is mess my mind up so badly I lose control and you can take over."

"That is not true," the bishop replied stiffly.

"It *is* true!" Myali laughed triumphantly. "I remember from last time. Your wonderful machine lacks finesse. It isn't a rapier, or even a broadsword. It's just a club, a primitive club! You turn it on, it invades my mind and knocks everything to pieces. There's nothing left behind but broken junk. Then you open me up and out it all pours, a babble of shattered trash. No order, no coherence, just disconnected fragments." She snorted derisively. "And then from the midden heap you've created, you try to rebuild some kind of order. That's stupid. The whole technique is stupid—stupid and destructive. And probably not even very successful.''

"No," Thwait shouted, anger reddening his face. "No! You do not, cannot understand. The Power is too subtle for mere mortals to comprehend. The machine is perfect. It works in accordance with the rules of the Power. It cannot fail.''

"Then the rules of the Power are primitive,'' Myali said quietly. ''The method you describe, the mere gathering of large quantities of data hoping some pattern will automatically emerge, is a crude version of the empiricism espoused by some of the early scientists on the home world. At first blush it seems to make sense. But it assumes the world is a much simpler place than it actually is. And it also assumes that the laws and rules which govern the world are equally simple and self-evident. No such luck, Bishop. The method didn't work. Collections of data are just that, collections of data. Until they're put into some kind of meaningful order, they're useless. So naïve empiricism was replaced by the technique of developing a hypothesis first, and then looking for the specific facts that prove or disprove the conjecture. The hypothesis itself generally came—''

"Enough!'' shouted the bishop. ''You speak blasphemy! The science of the ancients almost destroyed Earth. Only the Power was able to save mankind from certain doom. The old science and all its techniques are dead. The Power reigns supreme and cannot be questioned.''

"She's stalling, Andrew,'' Yamada interjected drily.

Thwait looked at him sharply. ''I can see that. But a Bishop of the Power cannot allow blasphemy to go unanswered. I have answered and now . . . Helmet,'' he called to the ceiling. The helmet lowered and fitted over Myali's head. "Isolation," the bishop demanded, and the flickering bubble formed around the chair and its occupant. "Begin," he ordered.

Myali began to twitch and strain against the straps that held her tightly to the chair.

Kohlsky looked at the display grid on the wall. Each man was a glowing dot. The black lines represented the bulkheads within the ship. Four levels, four grids.

Every member of the Power had been armed, mostly with the small, inconspicuous laser wands. They were quite deadly up close, even in the unskilled hands of novices and acolytes. His own men were armed with fully charged laser pistols, equal in every way to those carried by the marines on board. Here and there, at strategic points, he had hidden laser rifles. Key men had been assigned to pull them out when the signal was sounded.

He frowned slightly at the grid for level three. The dots in sector four were too bunched up. He hit the comm button. "Three-Four, spread out. Move around naturally. Don't group. You make easy targets and look suspicious." He watched with satisfaction as the dots spread out more evenly.

Smiling, he sat back for a moment and stretched. To anybody not paying close attention, it would look like everything was normal all over the ship. The robed minions of the Power were bustling about everywhere as usual. Perhaps there were a few more than ordinary on the bridge, in the comm room, and in the engine room, but not enough to make anyone unduly suspicious. No, to the unsuspecting eye, everything looked as it usually did.

It wasn't. All he had to do was reach out, hit the

comm button, say "Kuvaz," and all hell would break
loose. The marines' quarters on the second level, section one, would be isolated and gassed. The engine
room, bridge, and comm room would be seized at any
cost. The rest of the ship's crew would be forced to
surrender or would be burned down where they stood.
If surprise was total, and he expected it to be, he
estimated some nine or ten casualties for his own men,
perhaps twenty-five on the other side, not including
the marines. He was supposed to keep fatalities as low
as possible among the crew because the bishop felt they
were needed to run the ship efficiently. Screw 'em,
Kohlsky thought. We can run the ship on our own.
Anybody gets in the way, we burn 'em.

Sergeant Jackson, 3rd Marine Div., didn't like it.
Not one bit. That same friggin' novice had just passed
him for the third time. Something funny here. Jackson
was a fighting man, with all the subtle senses of one.
He'd survived quite a few heavy scrapes. More than
just luck, he'd always said; instinct. Right now his
instinct told him it was time to do a little scouting.
   Casually he began to saunter along the corridors of
second level, section one. He counted robes. Too friggin' many, especially along the periphery and at the key
points leading into and out of the area. He tried to
picture the layout of this part of the ship in his mind.
The result wasn't reassuring.
   He took the shaft up one level and went forward to
the bridge. He counted robes. Same result. Too many.
Not a whole mess too many; just one or two . . . with a
bunch more in easy running distance.
   Comm room turned out the same. No need to check
the engine room. He already knew. One last thing to
find out. A young one was coming toward him. He

ignored him and let him pass, then began to follow,
about fifteen feet behind. The brown robe turned into a
smaller corridor that led to some storage rooms.
Jackson paused at the mouth of the corridor. No one
around. He slipped the knife from his boot.

Five minutes later he knew everything. The acolyte
had been carrying a laser wand, and a rifle had been
stashed in the room. He had to find his company com-
mander soonest.

It rushed down on her like an avalanche. No, she
thought frantically, wrong image. No way to dodge an
avalanche. Must use images I can deal with. Human
comparisons aren't any good, though. It's too big, too
powerful to be anything human. It's like . . . like a
crazed Strider. All teeth and madness. Roaring down
on her. Yes! She twisted away and back. Another step
given up, she realized despairingly. Another step
toward . . .

The fight had gone pretty much the way it had last
time. Except now the machine was vastly stronger and
swifter. From the very first attack she'd known there
was no way she could hope to win or even keep from
losing. This battle would be to the finish. Her finish.

Nevertheless, she hadn't given up. Like a dancer,
she'd spun and swooped across her mind, diverting the
assaults of the machine, snatching important parts of
herself into her tight little sphere, abandoning others to
be smashed and ground beneath the ponderous charge
of her enemy.

Hold on, she told herself as another fond memory
slipped from her grasp to be blasted into chaotic fragments. Keep going as long as possible. Every second
counts. There's always a chance . . .

She remembered the tension she'd seen between the bishop and the admiral. The two men obviously hated each other. Clearly, there was some sort of struggle for power going on between them. They were almost at the point of breaking into open warfare. And if they fought, perhaps Kensho could be saved! If only, she thought, I can hold out long enough, perhaps their feud will come to a head and boil over into action. If only I can make it a little longer, there might be hope for Kensho. Might be hope for . . .

Kensho. The sun flooding a meadow. Forest looming deep green and cool around the edges. She and Karl, naked and warm after having made love. Now they started again, slow, slow, faster, faster, she felt it build into a rising wave, a towering wave, a . . . crashing in the forest, smashing of trees, darkness in the sky . . . There! There! Like a moving mountain! She fled, barely escaping as it roared by. The clearing was crushed, the memory shattered into a million pieces.

Back. Always back. She wondered briefly how Josh was doing with Dunn. He'd explained the problem to her, told her the danger the Way-Farer faced. And then he'd gone on to say how much he liked what was left of the man and how valiantly he was struggling against the spy. Myali had felt a warmth growing in her chest when Josh praised him. I've been in his mind, she reminisced. Even broken it was a wonderful place.

Oh, Josh. Will I ever see you again? Will I ever feel the warmth of sunlight on my skin? Or will I die here, strapped in a chair, sealed in a metal capsule, far from my people and my planet? Will they dump my body out into the vacuum? Or keep it and put one of their slave minds in it? Gods!

Her mother picked her up and held her, patting her

head and crooning a song that covered her tears and
pain. It hurt so much. Oh! Nasty biting thing! She held
up her hand, peering through misty eyes at the torn
finger. Bad, bad, biting thing! The pain was ebbing,
though, and the blood flowing more slowly now.
Mother's voice was so soft and . . . bellowing, raging,
through the wall it came, rending the memory. Clutching it she reeled back. Precious! She stumbled and lost
her grip. Oh! Lost, lost, lost forever!

She rolled out of the way. Too slow. A glancing blow
struck her and flung her to one side. She tried to stand.
Almost on her. Leap, fly! It roared past, just missing.

Three of them. In hoods. Dark, hidden faces. One
was Fear, one Despair, one Death. Only the three and
her on an empty road, in the middle of the Plain.
Coming closer. Fear pulled back its hood and she
looked into her own eyes. Despair showed its face and
she saw her own. Death reached a clawlike hand to the
cowl and she turned and fled.

Another step back. Closer to the place she feared.
And Death lifted its hand.

She spun to her left, off balance. Almost falling, she
reached out to steady herself. She touched the robe and
knew. Death lifted its hand.

No place to go. She stood at the brink and looked.
All, all empty. Dark, vast, hopeless, soundless, endless. And behind she heard the stealthy step, the ponderous tread, the roaring tramp. The machine.

No place to go. Give up. Yield. Allow the machine to
splatter the little of yourself that remains across the
desolate landscape, the smoking ruins of your mind.
Let the bishop have his way. Yield.

Never! Betray Kensho? Josh? Dunn? Kadir? Illa?
Jerome? Edwyr? Chaka? Yolan? Nakamura? Better the
abyss, the void, the eternal falling!

Death lifted its hand.

With a final, despairing scream of defiance she leapt into Nothingness.

PART FOUR

The opposite of a correct statement is a false statement. But the opposite of a profound truth may well be another profound truth.
—Sir Niels Bohr

XV

"Now, Dunn!!!"

The laser wand flashed from his pocket, its intense
beam cutting a hissing sweep of light through the air.
Dunn closed his eyes, unable to look. Dimly he heard a
muffled grunt of pain and surprise. He struck out with
every ounce of strength left in his mind and body . . .
then darkness hit him like a fist and he slammed back
into oblivion.

He opened his eyes. A ceiling looked back at him.
Inside. Slowly, without moving his head, he swept his
eyes back and forth. Small ceiling, small room. Maybe
ten by ten. A cell? Plain walls, beige, unbroken on left
and right. A door and window, unbarred, in the wall by
his feet. From the way the light lay in the room, another
window, unbarred, was behind his head. Not a cell,
then. Just a room.

To get a better look, he turned his head slightly—and
instantly wished he hadn't. The pain was like an explosion. In a swift gesture, he brought his hands up from

under the blanket that covered him to press against his forehead.

There was only one hand.

Pain was forgotten. He stared at his hands. Correction: hand. His right hand. On the left was a neatly bandaged stump.

He let his arms drop gently onto his chest again. With a sigh, he closed his eyes. One hand. Of course.

The pain began to ebb. I wonder if the rest went as planned? he thought. Cautiously, he probed his own mind. Spy? he queried. Myali? Face? There was nothing but silence and the retreating pain. He followed the pain for a while, pushing it every now and then, hurrying it on its way. When it was gone, he slept.

He woke, instantly aware of the other person sitting next to his bed. He opened his eyes and turned his head. The face was familiar, even though he knew he had never seen it before with his own eyes. It was her chin, firm, determined. Thinner lips, but just as ready to smile. The nose was thin and fine with slightly flaring nostrils. Her eyes, too. Brown and full of life. A higher forehead and lighter brown hair. The family resemblance was strong.

"Hello, Josh," he said quietly.

"Hey, Dunn," Josh replied. "How are you feeling?"

"Better. How are you?" he asked, noticing for the first time that Josh's left arm was in a sling.

Josh looked down at his arm. "Okay, considering. Pretty nasty gash; right down to the bone. Took twenty-seven stitches to close it. I'm gonna be moving kind of slow and careful for a couple of weeks. How's the . . . uh . . . hand?"

Dunn lifted the stump and looked at it. "Funny. Tingly. I can still feel the fingers. Weird."

"You did a very neat job. Nice clean cut right through the wrist bones. We only had to remove a couple of fragments and cover it with synthetic flesh. Our medical sciences are pretty advanced, so you'll be up and about in a day or so. And it'll heal faster than you can believe. Only problem is, we aren't quite up to regeneration yet. Takes too many machines, too much hard technology. We're trying to find a more natural approach, but . . ." he shrugged his right shoulder, "until we do, you're stuck with a stump."

Dunn laid his right hand over his stump. "Oh, well, win a few, lose a few," he said in a weak attempt at good humor. Then he grew more serious. "Actually, I think I won more than I lost."

Josh looked at him sharply. "Did you win, Dunn?"

Dunn nodded slowly. "Only one of us now. Me. Not very complete, mostly gaps and Myali's memories, but the spy is gone." Suddenly he sat bolt upright. "Shit, I forgot. Josh, get the hell out of here! Get everybody out of the area! Oh, shit, the belly bomb!"

The other man sat calmly, a smile spreading across his face. "Not to worry. We found the bombs first thing. They went off hours ago."

"Bombs? More than one?"

Josh nodded. "Three, to be exact. One at the base of your brain, one in your stomach, and one attached to your sternum. Man, they were going to make hash of you."

"They never use three." Dunn's forehead wrinkled thoughtfully. "Unless . . . unless there was more than one of them."

"Could be. Myali told me the bishop and the admiral

don't seem to be getting on too well. Could be both of
them put bombs in you, just to make sure each could
deny the other total control.''

"Sounds like the bastards," Dunn muttered as he
slumped back down onto the bed. "But that accounts
for two. Who set the third?" He paused for a moment,
then shook his head as if to clear it. Slowly, he raised
his left arm and looked at the stump. "Damn. Seems
like a miracle." He looked up at Josh. "Father Kadir?"

"He'll be along soon. Wants to find out what the hell
you did. So do I. I don't understand it, Dunn. I really
don't."

As if on cue, the door opened and Father Kadir
walked into the room. A slight smile played about his
lips as he saw Dunn begin to sit up to greet him. He
raised his hand to forestall the movement. "Rest," he
said gently. "You can talk as well lying down as sitting
up. As Josh says, I am consumed by curiosity as to
what you did and how you did it. I honestly thought my
final hour had come when I saw that laser wand come
out of your pocket."

Dunn chuckled. "It almost had. The whole thing was
a long shot. But there really wasn't any other choice.
Fact was, the spy had me pretty thoroughly under
control. Up to a point, I kept exhausting myself struggling against him, but it was hopeless. He simply had
more power than I did.

"Then one of the lessons Myali had taught me really
sank in. She learned it from the Master of the Soft Way.
Never meet force with force. Always use the opponent's strength rather than your own. Wait for the
moment when he is extended, when his power is off
balance, and then complete his movement, upsetting
him and establishing your own control.

"At first, it looked hopeless. The spy had all the

cards. But I had an idea. A pretty farfetched one, I admit, though it seemed the only one that even had a hope of working.

"So I pretended to continue the fight against the spy. I twisted and struggled, raged and fought—only never at full force. It must have seemed I was growing weaker and weaker. I was, but I was also saving as much energy as I could for one last attack, an attack that would take every bit of strength I had, an all-out, do-or-die attempt delivered at precisely the right moment.

"The problem was picking the right moment. Obviously the best time would be when the spy was least suspecting it, when his attention and energy were focused on something else. But even that wouldn't be enough, I realized. I needed something else, something totally unexpected, something that would stun him into momentary imbalance.

"Only one time and one circumstance fit my requirements. So we marched up the hill, stood in front of the Way-Farer, and pulled out the laser wand." He smiled at Father Kadir. "Sorry if I gave you a bad moment there, Father. But you see, I had to get his attention focused on something other than me. And in that moment, he was so sure of victory that he didn't pay attention to the fact that I had taken control of the muscles of the right forefinger."

Dunn chuckled happily. "There he was, in all his power, totally in the front of my mind, totally connected with my nervous system, gloating, triumphant. He screamed at me, 'Kill him, kill him!' All I had was that forefinger, the one on the firing button. And before the wand got high enough to hit the Way-Farer, I pushed and cut off my left hand.

"The shock hit him harder than anything I ever could

have mustered. It staggered him, knocked him over. That's when I struck—slammed into him with everything I had. I ripped and tore, destroying everything I could get my hands on.

"Actually, it was surprisingly easy. He was a tight system, very rigidly ordered. All I had to do was knock out a few pieces and the whole damn thing came tumbling down. Suddenly, I was all alone. The fight was finished before I hit the ground."

He looked thoughtfully at his stump. "Seems kind of strange now. Quiet. No spy hectoring and driving me, no Myali helping and guiding me, no Face taunting and frustrating me. Nothing much but silence and a little bit of me in a big, empty space."

The Way-Farer nodded. "Yes, it must be quite a change. But you're not really alone, you know. They're all still here. In time, you'll find them again. A piece here, a bit there. And you'll grow, too, to fill that empty space. You've got a lot of building to do, my son. Take your time."

Dunn looked up at him. "Do we have the time, Father? The bishop and the admiral aren't going to sit up there waiting forever. When they discover that their spy failed—"

"They've already discovered that," Josh interrupted grimly. "The belly bombs went off. Doesn't that mean . . . ?" He left the question hanging.

"Not necessarily," Dunn replied. "They would've detonated the bombs on completion of the mission in any case. Spies are considered expendable. Even successful ones are embarrassing and potentially dangerous to have around, especially if they fall into the wrong hands. So usually as soon as the mission is over, or when it becomes obvious failure is imminent, somebody pushes the button, and it's goodbye to the spy and anybody else in about a ten-foot radius.'' He paused, his brow furrowed in sudden thought. "Hmmmmmmm. What I don't quite understand is why they waited so long to pull the plug on me. You had time to find and remove the bombs. Strange. The spy was transmitting a detailed report of events right up to the second I struck; then communication must have cut off abruptly and totally. That alone should have been enough. Unless the very suddenness . . ." He looked at Josh. "How long was it between the time I collapsed and the bombs going off?''

"We knew about them from monitoring your mind during your trip here, Dunn, so we went after them at the same time we were working on your arm. Let's see . . . couldn't have been more than an hour between the time you cut off you hand and the explosions, right, Father?''

Kadir nodded. "Yes. We had them out of you in about twenty minutes. It was only about a half hour later that they went off. And that was, oh, perhaps two and a half or three hours ago.''

A malicious grin crept slowly across Dunn's face. "I just had a wonderful idea,'' he chuckled. The other two leaned forward in anticipation. "My transmitter probably still works. It has its own power source.'' His grin grew larger. "Yeh. I've got a real wonderful idea.''

He closed his eyes and reached his tongue back to activate the switch in his molar. The response was immediate.

What the !!!???

Reporting mission accomplished.

A stunned silence, then an equally stunned question: *Dunn?*

Reporting mission accomplished. Way-Farer assassinated. Have further discovered planetary defenses

are excellent. Some kind of exotic energy-beam em-
placements in small, rounded hills scattered seemingly
at random over the planet's surface. Passive until acti-
vated by attack.

Dunn?

They're almost here. Too many to fight.

How in Kuvaz . . .

Detonate bombs, imperative!

They've been detonated, damn you! You're dead!

Detonate before they capture me! Detonate!

Damn you! Damn you, you're dead! Dead!

Detonate! Deto— He hit the switch with his tongue
and cut the transmission.

For several minutes he couldn't stop laughing long
enough to let Josh and Father Kadir in on the joke.
They, of course, had been unable to hear the conversa-
tion between Dunn and the ship. When he told them the
details, they joined in his laughter.

Josh, in fact, laughed a little too hard. The gash in his
shoulder was still very recent and his strength limited.
His hilarity was cut cruelly short by a lancing pain that
brought tears to his eyes and drained the color from his
face. The Way-Farer immediately called for aid, and a
young woman came and helped the wounded man back
to his own bed for more rest.

When the younger man had left the room, Father
Kadir sat quietly next to Dunn for several moments.
Finally, he spoke.

"You're still weak, too. Don't try to overdo it,
Dunn. Losing a hand, even intentionally, is a dreadful
shock to your system. Just take it easy for a couple of
days."

"Do we have a couple of days, Father?"

Kadir fell silent again. Then he sighed. "Only the

Gods know, my son. This is the dark we could not see
into. All the lines of probability lie up there, now.'' He
gestured toward the ceiling. ''We have done all we can.
The rest lies in other hands.''

''Myali?''

''Myali, the bishop, the admiral, anyone and
everyone on the ship. We know only a fraction of
what's happening and so can't tell for sure what forces
are shaping the outcome.''

''But Myali's there, alone?''

''Yes. Alone.''

Dunn looked down at the stump. ''I know the feeling. But at least I had her to keep me company.''

''This is the path she must walk, that she walks for all
of us. No one knows where it will lead.''

''Isn't there anything we can do, Father? I mean, can
we talk to her?''

''Josh communicates through the network when he
has enough strength.''

''Can I . . . Can I talk to her?''

Kadir shook his head sadly. ''I'm sorry. You don't
carry the Mind Brothers yet. That will take time. No,
you can't enter the network. Besides,'' he added after a
pause, ''the last time Josh tried to call, he got no
answer.'' His voice sounded worried.

''No   answer,''   Dunn   echoed.   ''Does   that
mean . . . ?''

''We don't know what it means.'' He sounded puzzled. ''Even if she'd been sleeping, he should have
been able to get through. But there was nothing. Just a
dead silence.''

''The machine,'' Dunn muttered.

''What?'' the Way-Farer asked.

''The fucking machine. That bastard Thwait has her

under the machine.'' His voice rose in pitch, filled with both anger and anguish. ''They're trying to take her mind apart. Doing to her what they did to me. Oh, shit! Damn them!''

He brought himself back under control. ''The machine, Father. It's the way the Power maintains its control. If you step out of line, they put you under the machine. It scrambles your mind, sometimes even wipes it clean like it did mine. Then they just put in a new personality, like my spy, and you're theirs. They've got her under the machine. She can't answer. She probably won't ever answer again. They'll take her apart to get the information they want, then readjust her.'' Despair reduced his voice to a whisper. ''Myali, oh damn, Myali.''

The Way-Farer was thoughtful. ''This 'machine,' does it attack the conscious mind?''

Dunn nodded. ''Yes. And more. Memories, ideas, emotions. Oh, hell, it stirs it all up. Everything. Conscious, unconscious, the whole works.''

''No,'' the Way-Farer said gently, ''not everything. There is one place it cannot touch, cannot reach.'' Dunn looked up, hope and wonder lurking in his eyes. ''One place,'' Kadir mused. ''The abyss.''

''The abyss?'' Dunn asked. ''I . . . I don't know what that is. Could . . . Could Myali hide there? Would she be safe from the machine in the abyss?''

''Safe? In the abyss? Yes and no. In it lies total security . . . and utter danger. It is the source of both hope and despair.''

''Will Myali go there to escape the machine?''

''She would never go there of her own will. It's the one place she fears more than death itself. And yet, I think it's her only hope.'' He paused, contemplating. ''Her search has led her there again and again. And now, ironically, it leads her back, finally and irrevocably.'' He looked deeply into Dunn's eyes. ''How she faces it will determine the outcome of this entire thing. Yes, I can see that now. The darkness shifts aside just enough to see.

''And Mother Illa knew that. Saw it clearly. Picked Myali for the task. The task she has never been able to achieve.'' The Way-Farer fell silent, his eyes softening and losing their focus. For some time he sat there, staring off into nothing. Suddenly, unexpectedly, he stood, his eyes snapping back to life, his face purposeful. ''So,'' he said. ''It is as it is. I will let you rest now. I must go to see Josh for a few minutes. Then he, too, must rest. There is more for all of us to do yet, if I see aright. Yes, we need not be totally passive.'' He turned to leave.

''Father,'' Dunn's voice was pleading. The Way-Farer turned back. ''Father,'' he continued, ''Myali. Is she lost out there forever? Is there any way to bring her back? I mean, if the machine doesn't destroy her, can she return to Kensho?''

Kadir smiled. ''That is precisely what I want to see Josh about. He claims there is a way. I, for one, doubt him. But I'm about to go and see if he can convince me.'' His face became solemn, but kind. ''Dunn, we all want her back. You aren't the only one who loves her, you know.'' With that, he turned again and left the room.

Love her? Dunn wondered as he looked up at the ceiling. How can I love Myali when I've never even met her? He laughed quietly at himself. Of course I've met her. Known her intimately for years. Know her better than probably anybody in the whole universe. She's in me, in my mind and soul. Without her I'd be dead meat right now, blown apart by the bombs. Without her I'd never have found Dunn again.

Love her? Utterly. Her joy, her sadness, her goodness, her evil, her bravery, her fear . . . her in every sense that she is. I only hope that I have the chance to tell her so.

Without realizing what he was doing, Dunn prayed for the first time in his life. Please, he asked the universe, please let her escape the machine. And let her come back to Kensho. And to me.

There was no answer.

But he felt better all the same.

XVI

Falling.

No, not falling. Falling indicates motion, and here there is no motion. Here is only stillness.

Can one imagine total, utter stillness? Not the restful stillness of a late-summer afternoon when the day has played itself out and everything waits in a quiet stupor for the lively coolness of evening. Nor the pause just before the wind pounces down from the storm cloud to whip the grasslike growth of the Plain into a tossing sea of motion.

This stillness is deeper, going to the very core of things. It is the exhaustion of final entropy when all existence grinds to a halt and even the last subatomic vibrations fade away.

Nothingness. Transcendent emptiness that denies the very possibility of being. One by one the senses are drained of their sureness, and perception shown for a patchwork fraud. What we see, what we hear, what we smell, what we touch, what we know, the whole fabric of reality we weave so carefully to cover our nakedness in the face of existence is plucked, pulled, unraveled, dissolved, revealing the chaotic, ungraspable, seething turmoil that lies beyond. And beyond that . . . the stillness.

In the chaos all purpose dies. All attempts to give existence meaning, to impose order on the universe, coil and writhe in agonized frustration. And shatter. Existence simply is. All things are. Our knowledge is no more than a crude approximation, a reaching toward, never an arriving at. Explanation, justification are brought up short, here, there, always just shy of understanding. Nothing is left but a mere grunt of acceptance, an inarticulate acquiescence that merely dribbles off into the stillness.

The stillness. Once, long ago on the home world, a group of men declared that the world must be divided into two parts: what we can say precisely and clearly; and the rest, which we can only pass over in silence. They were right in one sense, but then went on to spend all their time turned toward the part of the world they could formulate, ignoring and finally denying the importance of the rest. Yet it would not go away, nor could they keep from casting worried glances over their shoulders at the darkness that loomed just beyond the feeble light their knowledge cast.

The stillness. Beyond the chaos, absorbing it, dissolving it. Lying in the very center of things. The Way does not "pass over" in silence those things that cannot be said. It does not turn its back on the unspeakable, the unknowable, the dark, the endless, wordless, meaningless, nothing. The Way dwells there and those who follow the Way sit in its center and become one with it.

That dwelling is silent. No Seeker of the Way speaks of the stillness any more than those who divide the world into the knowable and the irrelevant rest. But the silence of the Way is not an attempt to ignore or deny what cannot be spoken of. It is a finger, pointing, pointing, mutely focusing attention.

But how is it possible to dwell where nothing is? What can possess a person to take the endless leap into the unknown darkness?

Can knowledge, a sense of sureness based on even the most profound understanding, provide the confidence necessary to take that final step over the edge and into the abyss? No, for as we approach the abyss, all our knowledge is proven merely conditional, a fragile tissue of sense perceptions and our need to be in the world. We can comprehend, in a limited sense, *what* the world is. But the fact *that* the world is remains beyond us in the shadows of the unspeakable. To enter these shadows we must leave knowledge behind and step naked into the dark.

If knowledge isn't sufficient, can faith provide the motive force? No, for if one has dwelt in the light, one's faith can only be founded in the light. And no matter how firmly based in intellectual certainty or emotional conviction, its foundations shift and dissolve in the darkness. The abyss is endless, bottomless. The black stillness shatters the light and the things of the light. Faith becomes hollow, hopeless, useless in the face of eternal nothingness.

What, then, is left? Stripped of knowledge and faith, even hope cannot survive. Utter despair towers over us like a threatening wave. It breaks, beating us down, shattering us against the emptiness of an indifferent, entropic universe. The inarticulate sound we utter in the presence of the unspeakable becomes more than a mere grunt of acceptance. It becomes a cry torn in unspeakable anguish from the very essence of dissolving being.

This is the end, the last death, the final defeat.

And it is here the journey begins.

Here, in the abyss one can only say, "I believe." Not "I believe in" or "I believe because," but simply "I believe." Believing in or because implies something outside, something beyond the act of belief toward which it turns for justification. In the stillness there is no beyond.

"I believe" simply is. It depends on nothing outside itself. It is not subject to the unexpected twists of fate. It demands nothing, expects nothing, hopes nothing, knows nothing. A world can be built on it. If that world is swept away in an instant, it remains, as firm and solid as ever.

"I believe" does not create the world, does not change the world, does not make any demands on the world. It does not deny the stillness, nor does it transform it. It makes no difference in anything. Yet it makes all the difference in everything. It dwells in the stillness and is the stillness. It dwells in the world and is the world. It exists in both and is neither, in neither and is both. It does not question *what* the world is. It is content with the wonder *that* the world is.

Myali reached that place where everything ends. Stripped of knowledge, her faith shattered, hopeless and helpless before the power of the machine, she despaired. And in despair found that final ounce of strength that knowledge, faith, and hope had always failed to provide. With a cry of utter anguish, she flung herself over the edge, denying the bishop victory even as she accepted defeat.

She fell.

Falling.

No, not falling. Falling indicates motion, and here there is no motion. Here there is only stillness.

Can one imagine total, utter stillness? Not the restful stillness of a late-summer afternoon when the day . . .

"I believe." It had always been there, inside her, covered by layers of doubt and hope. Despair stripped her clean and let it free.

She waited.

Bishop Thwait glanced from the monitors to the figure of the young woman, quiet now, behind the isolation shield. At first the anomalies had appeared as before. Those queer spikes in the readouts, unexpected flatnesses where peaks should have been. It had worried him, made him begin to doubt the ability of the machine to subdue this strange being from the planet down below. But doubt was impossible. The machine was all-powerful. And eventually it seemed that indeed his faith was borne out.

The monitors were all normal now. As expected. Smooth, straight response curves, flattening out to neutrality. No more flickers. No more unpredictable bumps. Victory. The machine had won again.

He looked over at the admiral and nodded. "Finished. Her defenses have been overwhelmed. The machine has destroyed the structure of her mind, making everything in it accessible." He pointed to the master screen. "See how the response curve has flattened out? It is nearly neutral, indicating no remnant of conscious organization or will. Personality is gone, the ability to resist outside suggestion shattered. The mind is totally malleable. We need only drain it of its memories, correlate the data, and we have anything we need." Smugly, he smiled at Yamada. "The Power is in control, Admiral, as always."

Thomas turned his glance from the monitor to Thwait. The man's entirely too sure of himself, he thought. I don't like it. There's something up here, something that goes beyond this damn show with the girl and the machine. Andrew has something up his sleeve.

Casually, he stood and walked over to the chair. "Can you let the shield down now?" he asked. "When can we start with the questioning? I'd like to get on with it. Enough time's been wasted."

Thwait smiled again. "Everything is under control. Everything. There is nothing to worry about, Admiral. Absolutely nothing. I . . ."

The door slid open to reveal a very nervous Kohlsky. "Worship . . . I . . ." he stammered as Thwait swept him with a cold, silent glare. "I . . . wouldn't bother you but it's important."

"I would hope so, my child. The interruption is most untimely."

Kohlsky swallowed unhappily. "I . . . that is, we have lost contact with the spy, Worship."

" 'Lost contact'? What do you mean, 'lost'?"

"Worship, all communication ceased abruptly."

"All? Was there no report?"

"Nothing final, Worship. The running report simply ended suddenly, without warning."

"Have you reviewed the tapes? When did it end?"

"As the spy was about to strike at the Way-Farer, Worship."

"There was no report of success or failure? No summary on the defense capabilities of the planet? No findings or recommendations?" The bishop's voice rose on each sentence until he was almost shouting. "None? Nothing?"

"N-n-nothing, Worship." Kohlsky's voice was a frightened whisper.

The bishop looked grimly at Yamada. "He must

have been destroyed in the act of assassinating the Way-Farer.''

Thomas returned his look. ''He had a laser wand, if I remember correctly.'' Andrew nodded confirmation. ''Then they must have something more powerful than swords and bows and arrows. Damn! No report at all?'' he asked Kohlsky. ''Did you belly bomb him?''

''Yes, sir.''

''Immediately?''

''N-no, sir. We spent a little time trying to re-establish communication. It was so sudden and we wanted a report. So we—''

''How long?''

''Uh, about an hour,'' Kohlsky said weakly.

The admiral turned to the bishop, registering his disapproval with a silent, frigid stare. Andrew was angry, both at Kohlsky for his incompetence and at the spy for the failure of the mission. Damn you, Dunn, he cursed, even now you cause problems. Well, he sighed internally, at least the mission bought some time. Now I have the woman in my power and can get the information I need from her. Dunn is no major loss. Good riddance, actually. Hope the belly bombs did a thorough job of it.

He was about to turn back to the young woman in the chair, when he noticed that Kohlsky was still standing there, fidgeting. ''Yes, my child, is there something else?'' The tone of his voice was almost a threat.

Kohlsky's face drained of all its color. His hands began to shake ever so slightly. Several times he tried to open his mouth to speak, but no words came. Finally, making a terrible effort, he managed to croak out, ''Worship, I . . . there is . . . something . . . uh . . . else. . . . I . . .''

''Out with it, man!'' Yamada demanded harshly.

The man in the door began to shake. "A-about ten m-minutes ago w-w-we got a message f-from the s-spy," he stammered in a near whisper.

As soft and uncertain as the voice was, it fell into an absolute silence that made it ring and crash around the room. The admiral and the bishop turned to stare at each other, dismay and astonishment openly displayed on their faces. Yamada was the first to recover from his surprise. "A message? But you said he was bombed. What the fuck are you talking about? A message from a dead man?"

The security man nearly dissolved in fright. But from some hidden source, he managed to gather enough strength to answer. "Yes, sir. A m-message."

"You checked voice patterns to make sure it was the spy and not someone else?" demanded the bishop.

"Yes, Worship. There is no question. It was the spy."

"The message?"

"I-it said, 'Reporting mission accomplished. Reporting mission accomplished. Way-Farer assassinated. Have further discovered planetary defenses are excellent. Some kind of exotic energy-beam emplacements in small, rounded hills scattered seemingly at random over the planet's surface. Passive until activated by attack. They're almost here. Too many to fight. Detonate bombs, imperative. Detonate before they capture me. Detonate. Detonate. Deton—' Transmission ends." He looked up from the small piece of paper that he was holding with both hands to keep it from shaking too much.

The admiral exploded. "God damn it! This is just too fucking much. Exotic energy beams. Dead men talking. What kind of shit is this? What the hell are you trying to pull, you bastard?'' He rounded on Andrew, his face red in fury, his fists bunched, his body taut, leaning slightly forward on the balls of his feet, ready to attack. ''I don't believe a fucking word of it. Not one fucking word!''

Thwait took one involuntary step backward, then held his ground, glaring savagely at the furious admiral. ''How in the holy name of Kuvaz do I know what's going on? I'm as surprised as you are. Kohlsky, you idiot, have you triple-checked all this? Yes? Damn it, I don't believe a word of it either. Energy beams! What kind of nonsense is that? We have checked and re-checked every conceivable wave length, every possible source. Nothing!''

''Andrew,'' the admiral cut in, his voice hard and tight with control. ''I'm not waiting any longer. I'm ordering an immediate assault on the planet. We're going in shooting. And I don't give a shit what you or the Power thinks. I've had enough of your interference.''

''Kohlsky,'' the bishop commanded.

The security guard reacted as he had been trained, but his recent fear had weakened and slowed his reflexes. His laser pistol cleared its holster about a tenth of a second later than the admiral's; Yamada's beam hit him full in the chest and spun him into the door frame.

The two security guards outside the door were too stunned to move quickly, and the marines were equally slow to react. It was all too sudden, too unexpected. Thomas, however, kept firing as he dove for the floor and the door. One of the guards went down, his face a smoking ruin.

Bishop Thwait's laser wand cut a hissing path through the air just a second after Thomas's head left the spot. He shot again at the rolling body and missed a second time. There was no chance for a third shot, for the man was out of the door and pounding down the corridor before he could even take aim. The surviving marine ran with him.

Andrew ran to the comm panel and punched the general circuit. At the same time he palmed the door to the room shut. "Condition Kuvaz!" he screamed into the comm. "Attack!" Trembling, he turned to look at the unconscious Myali. "You," he muttered, "you will have to wait a while. I must take care of the admiral first. Then we will have our little talk and find out if this rubbish of exotic energy beams is true or not. That and a lot more. Yes."

He walked over the Kohlsky's body and looked down at the man. Chandra never would have been outdrawn, he thought. Right now I would have been looking down at Thomas's corpse if Chandra were still my chief of security. Damn the man! I could use his ability right now.

I must get to my quarters, he realized. That's the only place I can monitor the action and give orders from. With Kohlsky dead, I'll have to do it all myself. He leaned over and took Kohlsky's pistol from the stiffening grasp of the man's hand. He checked it: full charge, power on. Good.

Cautiously he palmed the door open, standing to one side so anyone outside wouldn't have a clear shot. There was no one. Carefully he peered around the door into the corridor. Empty. In the distance, he could hear the hiss and crackle of energy guns, but right here it was quiet.

He slipped out and palmed the door shut again,

locking it to his own thumbprint. Then he walked swiftly off toward his quarters.

Behind him, as the door closed, Myali opened her eyes and smiled.

XVII

Hello, Josh.

Hi, little sister. Got time to talk?

Time enough. Might as well spend it talking to you since there isn't much else I can do right now.

?

I'm strapped into a chair in a room. Until someone comes along and unstraps me, I can't do much more than wiggle my fingers.

Myali, Dunn's here and he's all excited. Says it sounds like they've got you wired up to the same machine that scrambled his mind. You okay?

Fine, Josh, fine. Tell Dunn not to worry.

You sure you're all right? You sound . . . different.

Different? Yes, I suppose so. But only in the sense that difference makes me more the same than ever. I'm me, Josh, in a way I've never been before.

Ah. The trees are trees, the streams, streams . . .

And the mountains, mountains again, Myali finished. *I'm not a Wanderer anymore, Josh.*

Huh, he snorted in reply, *about time you stopped running long enough to catch yourself. But don't you*

*think getting yourself strapped into a chair was a rather
extreme way of going about it?*

She laughed. *Oh, before I forget, tell Dunn his little
trick on the bishop and the admiral worked like a
charm. I wish you could have seen the looks on their
faces when they heard that last message from a man
they'd been told was dead! They thought I was still
unconscious and I didn't want them to realize I wasn't.
But I had all I could do to hold back the laughter.*

*Sounds like you're having a real fun time up there,
sis. Aside from the jokes and gags, is anything of
interest going on? You know, anything that might decide the fate of Kensho?*

*Well, the situation's deteriorated pretty badly. I've
been using my Mind Brothers to prod both Thwait and
Yamada whenever the opportunity occurs. Didn't take
much. The two of them hate each other like poison.
Things were already building toward a crisis, but
Dunn's little message seems to have blown the whole
thing wide open. The admiral killed Kohlsky, the
bishop's man, and then burned his way out of this
room. He took a couple of my Mind Brothers with him
and I let the rest loose for a while to help stir things up a
bit. From the sound of it, fighting must have broken out
all over the ship. In any case, the Brothers had a real
feast and are back, peacefully resting right now.*

Fighting among themselves? Josh chortled. *Wonderful!*

*Yes and no. Whoever wins will probably attack Ken-
sho. The only difference is that the admiral will come in
with guns blazing at any- and everything that moves
while the bishop will be far more selective in whom he
kills.*

There was a moment of silence. Then Josh said,
Dunn thinks that if enough men are killed, neither one

will attack. He says that if losses are more than about twenty-five percent, the winner will probably go back to fleet headquarters for help.

How long before they'd return to Kensho?

Dunn estimates about five of our years, two and a half each way, given the time paradox of the Sarfatti-Aspect drive.

Five years. That might be enough. Is there any way to make it take longer?

Well, our expert says that if you can knock out the comm before they call ahead, it'll add a year for mobilization of the invasion task force. And if a drive tube can be knocked out, another two. Total of eight, max.

Good. If I can get out of this chair, I'll take care of the comm. Can you activate the flagship? Just one of the laser cannons to knock out the tube?

Father Kadir says yes. But that puts you in a lot of danger, sis. I'd like to get you out of there before we start any shooting.

She laughed grimly. *I've been in a lot of danger for some time now, big brother. Don't be overly protective. We're trying to save Kensho, not Myali.*

I'm working on both.

First things first. Besides, there's no way to get me out of here. I knew and accepted that when I came.

Maybe, maybe not. Like I said, I'm working on it.

Okay, okay. Let's talk about that some other time, Josh. Right now I've got an idea I want to discuss with you and Father Kadir. Plus a lot of information about these people that could be very useful.

Okay, sis. We're all ears.

Myali smiled. *You look silly that way.* Then she began to talk.

$$* \qquad * \qquad *$$

Sergeant Jackson snapped off a quick blast down the corridor, then ducked back around the corner. Think I got the bastard. I better. Don't like being cornered here in this dead end. He heard a scrambling sound. Reacting, he popped around the corner and fired again. Two of 'em. He hit one and the other jumped back. Shit, he thought. Pistol's running low. He bent down to see if Nelson's had a better charge. Yeh. Old Nels bought it quick. Right in the throat. Pistol's good, though. Half charge left. He traded.

Got to get out of here, he realized. More footsteps. Must be three of 'em now from the sound of it. He sneaked a look up the corridor. It was about twenty feet long, ending in a main cross-corridor. About ten feet up, along the right wall, was a door. The door was what all the fighting was about, why Nelson and Jimmy had got killed. Not to mention old Tige up at the mouth of the corridor.

Doors critical . . . back way into the bridge. Once the fuckers get in there it's all over. Right now our boys are holding their own at the main entrance, but this one is vulnerable. Gotta keep it.

He snapped another shot around the corner just to let them know he was there. He wondered what would have happened if he hadn't seen that acolyte and found the laser rifle.

Damn! Might have surprised us. But it didn't work that way. No sir, not a bit. We were half ready for 'em. Shit, another ten minutes and we would have wiped their asses. Now, even if they make it, we've made 'em pay plenty.

More noises from the head of the corridor. Sounded like they were getting ready to rush him. Fuck, he thought, now I'll never be a lieutenant. Luck run out.

The pounding of feet told him they were coming. He dove out in the center of the passageway, low, firing up at them. The first two he cut off at the knees. Their shots went high, up where he should have been. If it had only been two, he would have won. But there were five. He burned one of the three others before they could adjust to his being on the floor. As he was swinging his pistol to bear on the survivors, a bolt of light hit him square in the chest.

Fuck. Doesn't even hurt, he thought as he fell into the darkest night he'd ever seen.

The bishop watched the display with growing dismay. It wasn't possible! The surprise hadn't worked. He cursed Kohlsky, the admiral, and every damn marine he'd ever known. The engine room had fallen, but he'd lost seven men in the process. Two was the estimated; four, the maximum. But seven! Holy Kuvaz!

Yamada's men still held the comm room and the bridge. The attempt to seal and gas the marines' quarters had failed miserably. Most of them had been out, moving in squads to key positions when it had happened. Not more than five had died in the gassing.

How had they known? Was Kohlsky really that utterly incompetent? Or was there still another spy in his system, another informer who told Thomas his every move?

Wait! Ah, ah, that's more like it. The bridge had been broken into from the back way. Now, now! Kill them! He switched on the visual monitor. Yes! The lasers spit deadly tongues of light. Damn, be careful of the controls! Two more marines down. Another brown robe tumbled, smoking, to the floor. He punched the comm button and spoke to the bridge. "Surrender! This is Bishop Thwait demanding that you surrender. Any one of you who dies fighting the Power is doomed to eternal damnation. We will toss your bodies into deep space and you will never know burial. Throw down your weapons and you will be spared. Surrender! The Power demands it."

For a moment the fighting stopped as the last defenders listened and considered. Suddenly a marine shouted, "Fuck you and your fucking Power," and began firing again.

"Damn, damn, damn," Andrew intoned helplessly. The marines didn't have a chance. Surely they could see that. The breaching of the rear entrance doomed them. But they refused to give up. More bloodshed, more death. More than he could afford.

The outcome was inevitable. In a few more moments, the last of the resistance had been silenced and the brown-robed members of his force moved in stunned wonder through the ruins of the bridge. For a few seconds he watched as they searched for the admiral. He wasn't among the dead.

Andrew slapped the switch and the picture died. He looked at the monitor. The fighting was still raging at the comm room and in many of the main corridors. Where the hell is Thomas? he wondered as he watched the display. Until that man is dead, I'm not safe. He must be found and killed.

But where is he?

The marine burned the door open, thinking: Must be important if it's locked. Three dead bodies right by it. Two guards and one of us. Must be important.

He kicked the smoking door and it collapsed on the floor. Cautiously, he peered in.

Shit. All kinds of computer crap. Consoles. That kind of stuff.

His eyes fell on a figure, its back to him, strapped into a chair. He brought the rifle up to ready and moved quietly into the room.

As he came around to the front of the seated figure, he realized it was a woman. A woman? What the hell was a woman doing here, tied up that way? She was awake, her eyes open and staring at him. Not fear, no. Something else.

Carefully he approached. Nice looking. Wore a robe, but not like the fucking Power bitches wore. This one was different. Yeh. Nice looking.

"You okay, honey?" he growled.

"Uh-huh. They tried to make me talk. Can you let me loose?"

He licked his lips, trying to decide. Not one of 'em. Shit, nice. He nodded and moved to unfasten the straps. It only took a minute. She pulled the wires off herself while he finished undoing the straps that held her legs.

The young woman smiled her gratitude. "Thanks. I won't forget the favor." He liked the sound of that. Liked it a lot. Nice. Pretty. Shit. He felt the warmth rise in his lower stomach. Been a long time since he'd had a girl. Shit. The barrel of his laser rifle dropped just a little and moved to the right. The girl stood, a little shakily and stretched. Nice. Damn fucking nice. The barrel moved another fraction to the right as his eyes focused on the way her breasts strained against the robe when she stretched. Shit.

Myali's foot came up and caught him underneath the chin. The force of the blow snapped his head back and broke his neck. She checked briefly to make sure he was dead.

She picked up the laser rifle, studying it. Pretty

simple: firing stud here; charge meter here; half
charged. Good. She walked to the door, leaned out
slightly and snapped a quick look right and left down
the corridor. Empty. Which way was the comm room?
She remembered that the admiral had bolted left when
he'd shot his way free of the room. Good enough, she
thought. Left it is. At a quick trot, she headed down the
corridor, rifle chest-high and ready.

"Can you really do it?" Dunn asked.

Josh shrugged. "I think so. We can snatch almost
anywhere on the planet. As long as there are Mind
Brothers at both ends, and more at the arrival end than
at the departure, it's pretty easy."

"But from that far? The longest distance you'd ever
have to snatch on Kensho is some five thousand miles,
right? From here to the scout's got to be a good five
times that far."

"I'm not sure distance, at least our distance, makes
any difference. Don't look so confused. I'll try to
explain.

"I have this theory about the Mind Brothers. It's
only a theory, and to be honest I don't even know how
to prove or disprove it. Anyway, I got to wondering
about them."

"I'll bite. What about them?"

"Maybe they're not 'them.' "

"What? Make sense, Josh. Remember, I'm not a
Kenshite and a lot of what you people think is profound
sounds like silly gibberish to me."

"No gibberish. I meant exactly what I said. I wonder
if the Mind Brothers are really 'them.' Maybe they're
'it' instead. Look, think of it this way. You're a fish,
right? I stick my hand in the water to catch you. What

do you see at first? Five separate wiggly things, fingers and a thumb, coming after you. But that's only because the rest of the hand, the part that makes it one thing instead of five, is not visible to you. It's out of your plane of perception, above the waterline.

"Let's carry the analogy in another direction. Suppose we're two-dimensional creatures on a plane surface. Again, a hand is plunged down into our plane. What do we see? Five individual and separate lines of varied length. If the fingers wiggle, the lines seem to move independently. No hint of anything bigger or more singular.

"If the hand comes farther into the plane, we begin to see the lines grow closer and closer together, until finally they merge into one large line. Many becomes one. If the hand pulls back up, one dissolves into many.

"Follow? Now what if the Mind Brothers are really a creature from another, higher dimension? A single creature. Oh, something totally alien and unimaginable in form, mind you. But still, in some sense, singular, a unit. It's quite possible that if that creature somehow got stuck partway into our space, we might see it as multiple beings rather than as it actually is."

"Suppose I buy that. What's that got to do with snatching? Or getting Myali back?"

Josh looked around for a second, then saw the piece of paper Dunn had used when figuring out how long the scout would take getting back to fleet headquarters. He picked it up and continued.

"Go back to the analogy with the creatures on the plane surface again. Suppose the plane is folded, not sharply in a crease, but just bent so that the two ends come close together." He demonstrated by bending the paper. "From our viewpoint, points on either end of the plane are quite close together if joined by a line that lies outside the plane. But to the creatures on the plane, the points are as far apart as possible. In fact, you'll notice that a lot of the points on the plane are closer in three space than they are in two space. Actually, those that are farthest apart in one space are those most likely to be closest together in the other.

"Well, of course, what happens in three space isn't of much interest to a creature in two space since he can't take advantage of it. But what happens if a creature from three space comes along and moves him from one side of the plane to the other, *through three space?* Assuming such a thing is possible, he jumps from one faraway spot to another by making a short journey."

Dunn nodded. "I get it. If the Mind Brothers are from, say, five space, then they, or it, might serve as a way of getting from one spot to another and distance as we perceive it might be irrelevant."

Josh grinned. "You've got it! We know we can snatch from anyplace on Kensho to any other place by using the Mind Brothers. Theoretically, we should be able to snatch Myali off the ship. The only apparent drawback is the distance. But if I'm right, it may not be a drawback at all."

"*If* you're right. That's a big if, Josh."

"I know," Josh replied grimly. "That's why I'm going to get as many people into the network as I can before I try it. I'm only going to have one chance."

She found a body about her size. The head was gone, but the robe was unburned. It took some doing, but she tugged the garment off and pulled it on over her own. Now at least the forces of the Power wouldn't shoot at her.

A pounding came from down the corridor. Several people, running. She leveled the rifle and waited.

Five brown robes came around the corner at a dead run. At the first sight of her, one screamed, "Don't fire!" and they all threw themselves flat. Myali held her fire and they rose, pale and trembling. The leader tried to speak twice before he finally managed a weak "Thank Kuvaz." He rose and trotted to her. "Come on," he commanded, "to the comm room. The admiral's holed up there. They're trying to rig a bypass on the comm to beam a message back to the fleet. Got to stop 'em before they do it." Myali fell in behind them as they started off again.

They attacked a side door while other units tried to smash a way through the main entrance. It took a good ten minutes, not to mention the lives of two of the five she was with, before they finally blasted their way in.

The admiral and two of his men worked feverishly at the comm controls right up to the last minute. All three died where they stood, never even bothering to turn around.

Myali walked over and looked down at Yamada. She knelt and turned his body over. From the front he looked fine, a feral grin still fixed on his lips. She left him like that and then looked up at the comm panel. This is how they communicate with the fleet, she realized. Without it, they'll have to hand deliver any message. An extra year, she thought, remembering what Dunn had said. If they can't send word ahead, maybe it'll take an extra year.

She stepped back into the center of the room. Everyone was busy checking the dead and wounded to make sure none were left alive. Calmly she lifted the laser rifle and blasted the comm panel. Then, before anyone could recover from their surprise, she turned the rifle on every other piece of equipment in view.

Myali didn't even see the blow coming, so intent was she on her work. It fell from behind, smashing into her head behind the right ear. The force of it spun her around to face the open doorway. As the blackness swept up and over, she saw the bishop standing there, his face twisted in rage as he took in the shambles she had made of the comm equipment. His eyes blazed with fury, but she also saw more than a hint of fear.

She smiled as the roaring darkness overwhelmed her.

XVIII

"We've activated the portside laser cannon on the flagship. That and the fire-control section of the main computer. From the initial readouts, it doesn't look like too difficult a task to knock out one of the scout's drive tubes. Could probably knock out the whole ship if we wanted to." The young Brother's grin was infectious. Dunn found himself smiling back even as he answered.

"Not as simple as you think. The scout has a passive shield that could handle the impact of a single cannon on a broad beam. You can punch through with a very narrow pin beam and go for the tube, but from then on, the full shield will be up and you'd need everything your ship's got to even scratch the surface." He shook his head. "Also, they'd head for deep space, crippled or not, at the first sign of hostility." Dunn paused. "Hmmmm. And knowing Yamada and Thwait, probably send a few robot missiles planetside while they were doing it. No. Best bet is just to go for the tube. It's a threat, a warning, but obviously not an all-out attack. Scare 'em, make 'em run, but don't try to corner and attack 'em. Scouts were built for just that kind of emergency and they're damn dangerous.''

Father Kadir nodded. "Sound advice, Dunn. Josh? All right, then, we'll just go for the tube.'' The young Brother gave them all another grin, then rose and left the room.

For a moment, Kadir considered Dunn. Finally he said, "My son, it's a lovely day outside. I'm sure your wound is well enough on the way to healing to allow you to at least sit in the sun a while.'' He rose. "Won't you join me?''

Dunn immediately reached with his right hand to pull back the covers on his bed. His left was halfway down to the bed to boost himself up into sitting position before he remembered it wasn't there. For a brief second, he floundered, then used his elbow to push, swung his feet over the edge of the low platform his mattress lay on, and stood. Josh grabbed his right arm to steady him.

"Whoosh,'' he breathed out, surprised. "Been a while since I stood. Guess losing a hand takes a little out of you as well as off of you.''

Josh and Father Kadir smiled. "You didn't eat a whole lot or rest much on your way here either, Dunn,'' reminded Josh. "I ought to know, since I had to keep up with you!''

The three of them walked out into the sunlight that bathed the courtyard just beyond the door of Dunn's room. It was a room, he realized now, not a separate cell. A room in a long, low building that stretched down one whole side of the courtyard. There were similar buildings on the other sides of the yard. One of them was two stories high.

In the center of the yard was a huge ko tree, its

branches casting an intricate pattern of light and dark on the ground around it. The sun, Dunn noticed, was high. Slept late again, he thought, amused with himself. Broken the habit of years. The Power never lets you sleep late.

The brightness of the sun was almost more than he could bear, so he began to move toward the shade of the tree. Only one tree, he thought. Not like the forest. He shuddered inwardly, remembering briefly the ordeal he had suffered while trudging through that endless green maze. I was insane most of the time, he realized. It was a miracle I made it.

Not completely a miracle, he admitted. A miracle and a Myali. The very mention of the name warmed him more deeply than the sun. It brought a brightness right into the very center of his heart. Myali. I know you in a way no person ever knows another. You're part of me.

I am myself. I am Dunn. I can no longer doubt that. The chase after the Face in the forest is over. I know who I am. Now I merely have to find out what I am. And what it means to be what I am. He laughed silently. That's all.

He looked sideways at Josh and Father Kadir. At least I'm in the right place to find out, he told himself. Careful to hold his left arm up, he lowered himself with his right so that he was sitting at the base of the ko, his back pressed against its trunk.

Good feeling. Secure. Like in the forest. It may be night, with infinite blackness all around. But behind me, it's solid and safe and feels good.

Without that little bit of reassurance, that small crumb of faith, the darkness could easily overwhelm you. He knew. He remembered.

Yes, the ko's trunk felt good. But it felt even better having Josh and Kadir there. Friends. Not just people you associate with, people you are thrown together with because you are in the same class at the Temple of the Power or part of the same crew aboard ship. Friends. People who are with you because they *want* to be. It was hard to describe. He'd never really had any friends before. Not in the Power.

He remembered Yoko, his mate. Not a friend. A need, yes. A release, definitely. But never a friend. Oh, he'd wanted her to be more than just a partner for releasing sexual tension. He'd wanted, God, *needed* someone to share his dreams and hopes with. But, then, dreams and hopes were not allowed in the Power. And when he'd tried to share his, Yoko had become so frightened she'd turned him in. Not a friend.

Myali. So much more than a friend. He didn't even have a word to describe it. "Love"? Weak. "Love" seemed so limited a word. Or not limited enough. Too broad. It could be used to describe so many things, such different things. Sexual lust for a woman or a man, feelings toward a brother or sister or parent or child or friend or thing or hobby or sport or idea or . . . Why do we only have one word? Why not a word for each shading, each object, each relationship?

Yet at the same time, only a vast word would do to describe the swelling in his chest, the warmth in his stomach, the brightening in his heart, every time he thought of Myali. It isn't just sex or friendship, damn it, he thought. It's bigger. I don't know how or when it happened. But now it's there, everywhere, and I can't imagine how the hell I existed before it was there.

And what if Myali can't come back to Kensho? What if she's already dead, up there in the scout? What if she's dragged back to fleet headquarters aboard the

ship? What if the bishop . . .? He pulled his thoughts
to a sharp halt. Enough. Those are useless paths that
cross and recross and lose themselves in a morass of
worry. It's a beautiful day.

But, dear God, let her come back, a small voice deep
inside him pleaded.

The fear was still in the bishop's eyes, and so was the
anger. Her head hurt and she could feel the lump over
her right ear. She was in a chair—not *the* chair—and
her hands were tied, *tied*, in front of her. And that was
all. It almost made her smile. No room, no chair, no
straps or wires. No machine. No wonder there was fear
in his eyes.

"I know you are conscious," he said harshly.

Myali smiled sweetly. "I hope you find yourself in
as good a condition." Play with him, irritate him, keep
him off balance.

The bishop's lips tightened. "Woman, somehow
you seem to have . . ." he had trouble saying the
word, "beaten the machine. I do not understand this.
Perhaps it is simply because the machine on this scout is
somewhat limited. Back at fleet headquarters there is a
much larger one with many more resources. There we
will see. We will see. Afterward, I will personally
dissect your brain to discover how it functions. A vivi-
section, of course." His cold eyes bored into hers,
looking, hoping to see weakness in her.

She laughed. "Back at headquarters? And what
makes you think we'll ever let you leave? Or do you
even have enough of a crew left to leave?"

The tightness in his face increased. It almost seemed
as if the skin was shrinking closer and closer to his
bones. "What do you mean?" he demanded tersely.
"How can you stop us?"

Myali laughed again. "Look around this ship, Bishop. Count the bodies. With my own hands I've killed seven of your people. And destroyed your comm room. With my own hands. Me. One little lady from Kensho.

"You think you captured me. You think it was just chance that I happened to be right there when your ape Chandra came along. You think it was just a strange fluke of fate."

She shook her head. "No, Bishop. You've been buried in your machines for too long. It was all planned. Every bit of it. Even this." She gestured with her bound hands to indicate the whole debacle on board the scout.

"That is not possible," he said slowly.

"It is one of many possibilities. And it's the one you have to deal with. We've been playing with you, Bishop. With you and all your little toy machines and missiles and lasers and starships and marines and computers. Playing. Like children teasing a sand lizard."

"No."

"Oh, yes. We can smash you any time we wish. But we wanted to learn more about you, see what it was that makes you tick, find out all your weak points. I was sent up here for that job.

"It was so easy. You're such fools. So gullible. So overconfident."

"No! Be quiet! All I have to do, you little fool, is raise one hand, thus, and push one button, this one right here, to inundate your worthless little planet with fire. Missiles, with warheads of a power unimaginable in your primitive society. Death. Destruction. I have that power, fool! I have it!"

The young woman snorted derisively. "Oh, I don't doubt you have the power to push the button. A small lizard has that much power. But to rain missiles on Kensho assumes the missiles can reach the surface of the planet. They never would.''

"You lie! You have no defenses! Even now, even with the remnants of my crew I can destroy you!''

"One of us has brought you to this situation, Bishop. Don't make the mistake of getting the rest of us involved.''

Thwait's face began to turn deep red. He seemed to be grasping for control, missing, and trying again. Myali could sense the building of an explosion. The little man's entire body was rigid with the effort to force his aroused emotions to bend to his cool will.

"Damn you!'' he suddenly shrieked as he leapt up. "Damn you and your stinking little planet! I will destroy you! Now! Now!'' He waved his bunched up fist under her nose. "You, you bitch, I will personally dissect, bit by bit, keeping you alive, without anesthesia, to the very end. I will leave the pieces of your body scattered across deep space, far from any planet or star. And I will burn your planet and everything on it to a cinder. I will make Quarnon look like an act of benevolence!''

He spun around and poised his finger over the missile-firing button. "This,'' he said triumphantly, "will only be a beginning of the death your people will suffer!''

A sudden shock hit the ship and threw him sideways, slamming him into another console. Myali was almost thrown from the chair. The lights flickered then failed, then came up again lower, redder. Sirens sounded and lights began to blink wildly in several panels.

Bishop Thwait leapt to his feet as several acolytes tumbled in through the door. "W-w-worship,'' one of them stammered, "the flagship . . . it opened fire and hit our number-four tube. All shields are up maximum. They want you on the bridge."

His face drained of all emotion, Andrew turned and looked silently at Myali. She returned his stare calmly, coolly. The anger was gone from his eyes. But the fear was there, stronger than ever. And deep beneath that, a glimmer of madness flickered to life.

He spun on his heels and ran from the room, the others following.

Myali looked around the room in the dim light. Over by the door, a body. She stood and walked to it. Brown robe; hands empty, spread out. Took the blast right in the chest. She searched in the direction his right arm pointed. There, at the base of a console. A laser wand. She picked it up. Not much of a charge left.

For a moment she stood and considered. Not enough energy left to do both things. Choose. She decided. Walking over to the panel the bishop had been standing in front of just before the flagship had struck, she blasted the missile-firing controls until the wand was empty.

Kensho is safe, she thought. For eight years. That's enough time. I hope.

Dropping the useless wand, she turned to sit once more in the chair. The turn brought her facing the door.

With a start, she saw Bishop Thwait standing there, a laser pistol in his hand. His eyes were staring at the burned ruin of the missile-control panel. Slowly they rose and met Myali's.

No anger. No fear. Just madness.

There were at least thirty of them seated around the ko tree now, and a few more were arriving. Dunn could feel a strange tingling sensation in the air. The Mind

Brothers, Josh had said. More Mind Brothers than had ever been brought together in one place since the original assault of the Mushin on the Pilgrims at First Touch.

Everyone became still. Father Kadir spoke softly into their silence. He welcomed them all, thanked them, warned them of the danger of what they were about to do. No one, he said, especially not Josh (a chuckle from all), knew exactly what would happen with a network of so many Mind Brothers. Ever since Jerome had devised his plan for keeping the Mushin in the 'hoods, separated and under control, ever since Edwyr had discovered men could carry the Mind Brothers, the creatures had been isolated in small groups. Now they were bringing them together again, recreating something approaching totality. The results . . . ?

But the need was great. Myali was alone and helpless on the scout. It was time to act. The flagship had been activated and had knocked out one of the scout's drive tubes. They would not stay around much longer. If they were ever to save Myali, now was the time to act. If . . .

And he began to chant:

"Moons, moons, shining down on
    waters,
    waters moving slowly, moons moving
    slowly,
    yet being still.
    Still the waters, still the moons.
    Movement, strife, all longing is but
    reflection, passing to stillness
    when the mind is calmed."

The chant went on as all of them joined in. It wrapped around Dunn, enfolding him, lifting him, carrying him.

He lost touch with anything but the flow and rhythm. Not quite able to merge with the others, he drifted near them, buoyed up and swept along. Myali, he thought, we're coming.

For a long time the bishop didn't speak. Then he laughed, softly, with just a tinge of wildness in the high end of his voice. "So," he finally muttered. "So, once more you outwit me. Yes, yes. Again. But never more. Noooooo. Not again. Now I know about you and your people. Oh, I should have guessed from the very beginning. Nakamura, that was the clue. Nakamura." He gestured with the pistol, demanding she sit in the chair. As she obeyed, he stepped into the room.

"Yes," he continued, muttering almost as if to himself. "Zen. Enemy. Haters of the Power. The Arch Fiend. The holy Kuvaz fought you and won. Now you try again.

"He is gone, the holy Kuvaz. But I, Andrew, the holy Andrew," he laughed shrilly, "I am here to save the Power. Power. Yes. One tube gone. Less power. We will limp back to the fleet. Limping, limping, limping." He bent his back and moved farther into the room, limping in mimicry as he came.

"But," he straightened up suddenly as he stopped, "we will come back! With a fleet of ships and fiery death for the enemy! And holy Andrew will rain death down, down, down on the Fiend!"

His eyes bored into Myali's. "And you my dear, you will stay alive and become my slave. Yes. I will destroy your mind, but not your body. No, not the lovely body. So lovely. I will burn off your feet with this laser pistol. Burn off your unholy, demon feet. And your foul, fiendish hands. Yes. Then you cannot run away ever again. Or do bad things with laser wands. No.'' He laughed, the sound ricocheting strangely off the walls of the room. ''No, you will just lie there and watch the things I do to your body and your world. Oh, yes. The things I will do!''

Slowly, Thwait lowered the tip of the pistol until it pointed at her left foot. ''One foot now. Another later, when you recover. Then a hand. Then another. Maybe I will even burn off your arms and legs just to while away the time on the trip back to headquarters. Such a long trip now, thanks to your friends.''

Myali could see his finger tensing to push the firing button. In desperation she did the only thing she could think of: She threw her Mind Brothers.

The bishop went rigid as they struck, his finger hitting the firing button. A blaze of light flashed out. The motion had been enough, though, and the beam hit the leg of the chair rather than her foot. It collapsed as she sprang to her feet. She raced for the door.

In despair, she ran down the corridor. There was no real escape—except perhaps through her Mind Brothers. But they were no longer with her.

Alone, she fled.

Riding the crest of a mighty wave, Dunn swept on. Myali, he called. Myali!

Now the wave became a beam of light, burrowing its way through a vast blackness that stretched out and on forever. No other light relieved the darkness in any direction. Deeper and deeper the beam tunneled. And became thinner and dimmer the farther it went. Still Dunn rode it, right at the leading edge, his eyes straining to pierce the night that lay ever ahead. Is there no end to it? he wondered.

There! A dim glowing up ahead. He felt a surge of recognition all around him. Mind Brothers! those in the network cried. Myali! he replied.

He reached, yearning as the beam sped on to meet the small dot of light. They merged and he shouted out his dismay. It wasn't Myali!

Breathless, she sank against one of the bulkheads along the corridor. Twice she had barely managed to escape patrols of the brown robes. It wouldn't be long now. They'd catch her. Already she'd heard the warning bells that told they were readying the drive. There was nowhere to go. And soon Kensho would be lost far behind in space.

Kensho, she moaned inwardly. Josh, and Father Kadir and Dunn. All gone. All left impossibly far behind. Oh, Gods!

But left safe. With a chance. With hope. I give them mine, for I have none.

She took a few more deep gulps of air and pushed herself from the wall. It hurts, she admitted, but I have the strength to go on. I've always had it. Just never realized it. Mother Illa saw it. The strength. To save Kensho. Nothing else mattered.

Dunn could feel their despair. They'd found the Mind Brothers, but not Myali. The creatures had been attacking the mind of Bishop Thwait. They were quiet now, under the control of those in the network.

Josh and the others were trying to decide what to do. The strain of holding the path open to the scout was beginning to tell. They couldn't keep it up much longer. If Myali didn't show up or didn't call her Mind Brothers to her, they'd have to abandon the rescue mission.

Dunn couldn't participate in the discussion because he wasn't really one of them, didn't know how to use the Mind Brothers in that strange, wordless, mind-to-mind communication they used. But even if he couldn't converse, he could hear them, could feel what they were saying. It stunned him. Leave Myali? Pull back to Kensho and leave her alone on the scout? Never!

Myali! he cried out, focusing every ounce of his energy on the woman whose mind was part of his own. Myali!

She came around the corner and knew it was all over. Strangely, she felt relieved. As the bishop raised the laser pistol, she looked up and smiled into his face.

His features were a twisting, writhing horror. He was totally, hopelessly mad. The Mind Brothers had driven him to the Madness, but for some reason hadn't finished the job and sucked his mind dry. Strange. Why? And where were they?

The call came from deep within. Soft, urgent, it trembled at the edge of awareness. Just one word, "Myali," her name, filled with urgency and longing. She'd never felt anything like it before. Not even the direct communication of the network came from within. It was . . . It was . . .

Suddenly she knew. The bishop, the missing Mind Brothers, the call, it all fell into place.

With a laugh that shook the whole corridor and stopped Thwait dead in his tracks, she called out, "Dunn! Josh!"

And disappeared.

Andrew Thwait, Bishop of the Power, stood and stared at the spot where she had been. Then with a scream of rage he flung his laser pistol at the wall. Still screaming, he ran to the place and jumped up and down, stamping and smashing the floor again and again.

He didn't even hear the final warning bell. As the drive started, the ship jerked awkwardly and he lost his balance. With a thump, he careened into the wall and slid to the floor. Tears poured down his face, his voice muttered hoarsely, dulled from all his screaming. His fists pounded the floor weakly, hopelessly. Nothing he said made any sense. Just a stream of words, disconnected, meaningless.

"Damn, holy Kuvaz, Thomas, oh, Thomas, ah, ah, Kensho, damn, hate, bitch, bitch, Kuvaz, can do it, find them, kill, ah, ah, Chandra, I . . . I . . ."

Slowly the scout moved out from behind the moon, heading for deep space. It would have to get far beyond the gravity well of the system before it went into Sarfatti-Aspect drive. With one tube missing, it couldn't take the chance of jumping in a spacetime that was too strongly curved. That would make the trip longer, but it was the only safe way.

Home and security were a long way off. Like a badly wounded animal, the scout limped toward them.

EPILOGUE

Dunn sat in the shade of the ko. The late afternoon sun slid over the wall of the 'hood and beneath the branches of the tree to warm his face. It felt good.

Most of the others had already gone. Only Josh, Father Kadir, and Myali remained. "I can't explain it, Father," the young woman said. "It wasn't like anything I've ever felt before. Not like talking through the network. More internal. Like it came from inside me. As if one part of me was calling the rest."

Kadir nodded. "Hmmmmm. Yes." He looked at Dunn with considering eyes. "Like one part of you called the rest. My son, you're being awfully quiet."

Dunn grinned. "Happiness doesn't need a voice."

Josh laughed. "Ha! You're already beginning to sound like one of us!"

Myali looked serious. "Dunn. Does love need a voice?"

He met her eyes. "It has one. But not everyone can hear it. Those that can, know. It speaks even when it is silent."

"And its smallest whisper is a mighty shout," she murmured quietly.

"That can be heard across space and time," he finished.

For several moments they all sat in companionable silence, enjoying the late-afternoon sun on their faces. Finally Father Kadir stirred with a sigh. "We walk in new places. But they are places of great beauty. There's no need to hurry, and much reason to linger."

"Dunn, will they be back?"

"Hopefully, yes."

"Hopefully?" asked Josh.

Myali answered. "Yes, Josh, 'hopefully.' " He looked at her, unsure of how to take her reply.

"Josh," she began, "do you remember the Council meeting and that merchant?" He nodded. "He was right, you know. It is time for us to move out into the universe. We've just learned what can happen if you sit and wait for it to come to you.

"We were lucky this time. What came was our own, people we could understand and deal with. Next time we might not be so fortunate."

"We may not be so fortunate when they come back, sister. I've a strong feeling they'll arrive shooting."

"Not quite," Dunn replied. "They'll arrive, ring the planet, and deliver an ultimatum. If we say no, then, poof, no more Kensho."

Myali nodded to Dunn. "Yes, I agree. We'll have at least a full day after their arrival."

"Will that be enough?" Kadir asked.

"If we're ready," Myali answered. "We have eight years to prepare."

"Ah," he said as he rose, "eight years. It took Jerome eight years to pen up the Mushin and free our people. If such a thing as that is possible, surely this is, too. Come, Josh, we have things to discuss.''

As the two of them left, Myali and Dunn fell silent. For many minutes, quiet pervaded everything. Then, as the sun eased itself beneath the wall of the 'hood and covered them both in shadow, the air was filled with the evening song of a lizard.

They listened, their eyes finding each other. As the last notes died away, Dunn smiled. ''Why does the lizard sing?'' he asked softly.

Myali smiled back. ''We walk in new places.''

''Then let us walk slowly.''

''Yes. Slowly.''

''And for a long time.''

''Yes. A long time.''

Her eyes drifted up toward the sky. Two moons were just becoming visible. ''They will come,'' she sighed.

He nodded, looking up too. ''They will come.''

''And then will the universe be ours, Dunn?''

He reached out with his right hand and covered her left where it lay on her thigh.

''It already is, Myali.''

FRED SABERHAGEN

Classic stories by America's most distinguished and successful author of science fiction and fantasy.

☐ 12314	**CROSSROADS OF TIME**	$1.95
☐ 33704	**HIGH SORCERY**	$1.95
☐ 37292	**IRON CAGE**	$2.25
☐ 45001	**KNAVE OF DREAMS**	$1.95
☐ 47441	**LAVENDER GREEN MAGIC**	$1.95
☐ 43675	**KEY OUT OF TIME**	$2.25
☐ 67556	**POSTMARKED THE STARS**	$1.25
☐ 69684	**QUEST CROSSTIME**	$2.50
☐ 71100	**RED HART MAGIC**	$1.95
☐ 78015	**STAR BORN**	$1.95

H. BEAM PIPER

MORE TRADE SCIENCE FICTION

Ace Books is proud to publish these latest works by major SF authors in deluxe large format collectors' editions. Many are illustrated by top artists such as Alicia Austin, Esteban Maroto and Fernando.

Robert A. Heinlein	Expanded Universe	21883	$8.95
Frederik Pohl	Science Fiction: Studies in Film (illustrated)	75437	$6.95
Frank Herbert	Direct Descent (illustrated)	14897	$6.95
Harry G. Stine	The Space Enterprise (illustrated)	77742	$6.95
Ursula K. LeGuin and Virginia Kidd	Interfaces	37092	$5.95
Marion Zimmer Bradley	Survey Ship (illustrated)	79110	$6.95
Hal Clement	The Nitrogen Fix	58116	$6.95
Andre Norton	Voorloper	86609	$6.95
Orson Scott Card	Dragons of Light (illustrated)	16660	$7.95

145